Witches of Moondale: Book Four

A Hex to Remember

Lou Wilham

Midnight Tide
PUBLISHING

To those who are scared right now.
May this book bring you some measure of peace, and
just know that you're never alone.

Chapter 1

"You bring him back to us!"

The words echoed in Azure's head over and over again. It wasn't the words *themselves* that made them stick there, but the fire in Tony McMahon's eyes as he said them, as he hunched over the body of the man he loved and demanded Rus bring Eric Marcelino back from the dead. Not just for himself but for Hunter as well. Azure understood it, perhaps better than she'd ever be able to express in words. After all, she would do the same were she in his shoes, clutching the body of Rus in her arms and demanding the universe bend to her will, give her just one more day with the woman she loved.

Especially now that Rus was back in her life after so long. Azure would not give her up so easily. Even if it were a consequence of the job, as it was for a vampire hunter like Eric.

"I know you don't approve," Rus said, dragging Azure out of her own head. She was on her tiptoes, trying to reach something on the top shelf at the back of their wardrobe. Her fingers scraped against the wood in the silence of their home—like nails on a chalkboard.

"Hm?" Azure asked, her steps soft and careful on the dark-stained floorboards as she joined Rus in front of the oversized piece of furniture. Peering through the darkness, she found a worn duffle stuffed onto the back of the shelf, far out of reach of little hands. Maybe even out of sight and out of mind.

"You don't approve of what I'm about to do," Rus repeated. Finally, her fingers caught on the long strap of the bag, and she was able to yank it from its hiding place down into waiting arms. It landed with a muted *thump* before Rus dropped into a squat to dig through it, pulling items from the dark recesses. A switchblade, looking as unceremonial as a kitchen knife. A few vials of dark, congealed blood that Rus uncorked, sniffed, and curled her nose up at. A notebook with pages falling from it. Some chalk pencils that were sharpened down to nubs.

Azure had to shake herself and return her mind again to what Rus was saying instead of the capable, sure way Rus handled this kit of items Azure had never seen before. "I don't believe I said that."

"Yeah, but you didn't have to, did you? It's necromancy. I know how you feel about that, Az." Rus exhaled a short breath, her shoulders hunching as if readying for a blow that would never land. "You don't have to be there when we do this. I'd understand if you weren't."

"I'm coming with you. You are not doing this alone." Which seemed obvious to Azure. She couldn't let Rus face this by herself. They were coven. They were a team. They would stare down the reaper together and bring their friends' friend back. Azure may not know Eric at all, but she knew Hunter and Ava. They were coven, too, and anyone who meant enough to them to demand a necromancer bring him back must be the best kind of person. And even if he weren't? Azure could hardly deny that she would do anything to mitigate the reminder of that pain in Tony's eyes for fear she'd find it mirrored in her own one day.

"Well, not alone, obviously. Ava and Hunter will be

there. And Tony, I'm sure. I don't think he'll leave Eric alone for a—"

"Icarus," Azure said her name on a sigh as she reached for Rus's trembling hands. It took her a moment, but when Rus finally lifted her gray eyes to meet Azure's, there was an uncertainty there that would not stand. "I was wrong, before, when I parroted the things the elders said about your magic," Azure assured her softly. It was something she had wanted to say to Rus for months now but hadn't yet found the opportunity. "There is nothing dark or evil about what you do. There is nothing wrong with giving life to those whose time has been cut short. Nothing wrong with helping the dead when so many of us ignore them. I understand you and what you do better now, and I would like to continue to learn more. I apologize if I ever made you feel otherwise."

Rus blinked, mouth falling open in a stunned silence that was so beautiful, Azure wanted to lean forward and taste it on her lips. She'd done that. She'd said something so deep, so wonderful—at least, she hoped that's why Rus was shocked—that it had stilled Rus's tongue for perhaps the first time in her entire life.

"Az, I—" Rus inhaled sharply, leaning in to where Azure lifted her hand to brush her thumb against Rus's cheek like a cat seeking warmth. Ravishing and pliant. Azure could close the distance between them, swallow her whole. She could—

The back door creaked open, and Nando's soft voice carried up the steps of 157 Mourning Moore. "Rus. Azure. We've got everything together."

"Shit." Rus hissed. Then she spun to shove things back into the bag, and Azure noticed that her hands no longer trembled. "What time is it?"

Azure checked her watch. "Quarter to three."

"We need to hurry. It'll take time to set up the array and the sheeting and stuff." With that, she pushed to her feet and slung the bag over her shoulder before heading for the door.

"Do you need me to grab anything from the pantry downstairs?"

There was a helpless feeling settling into Azure's chest she didn't care for. She didn't know enough about what Rus was going to do to be of any real use. Her magic wasn't geared toward this sort of thing. And even if she accepted Rus and all that she was, there was still a nagging discomfort that went along with the idea of dragging a soul back to the plane of the living. A feeling that she was sure would linger, perhaps for years, because it was so engrained in her from a lifetime of listening to the elders speak of mediums and necromancy as if it were taboo, forbidden, dirty. She knew better now, of course, but that gut reaction stuck with her.

"No. I have everything I need in here." Rus patted the bag hanging at her hip. Then she held her hand out to Azure, and Azure was helpless but to take it, to let Rus lead her down through their sleeping home, out to the quiet of the yard, and across the crisp grass toward the house next door—155 Mourning Moore, their coven house.

When they arrived, someone had already covered the worn floorboards and the minimal furnishings they'd managed to move into the living room with plastic sheeting. Standing in the center of the big open front room, right next to the fireplace, was a calf. Azure didn't want to think about how Ava and Vanessa had gotten the animal inside without being seen, nor where it'd come from at this time of night. Darcy—Rus's crow familiar—sat on its shoulder, chittering softly and soothingly to the creature.

Explaining to it why it was there, asking it if it would go willingly.

"Does Darcy always do that?" Azure asked in a whisper, hoping not to draw the attention of the others in the room as they entered. Not that it mattered. The moment Rus stepped over the threshold, all eyes turned to them. Ava and Vanessa, where they huddled in one corner, Ava's eyes red rimmed and puffy. Hunter and Tony, where they were crouched on the floor, unwilling to leave the still form of Eric for a single moment. Even the calf next to the hearth. All attention shifted.

Rus shrugged. "The last time I sacrificed an animal to bring someone back, it was *for* Darcy."

Evasive as ever, but Azure would let it go, at least for now. Rus had once said that she'd only brought two beings back from the After that mattered: Darcy and Aihuan. But that didn't for one second mean those were the only two times she'd performed this ritual. And considering the state of her kit for it...

"You're going to have to step away from him," Rus said, dropping Azure's hand and crossing the room to where Hunter and Tony cradled Eric's lifeless body. Her hands lifted to brush their shoulders in a gesture that was likely meant to be comforting, but both men flinched away. "I'm sorry."

"Come on, sweetheart, let's let the lady work," Tony murmured. He settled Eric gently onto the floor and reached for Hunter instead, his hands shaking much the same as Rus's had been not but a few minutes ago as he peeled Hunter's fingers away from the material of Eric's shirt. "Let's let Ashthorne do her thing."

Hunter nodded but didn't speak. There was a quiet to him unlike Azure had seen before. When he looked up at

Tony, it was as if he weren't really seeing at all. Grief had stolen so much from him, Azure hardly recognized the quick-witted, tattooed Black man who helped them overcome a soul jumper.

"He'll be back," Rus promised with a conviction Azure admired. Icarus Ashthorne might be unsure about other things—about their relationship and her place in the world—but she knew her capability. She knew her magic. And she knew she could bring Eric Marcelino, vampire hunter, back from the dead. It was super sexy. Azure would have to address that later.

Hunter nodded again and let Tony lead him to one of the plastic-covered couches pushed against the curtained windows.

"Az, can you put up a security ward to make sure no one does any peeking?" Rus dropped down beside Eric. She pulled out a notebook and pen from the bag to hold out to Azure before getting everything she needed together while Azure turned to the windows without a word.

The setup took much less time than Azure would have thought. Between Rus and Nando, they moved like a well-oiled machine, which again, made Azure wonder how frequently Rus had done this.

Three intersecting protection circles were drawn in dry-erase marker around Eric, the calf, and Rus. Candles were lit around the room, and the house took the initiative to lower the lights. Rus settled into her circle, hands resting on her knees, Darcy on her shoulder, eyes closed. Green magic twisted around her, whispers growing louder and louder as Rus plunged herself into the After with only Darcy to tether her to this plane.

Azure's hands itched to reach for her, to pull her back from the brink. She knew what she'd have to do if Rus got lost in there, if she couldn't find her way back. She'd done it before.

It seemed like it was taking too long. Seconds ticking by into minutes.

The shine of the pendant around Rus's throat—the one Azure forged for her—would ensure Rus couldn't get trapped there easily, not the way she was once in danger of doing. Things would struggle to cling to her. But would it be enough? It never seemed like enough. Nothing Azure could do would mitigate all the dangers of this kind of magic. But she also wouldn't keep Rus from doing it. Not anymore. She wouldn't push Rus away like that. Not again.

It took several minutes. The only sounds were the soft breathing of the people around her and the calf shifting slightly against the plastic sheeting, before Rus finally came up for air. When she opened her eyes, they glowed the way a glow stick would, and a thin sheen of sweat glittered against her skin.

"He's here," she said in a voice that echoed with those of the dead, her magic swirling more quickly around her. Not violent and volatile the way it did when it was ready to go on the offensive. But not slow and lazy either, as it did sometimes when Rus was just checking in with the spirits that surrounded them on the daily.

Hunter lifted his head and looked around, like he could see the spirit of the deceased vampire hunter floating right there in the middle of the room. But there was nothing. Just the glow of candles and Rus's magic glinting off the sharp edge of the athame as she rose and moved toward the calf.

Darcy cawed softly, a question.

The calf answered, bowing its head and lying down.

Rus rested her hand on its shoulder, murmuring softly

to it, her magic swirling around it, lazy and comforting. Lulling the creature into a state of twilight.

A spell lingered in the air that Azure recognized. One of sleep, of rest. Something to send the creature into the After without the trauma usually associated with ritual sacrifices. A kindness that made Azure's heart leap into her throat.

Then in a movement so swift Azure couldn't track it, Rus cut the main artery in the calf's neck, and blood dripped steadily onto the plastic beneath it. Rus did something with the blood Azure couldn't see over her shoulder, her finger swiping through the viscous liquid. It took a few moments, but once all breath stopped in the creature, she turned back to Eric.

Blood dripped from Rus's hands, her eyes glowing still, her magic making her hair float around her face. Azure's breath caught in her throat. She'd never seen something so beautiful in her entire life. That was *her* Rus. Her partner. Her girlfriend. And one day, her wife. Azure wouldn't rest until Rus agreed to that.

With her clean hand, Rus tipped Eric's chin, opening his mouth, then dripped some of the blood inside. The whispers hit a fever pitch, so loud the entire room covered their ears. And Azure might have been imagining it, but she would swear she saw a pale-blue wisp break off from Rus's magic and settle onto Eric's tongue just before Rus slammed his jaw closed and held it shut.

Eric started struggling.

Arms flailed, smacking Rus. Nearly knocked her hand away, but she held him firmly even as his breaths came in ragged sips. Even as tears streamed down to his temples.

Hunter let out a soft squawk of upset and leapt forward as if to stop her, but Tony held him fast, and Azure took a step in between them, protecting Rus from whatever Hunter thought he might do to put an end to this.

Sweat gathered in thick drops on Rus's hairline. Her cheeks flushed. Her chest heaved in hard pants.

The silent battle between Eric's body, his spirit, and the necromancer forcing them back together went on for an agonizingly long time. Every second that ticked by, Rus looked paler and paler, her magic growing more violent around her, the whispers and the wind picking up. The candles guttered. The room grew so cold, Azure could see her breath. A shiver raked its fingers down her spine.

And then everything stopped.

The candles went out.

Rus's magic died away.

Plastic no longer crinkled.

Someone gasped. Eric, probably. The sound wet and guttural as he reached for the newly stitched wound on his throat, his movements just visible in the dim light coming through the curtains from the streetlights outside.

"Where am I?" a man asked into the silence, a voice Azure didn't recognize, so it could only be Eric. It was wreaked, and choked either by the wound he'd suffered, or by something else.

"Take it easy," Rus said gently as she helped him sit up. "Slow, shallow breaths. That's it."

Azure snapped her fingers, and the candles relit, their flames rising so high and so bright, they were near blinding, her magic overreacting in her panic. But once she could see clearly again, she found Rus sitting next to Eric, both looking drawn and tired but upright, nonetheless.

"Where am I?" Eric asked again, his voice raspy.

Rus gave his hand a squeeze and met his gaze. There was something twisted and lost in Eric's expression, something Azure didn't think she was equipped to identify, much less understand, but Rus gave a subtle nod as if she did.

"Oh," Eric said. His eyes flicked to meet Hunter's and Tony's over Rus's shoulder. The smile that lifted his mouth was slow, strained, but it was honest. "Can I get a hug?"

"You're home," Tony whispered, a little disbelieving. Then, "You're home!" He, Hunter, and Ava rushed from their respective corners to tackle Eric. To pull him in close. To check him over to make sure he was all right.

Rus pushed herself out of the way, skidding across the plastic on her ass until she could press her back into Azure's knees and look up at her with a tired, lopsided smile, blood smeared across her cheeks and in her hair. "Hey, Magpie, you ready to head home?"

And Azure... Well. Her heart was in her throat, her cheeks on fire, her blood pumping so loud and so quick she could hear it. And she was so, *so* in love with Icarus Ashthorne. What else could she say but "Marry me?"

Chapter 2

S he couldn't.

She *shouldn't*.

But that didn't change the fact at all that Rus *wanted*. She had spent a fair portion of her formative years imagining the moment when Azure Elwood would propose to her. Daydreaming about the family they would have and the life they would live. Even before they were anything more than best friends. Even before romance ever came into the equation. Rus always knew, for her, it was Az and Az only. Sure, there were years while she was away when she'd settled for something, someone, that she thought she deserved. But she knew better now. Knew that Kaytee was a mistake in so many more ways than one.

And there Az was, looking all kissable and soft, smiling down at Rus and asking her the one question that had echoed through Rus's brain since she was six fucking years old.

Marry me?

It was just as beautiful falling from Az's lips as Rus always imagined it would be. And doubly as heartbreaking, because Rus knew she shouldn't, couldn't. Not until Az knew everything. Not until Rus had come completely clean about what saving Aihuan cost her. Laid her whole bloody, black heart on the table for Az to determine its worthiness, or lack thereof.

"Really, Az? *Now?*" Rus joked, her tongue thick with all the things she couldn't say. Not here where other people could hear, where other people could judge. "I'm covered in blood and half drunk on necrotic magic."

It wasn't a lie. The metallic scent clung to the inside of her nose. Her skin was sticky with crimson. And she could hear herself slurring, her body listing heavily against Az, even as she tried to hold up her own weight. Her fingertips were tingling, feeling oddly disconnected from the rest of her body, just like the times she'd had too much schnapps when she was a teen.

"And you just did something unbearably sexy," Az countered, her lips twitching at the corners as if she was laughing at Rus. Which was fair, Rus supposed. She made a pathetic sight for an all-powerful necromancer.

"Oh. She's got jokes." Rus snorted and rolled her eyes.

"Who's joking?" Az asked with a brow raised so high, it nearly disappeared into the plum-colored hair falling across her forehead. She didn't sound like she was joking. She didn't *look* like she was joking.

Rus's heart couldn't take it. It lurched into her throat, and she swallowed around it with an audible gulp in her ears. Hopefully all the blood covered the flush that heated her cheeks to a blaze. It was always so easy to flirt with Az. The subtle push and pull of their relationship that wound up drawing them closer together, even when they were already so close, Rus could feel Az's breath on her skin.

Fuck.

"We should get back," Nando said, a note to his tone like he was sorry he had to break up whatever moment Rus and Az were sharing. Or maybe he was afraid to, given the glare Az leveled at him. "The girls will be getting up soon for school."

With a nod, Rus held her hands up to Az, begging for help to her feet. Az let out a soft scoff of fondness and pulled her up by her underarms the way someone might an errant toddler. Then when Rus's legs wobbled and threatened to give out on her, Az didn't let go. Goddess, she was amazing.

"All right, home." Rus leaned heavily on Az's shoulder, letting Az take the majority of her weight with her shorter height. Then with a nudge, they moved as one so they could turn to look at the five others in the room, all huddled together the way a family would when someone returned home. "Do you think you can handle the cleanup?"

Vanessa poked her head up and offered Rus a sly grin. Her eyes darted between Rus and Az knowingly. "I think we've got that covered. Do you mind if we stick around for a bit?"

"Nah. Just make sure no one sees you guys disposing of everything. This house is under my name." Well, hers and Az's. The purchase for 155 Mourning Moore had only just finished going through. Rus wondered if Nesta—her real estate agent and dear friend—would ever figure out that the first act Rus and her coven had done inside their new coven house was bring someone's boyfriend back from the dead. Probably better they didn't. Not that Nesta would judge. It was simply better if they had plausible deniability.

"I think we can manage that." Vanessa nodded, speaking for the entire group. The others were whispering softly and brokenly to each other, holding each other close. Ava was sandwiched in between Tony and Hunter right along with Eric, glued to his side.

"Nando," Rus said, turning back to her best friend and partner in crime. "You'll stick around and see that it's done right?"

"Of course."

"The rest of you, meet me back at 157 after I get the girls out the door. We've got to have a chat." Rus chewed on her lower lip. The girls might ask where their uncle was this early in the morning, but that'd be okay. They could make up some story about the milk steamer breaking at Necromancer's and him having to go in early.

There was a collective nod, then everyone turned to their tasks.

Another light nudge, and Rus and Az were headed for the door, out into the slowly lightening dawn of Moondale. Dew clung to the grass, mist hovered above the graves as they passed through, and the world was quiet. But for how much longer, Rus didn't know. There was still so much they hadn't solved, so much they hadn't dealt with. The centennial was in a few days. The prophecy was still indecipherable. And they were no closer to understanding why Az had an ancestor—Mazarin Elwood—who'd been stricken from the Elwood family records. This and more weighed Rus down, adding to the sluggish exhaustion post-necromancy, and she was still stumbling by the time they reached 157 Mourning Moore. Home.

"I'll go get the girls up in a minute if you start making their breakfast," Az volunteered, accurately assuming that Rus wouldn't be able to take the stairs in her condition.

"Meiling is trying to get herself up, remember?" Rus slumped into one of the dark-stained kitchen chairs and leaned back until she was blinking up at the ceiling. "Give her twenty minutes. If her alarm hasn't roused her, then we'll deal with it. I should be able to walk by then."

Az snorted and headed for the kettle. "I'm making you some tea."

Rus's eyes followed her as she gnawed at the inside of

her cheek. Az was acting like the proposal hadn't even happened. Like it was just a normal part of life, and the fact that Rus had essentially said no didn't bother her in the least. Should Rus be worried about that? Should she say something? Was she completely fucking this up? She didn't know. There was no way to know. Az was a carefully sealed vault. Always had been.

"Tea sounds spectacular." Rus sighed and scrubbed at her crusty face, flaking away some of the dried blood onto the floor. "Tea and a bath."

"I'll get you a washcloth to remove most of the blood. We wouldn't want the girls to—"

"Magpie." Rus tilted herself so she was sitting up again, fixing Az with a small smile. Az's hands stilled where they were filling the kettle, heat rising in her cheeks at the term of endearment. And fuck it, Rus needed to at least start laying herself bare to this beautiful, wonderful, perfect woman. This woman who wanted to be her wife. She couldn't do it all this morning—she didn't have the strength —but she could start. "The girls won't be worried about the blood. They've seen it before."

Az tinkered for a moment with the lid on the kettle, popping it off, shoving it back on, popping it off again. The sound was strange and echoing in the quiet of their kitchen as their home slept around them. "They have?"

"They have." Rus nodded. Although she wanted to drop her gaze and look away from the intensity of Az's deep, dark eyes, she didn't. It was important for Az to understand, to see how serious Rus was. And Rus needed to be able to gauge Az's response to this, and to every other confession she might make in the coming days. "You said you wanted to marry me."

"I do." Az said the words like they'd been locked up in

her chest for her entire life. Like they'd sat on her tongue, blistering and too hot, the way a Hot Pocket straight out of the microwave would be.

"Then there are a lot of things you need to know about me. About my time away from Moondale. I'm not—" Rus paused, sucked in a breath, and reminded herself that communication was good. It was important. That she wasn't going to let herself and Az fall into the trap of not talking again. Even if it wound up hurting her. "I'm not the witch I was before I left. The Board of Magic didn't like me then, but if they knew half the shit I got up to while I was away, they would have locked the wards against me, and I'd never have been able to come back home."

A slow inhale and exhale was Az's first response, calm and measured. She didn't drop her gaze, though, and Rus couldn't read anything there that would lead her to believe Az was about to take her proposal back. About to set the kettle in the sink and walk out the front door without a backward glance. "I want to hear about it," she said in a voice that was quiet but carried. "I want to know all of you."

"Okay." Rus nodded. "Okay."

Somehow, she'd known that's what Az would say. Hadn't dared to hope but had known down in her bones that Az wouldn't cast her aside. Not so easily. Not before she had all the facts. Maybe after she did, she'd light the torches herself that the board would use to burn down everything Rus loved. But not yet. Not before she heard what Rus had to say.

It was a relief. It left Rus feeling small and vulnerable.

She was so used to her past relationships, like Kaytee, where she'd lay things on the line like this and people would tread on them. Tell her she was being ridiculous. Ridicule her. Make fun of her. Shout their beliefs louder over the sounds of Rus's protestations until Rus stopped protesting entirely because it was just easier. But Az wasn't like that. Not anymore, at least. There had been a time where she would have chastised Rus for her actions, where she would have tried to urge Rus toward the "light" side of magic. Where she would uphold the board and their laws without a second thought.

Eleven years—almost twelve at this point—was the distance between that girl and the woman who stood before Rus now. And Rus was... She was grateful they'd had that time apart. To grow. To learn. To become the people they were now. The ones who could look each other in the eye and be honest with each other even when they were afraid.

"Aihuan and Darcy aren't the only ones I brought back over the years." This was the truth that hurt the least to say and the one that would have driven past-Az away the easiest. "There have been others."

Az chewed on this information for a moment, her jaw working in tandem with her thoughts. For a second Rus thought maybe she'd ask her how many, and Rus would have to be honest and say she wasn't sure anymore. That sometimes she blocked the rituals out to the point where she didn't even know if they'd been successful. But that there'd been enough of them that should the board find out, they might burn her at the stake á la Salem-witch-trials.

But instead, she merely nodded. "You'll tell me about the others?"

"In my own time, if that's all right. They weren't always so peaceable as this one." And sometimes someone else had to die to make them work. The logistics were something she wasn't ready to discuss with Az. Not right now. "And I'm very tired." She pouted a little for the sheer dramatics of it.

Az rolled her eyes and returned to filling the kettle.

With it full and on the burner, she turned back to Rus, her arms crossed over her chest, her jaw set. "I still want to marry you. And you never did answer me."

Rus blew out a breath, fond and annoyed all in one. Goddess, if there was one thing about Azure Elwood that hadn't changed, it was her stubborn streak. "Don't you want someone better than me?" she teased, although the words left her feeling raw, rubbing against her skin like sandpaper. "Someone who the Board of Magic won't run out of town if they find out all of the shit they did."

"If they run you out of town, I'm coming with you," Az said with an air of finality that Rus could hardly argue with.

"Goddess." Rus laughed, exasperated. "In all the best ways, you haven't changed at all."

Az tilted her head, her lips twitching at the corners in a small, fond, secretive smile. "And in all the best ways, you have. You wouldn't have talked to me about this before. You'd just have hidden it."

"*Hidden* is such a strong word." Rus chuckled to herself. "I never hid what I did from you or the board."

"No. You hid what it cost you. You refused to show me your weakness and let me help." It was an accusation as much as it was a statement, but it didn't sting. Not the way the truth normally did.

Still, Rus winced. It was too close to the things Rus didn't want to say.

"I'll keep asking until you give me a definitive answer," Az said. "You can feed me all the excuses you want. You can say it's a Wednesday and you've never wanted to be proposed to on a Wednesday. You can tell me that I ought to look to one of the traditional witch families. Argue that I won't want to be with someone who's literally haunted. Any ridiculous notion that strikes, you can throw at me. Tell me all your insecurities. Tell me everything you're worried about. Anything that stands in the way of us being together. I want to hear it all. But until you say the word *no*, I will keep asking you."

Rus blinked at her, wide eyed, shocked. Her jaw slack, her breath lodged in her throat. She'd known Az was stubborn. It was the thing she loved most about her. But... but she'd never thought Az would be this stubborn about *her*.

"Have I made myself clear?"

Goddess. What had Rus ever done to deserve this woman? Who had she been in her former life to warrant someone who wanted her so fiercely that she was willing to face down the barrel of rejection like this? She must have been a saint. She must have saved millions. She must have been the kind of person who was in history books. That was the only explanation for this.

"Icarus. Have I made myself clear?"

Rus nodded numbly. What else could she do? Because the truth was, as much as she rightly believed that Az deserved more, better, Rus was too fucking selfish to actually say no.

"Good. Then, here goes a second attempt." Az crossed the kitchen in what felt like a single step and tilted Rus's chin back with careful fingers to look up at her. "Will you marry me?"

Rus's mouth was dry. Her eyes darted around Az's face. Goddess above and below, Az was serious. She was *so* fucking serious. And Rus loved her so fucking much. But... but Az still didn't know the whole of it. "Az, you don't even have a ring!"

Az smiled, blindingly beautiful and bright. "I can fix that." Then she dipped down to kiss Rus, pressing their lips together with just the right amount of pressure, her teeth snagging on Rus's lower lip as she pulled away. "I'm going to go get the girls up. Should we do eggs for breakfast?"

"Eggs sound nice."

"IT'S ONLY TEMPORARY," Rus said as the group of them all crowded around the little kitchen table of 157 Mourning Moore. Eric sat in the middle of Hunter and Tony, with Ava's chair pushed so close to Hunter's that she was practically in his lap. Vanessa was beside her, though she was keeping a more respectable distance. Rus's kitchen had never felt so cramped before, and she'd never been more thankful about the fact that her girls were morning people and thus didn't require a lot of prompting to get them off to school. Az piddled around the kitchen, making tea, while Rus faced them with a tired kind of determination.

"What do you mean *temporary*?" Tony snarled.

"I mean, I bought you six months." Rus scrubbed at her face, it still itched from the blood. She hated having to give this kind of news. It wasn't fair, but it was the way of things. And it was better they know now than have their time run out on them.

"I don't understand." Hunter's voice was quiet, lost.

"Necromancy is about balance," Rus explained, her fingers threaded together on the table to keep her hands still. They were overwhelmed enough—no sense adding to it. "It's hard to explain, but the easiest way to understand it is that it's about possibility. People like to think of it as a life for a life, but that's not really how it works. Every life has its own cosmic value. One isn't better than the other, but—"

She paused, sucking in a breath. "Think of it like stones in a stream. Some stones displace more water than others. Some take up more space than others. And some can divert the current entirely to erode the shore. In order to keep the stream flowing as close to the way it had been before to keep rip currents from forming, and damage from being caused, every life I bring back to the world, I have to remove another that's almost exactly the same."

"So a cow wasn't enough," Tony grumbled.

"No. A cow wasn't enough." Rus shook her head. "The only creature that would have been close to equal value was another Venator. And as there are so few of them, and I don't think you really wanted us to go out and murder—"

"No," Eric said.

"Then what do we do?" Ava whispered. She hadn't looked away from Eric this entire time, like she was afraid he'd disappear right before her eyes. They all were doing that. Rus wished she could give them better news.

"You're going to have to cheat death." Rus's mouth ticked up at one corner in a smirk.

"How?" Hunter frowned, his brows knitted together.

"Easiest method? Go find a vampire and have him turned. Given the nature of being a Venator, I'd suggest finding an old one. The older the better, in fact. Less likely your Venator blood will attack the virus and just wipe it out." Rus reached into her pocket and pulled out her phone. "I'll put you in touch with Bat, she might be able to help you find someone."

"Okay," Hunter and Tony said as one, nodding their understanding, grave determination lining their features.

Chapter 3

Rus was still shaky two days later when the new moon rolled around. The date of the induction ceremony for Ava and Hunter, the newest members of her coven. Their tattoos were already drawn on their skin. Their pledges were already made to the Coven of the Forgotten. All that was left was to ask Moondale for her blessing. To bow at her feet and pray she approved of the decisions Az and Rus had made to expand their coven. That she didn't reject Ava and Hunter because they called Ironport home, not Moondale.

There was no way to tell for sure that she would. Moondale had always been fickle, and arguably Rus could have taken Hunter's boyfriend being killed by a vampire as a sign that perhaps Moondale didn't approve. But that happened in Ironport, and when she'd done the ritual to bring Eric back on Moondale land, Moondale hadn't fought her on it. In fact, it was perhaps the easiest necrotic ritual she'd ever done. Sliding into the After and finding where Eric had settled had been like cutting through butter with a warm knife.

It was unclear to her what his resting place had been like, but getting him back into his mortal shell was more of a struggle than she'd been prepared for. Almost like he didn't want to return to the plane of the living. Like he didn't want to go back into the body that had failed him. If it had been anyone else, she wouldn't have forced it the way she did. If the dead wanted to stay dead, that was their business.

But looking at Hunter now, where he stood across the clearing from her in black jeans, a black dress shirt, and a crimson velvet blazer that looked like it might be Eric's—given the width of the shoulders—she could see that she'd made the right decision. Eric and Tony weren't allowed to stay for the ceremony, but they both hovered around him, moons in orbit. Tony refused to leave Eric's side while Eric futzed with a crimson pocket square in Hunter's jacket.

The look suited him. Black for his coven, for the people he would tie himself to in a magical sense. Red for the vampire hunters—the Venator—he'd given his heart to. Rus approved.

Hunter shifted nervously, his brows drawn up, but he also looked relieved. His hands lifted but didn't touch Eric. Like he was still not sure that he was real.

"We need to begin soon," Az said softly, her voice carrying across the clearing.

She was in the same black velvet dress she'd worn to their last induction ceremony. Rus and Nando had reworn their own black velvet attire as well. Between them, Hunter, and Ava's tea-length black velvet dress, they looked like a murder of five crows against the browning grass that surrounded the Heart of Moondale.

Hunter dipped to press a kiss to Eric's lips, his fingers brushing against his jaw, and Rus turned away to focus instead on ushering Aihuan and Meiling back to the edges of the clearing where they'd stood during the last ceremony. Indigo stood waiting for them, a soft smile on his face as he watched, like he couldn't be prouder of his sister and her coven. Perhaps he couldn't be. Perhaps he saw what Az had done for Rus and her family and thought it was the right thing. Rus would have to ask to know.

"You really didn't have to come," Rus murmured to Carmine Elwood as she brushed past Indigo and followed her to the large moss-covered stone at the center of the clearing. The moss was purple now, thanks to the warmer weather and the shifting magic, but its colors would change as the season turned colder.

Carmine still looked sickly after her close call with the soul jumper a few weeks ago, but she didn't back down from Rus's raised brow. "As if I'd let Azure's coven proceed without my blessing."

"You already gave us your blessing when we had the first ceremony." But even as Rus said it, warmth blossomed in her chest. It was good to know they had Carmine on their side. That even if Violet still wasn't speaking to any of them, the Elwoods hadn't disowned Az simply because she left their coven for Rus. It felt oddly like family in a way Rus had only known with Cagney and Phyre growing up.

"I did," Carmine agreed. Their clothing shushed softly against the grass as they approached the rest of the group, passing Eric and Tony on their way.

"Thank you." There was so much more that Rus wanted to say. She wanted to tell Carmine that Az had proposed to her. That someday soon they might officially be family. She wondered what Carmine would make of that. Whether she'd approve or not. She had to have known that Az planned to do it. Az wasn't exactly subtle. But that didn't change the fact that maybe she wouldn't give her blessing for that particular change.

Carmine tilted her head to look at Rus, her eyes narrowing to drink her in, to assess her, and find her...

worthy? If the slight uptick of her mouth meant anything, then yes, worthy.

Huh. Rus was worthy.

She couldn't remember the last time someone had done that. Looked her over as if to weigh her worth and not found her wanting.

"Of course," Carmine said, simple as that, then turned back to where they'd been headed and pulled her athame from a sheath at her side.

The rest of Rus's coven moved into a circle around the Heart of Moondale, the pale stone gleaming in the moonlight through the moss. Its magic felt different today than the last time she'd been there. There was a quiet to it that didn't settle right with her. Like the eye of a storm. The lull between one set of events and another.

It felt as if life had been near nonstop chaos since she'd returned to Moondale almost a year ago, the cooling October air reminded her. Witch hunters. Possessive—literally—exes. Soul jumpers. Rus didn't think she wanted to know what the tiny town of Moondale had in store for her next, but as she lifted her head and looked at the group of witches that surrounded her—coven—she knew that she'd be all right. They would face down whatever this next threat was together.

"Let us begin." Carmine sliced into her hand, the blood leaving a red streak that glittered in the moonlight as she passed the blade to Az at her left before it was passed back to Rus at her right.

The order of things was important, Rus knew that. To establish the connection with the Heart for the new members, they needed to ensure someone paved the way, and the easiest method to do that was by those who had been a part of this place for longer going first. Those with the deepest connection to the heart would open the path. Rus didn't mention that she'd come up to the Heart by herself and asked questions of it without the permission of the board not but a few weeks ago.

Once the blade had been passed between all of them, and the subtle drip, drip, drip of blood against stone echoed through the silence of the clearing, Carmine started the soft chant that would wake the Heart. Az, Rus, and Nando, who had done this already, joined her, followed by Hunter and Ava once they'd picked up on the rhythm and words.

The stone glowed more brightly in the moonlight.

The wind picked up around them, rustling through the slowly drying leaves.

A chill slipped up Rus's spine, tickling the back of her neck.

That wasn't good. She took a moment to breathe, then glanced to her left and right from the corners of her eyes. There were no visible signs of a shade lurking around them. Not that she could see from her limited perspective. But with the way the cold lingered on her lower back, she'd lay money that it was behind her. Waiting. For what?

She could stop the ritual, but she knew if she did that at this point, they'd have to wait for the next moon cycle to try again. This one would be a wash. And with the prophecy hanging over their heads, she didn't like the idea of not having her entire coven at their full capabilities when it happened. Even if Ava and Hunter wouldn't be in town, technically, should shit hit the fan.

No. She couldn't let whatever it was interrupt them. But what if that's what it wanted? What if it was waiting for them to be at their most vulnerable, pressing magic into the Heart of Moondale to attack?

And how had it gotten into the clearing to begin with?

There was so much warding magic guarding the Heart of Moondale, it didn't make any sense that a malevolent spirit would be able to get close enough for her to feel it. Maybe it was attached to one of them? Maybe it was already there?

Keeping up the soft chant, she shifted her attention to her girls at her back, listening for any chatter or discontent, but there was nothing. No sound at all from the two little mediums she'd been raising for the last year and a half. Then whatever it was, it was remaining hidden. That didn't bode well either. She didn't like this.

If she were closer to Az, Rus might be able to ask her to throw out some warding talismans just in case. She always had some on her. Az was constantly prepared. It was one of the things Rus loved most about her. But Carmine stood between them.

The chant died slowly, those who had started latest ending first while Carmine kept on for at least a half minute after Az stopped. Then she leaned forward and pressed her bleeding hand into the stone. The others followed. The harsh rock scraped against Rus's already-sore palm. She really hated the ritualistic bullshit of cutting one's palm. It didn't make sense, and it was always a bitch to heal after, but she wasn't going to question the requirements of this ritual.

The chill at the base of her spine burned colder, making Rus shiver. Her muscles jerked. Everyone looked at her as if worried.

The stone beneath her hand glowed brighter. Brighter. Brighter. *Blinding.*

Power zipped from her veins into the rock and then back into her, an endless loop that wasn't completely foreign to Rus. It was the amount that was staggering. She buckled under it, tried to pull her hand back, but it was like when someone touches an electric current. She was stuck.

Someone screamed. Something hit the ground.

A jolt sparked in her knees.

Still the Heart refused to release her, the magic flowing in and out of her like a live wire.

She couldn't help but think it was trying to tell her something. Trying to show her something. Moondale just didn't have the power right now to do that. That's why she kept taking Rus's magic—the witch with the lowest barriers after her recent dally in the After—then cycling it back to her.

Finally, someone grabbed her by the wrist and ripped her hand away from the stone. Rus trembled in the cold, pressing herself to the warmth of Az's chest. She'd sunk to her knees in the grass right alongside Rus, likely ruining her beautiful gown.

"What *was* that?" Ava asked, her voice shaking with fear.

Right. The newbies. They didn't know Moondale the way Rus did. They hadn't seen down into her. Hadn't chatted with her. Didn't yet know her ghosts and her idiosyncrasies. Of course they'd be shaken by what just happened.

"I think Moondale was trying to tell me something." Rus brushed her sweaty hair back from her face, taking a deep breath that shook only slightly on the exhale. "Did the rest of the ritual go through?"

"Yes," Carmine answered. She was close, her hands extended as if she, too, had reached for Rus when she realized what was happening. "Your new initiates won't feel the power increase yet. Not until after the centennial."

"Right. Okay." The centennial. Of course. Moondale was low on her reserves, Rus knew that. But that also meant so were her magical creatures. They all were suffering from the slow draw it took to keep the town running for a century. Maybe even more so now than in previous years, considering the rise in population.

"We should head back," Nando said when no one else spoke for what seemed like too long a time.

"Are you all all right?" Eric asked once he'd been given the all-clear from Indigo to rush across the clearing like a stag on wobbly legs. "That was scary."

"We're fine, hon," Hunter assured. He looked shaken, though, like maybe he had seen more than he should have. Had the Heart used Rus as a means to communicate something to the others? Or was Hunter just wigged out by what happened?

"Back to the house then." Az reached down to help Rus to her feet, supporting much of her weight even once she was there. Fuck, when had Rus become so dependent on her? "There's snacks and drinks there. That will help settle some of the afterburn."

She met Rus's eyes, and Rus could practically hear what she wasn't saying. *And we can discuss what the fuck just happened as a coven.* And yeah... yeah, Rus liked the sounds of that.

"Az is right. It's late enough as is, and we've all still got centennial prep in the morning. One last hurrah before the gates open and we're flooded with normies. Let's go back to the house and chat." Rus pasted on a smile, but she was pretty sure everyone saw right through it. Especially Carmine, who was looking at her like she wanted to shove Rus into one of Greer's interrogation rooms down at the police station and get some answers. Yikes.

A collective grumble of agreement went through the group, and they moved as one toward the cars parked at the edge of the wood.

Chapter 4

Azure didn't know what the people who lived in 155 Mourning Moore prior to it becoming their coven house had been like, what sort of life they'd had. They may have been quiet, well-mannered folks, or they might have thrown parties. For all that she'd lived her entire life down the street from the house, she knew surprisingly little about her neighbors. But that didn't matter as the house belonged to the Forgotten now, and it seemed to relish this new hustle and bustle.

Plates and cups appeared aplenty for the lot of them. The rooms were free of dust and any evidence of the ritual that had taken place there a couple days prior—including the lingering metallic scent of blood. The house so pleased to have people within its walls, it practically hummed its approval.

Azure leaned on the doorframe, watching her coven, her family, chatter happily, the way Rus had reacted to the ceremony momentarily forgotten. They'd have to talk about it at some point, if not tonight, then tomorrow. Azure wasn't going to let Rus weasel her way out of explaining. Not when she'd seen the way Rus buckled under whatever that was back there. Not when she'd nearly lost Rus enough times over the last year to know that sometimes Rus kept things to herself until they festered, until they ate away at her, until there was almost nothing left. She was a self-sacrificing idiot who didn't want to bother anyone with her pain. But they were working on that.

"Get in here, Az, we're toasting our success," Rus called from the living room, an antique coupe glass filled with champagne in her hand. The glasses had appeared with everything else. Azure wasn't sure where the house had gotten them from. She hoped it hadn't conjured them from its previous owners, who were now living across town.

Shaking herself, a smile tilting one corner of her lips, Azure made her way over to Rus and took the glass from her, leaning in to brush a kiss to Rus's cheek that left Rus blushing. Silly, really, considering all they'd done since Rus had been back.

Rus cleared her throat and reached for another glass off the coffee table before holding it aloft and saying, "To the Forgotten."

"To the Forgotten," the group echoed, clinked their glasses, and drank.

Power buzzed around them, making Azure's hair stand on end. She'd been a part of a coven before, but it had never felt this electric, this close. The Circle of Jade Waters was too large to feel this tightly knit with her fellow witches. It had even expanded beyond the boundaries of Moondale, which made it more powerful but changed the dynamic. Azure liked this better.

As the group fell into soft chatter, companionable and easy, Azure took a step back to lean against the mantel and silently watch, a smile gracing her lips. It was good to be here like this with these witches. Good to see Ava and Hunter settling in so easily with Fernando and Rus. Good to know that they were no longer alone in this. Whatever came for them next, they wouldn't have to face it by themselves.

"We did good, didn't we?" Rus asked, bumping her shoulder against Azure's just before she reached down with her free hand to thread their fingers together. A pleasant hum of magic welled between them. Their innate power recognizing each other now as something important to one another. Not quite family, but well on its way to being that and more.

"We did," Azure agreed. The urge to drop to her knees and ask Rus to marry her again swept through her, but she still hadn't gotten the ring cleaned, and she wouldn't ask again until then. Good thing she had an appointment with Phyre after her meeting about the centennial for the final prep phase tomorrow. She wasn't looking forward to walking through town to ensure everything was exactly where it was meant to be early in the morning with the others, but she couldn't snub her nose at her duty. Especially not now. The Coven of the Forgotten depended on them keeping up appearances, which included her performing her responsibilities as an elder. "I think Hunter and Ava fit quite well into the tapestry of a coven we're weaving."

Rus scoffed fondly. "Only you would try to sound all wise and poetic at a time like this."

Azure lifted a brow in question but didn't say anything. She was used to Rus's teasing by now, and it left behind the faint tingle of warmth in her veins. They weren't getting back to normal, not really, as they'd never been this free, this open, this comfortable with one another when they were first dating in their late teens and early twenties. Rus had always been holding something back, and Azure could hardly blame her for it. She'd been less than accepting of Rus and all that she was. Things were different now.

Still, what happened at the Heart of Moondale hung in

the air between them. An unsaid, unquestioned thing. A silence spread between them as Rus watched the others and Azure watched her, waiting. She'd push if she had to, but some idealistic part of her hoped they'd grown past that.

Rus seemed to sense it, too, because she sighed. "I'm not sure what happened back there."

"But you have a theory."

Rus always had a theory. She was too bloody smart not to. And maybe Azure was biased, but it seemed to her that Rus had only gotten more intelligent since returning to Moondale. It was like she applied everything she'd learned while out in the big wide world to the study of Moondale and how she worked. And—again biased, but not untrue, opinion—it was super sexy.

"I think she was trying to tell me something." Rus rubbed at her eyes tiredly. She'd set down her glass of champagne at some point, but Azure wasn't sure when. She likely hadn't even finished it, too exhausted from the ceremony to drink anything that would only make her drowsier. Azure should really take her home. They had a long day ahead of them.

"Something about the centennial? About what's coming?" Azure pressed. The world had been too quiet since Taryn disappeared. Even the spirits of Moondale had settled. It wasn't right. Not with how chaotic things had been before Taryn was defeated and with her body never being found. She wasn't gone. Nor was the soul jumper. And whatever hung over their heads with the warning of the prophecy wasn't going anywhere either. So why were things so quiet?

"I think so. But she didn't have enough power to tell me. Not during the induction ceremony, at least." Rus scrubbed at the tip of her nose, a thoughtful gesture.

"You want to go back out there and see what she has to say." It wasn't a question. Nor was it an accusation, honestly. Azure could see the benefit to doing something like that. She wanted answers as much as Rus did. The more they knew about what was coming for Moondale, the better off they would be. "We can go tomorrow night, after our classes."

"I could just go up there while—"

"No." Azure shock her head. "We'll go together. You're not doing this alone anymore, remember? I'm here. We all are. And if something is coming for Moondale, it's not your sole responsibility to fight it. We'll fight it together."

Rus tilted her head for a moment, her eyes still focused on their small group clustered together in the living room of 155 Mourning Moore. Eric, Hunter, and Ava were stuffed on the couch together while Tony sat on the coffee table, facing them as they talked. He wasn't saying anything, but Azure could see the way he refused to take his eyes off Eric. The desperate need for them all to remain close. She understood it, perhaps better than they'd ever know. Fernando, Indigo, and Vanessa were in three armchairs that they'd pulled close together as they talked, Aihuan asleep on Fernando's lap, and Meiling leaning against the leg of the chair, her head listing like she might pass out at any moment.

Their coven.

"It's hard to break the habit of doing everything myself," Rus said after a long silence. She turned to look at Azure, her gaze pleading for Azure to understand. To not be angry with her about this small slip.

"I understand that." Azure reached for Rus, and Rus came willingly, wrapping her arms around her middle. "And I'll keep reminding you as frequently as you need."

Rus nodded, hooking her chin over Azure's shoulder as she curled around her like a cat. She was nearly a full head taller than Azure, lean and willowy, but that didn't mean she didn't seem small sometimes when Azure held her close. Fragile in a way Azure had never noticed before she'd left Moondale all those years ago. Whether that was because Rus let her see it now, or because Azure wasn't blinded by her biases anymore, there was no way to tell. And it didn't really matter anyway.

"We'll go tomorrow. I get out of class just before dinner. We'll head back to the house, get the girls settled with their homework, and then Blue can take us up the mountain. Do we need to prepare anything to make the conversation easier?" *And safer*, Azure didn't say. Because she knew how Rus felt about such precautions, especially when they came to herself. They were working on that too. On Rus realizing that she couldn't throw herself to the wind just because it made some things simpler. She couldn't leave behind her girls, her family, her coven, her Azure.

"I'll give it some thought tomorrow," Rus promised. "When I spoke to the Heart last time, I just gave it blood and set my intentions."

"But it wasn't as drained then."

Rus hummed thoughtfully, turning her head, her chin digging into Azure's shoulder as she shifted so she could look at their group again. "We could ask the coven to charge some crystals, maybe. Then the Heart would have something to draw on besides me. It was creating a feedback loop up there, because it wanted to draw on me, but it also wanted to give me its power."

"That should alleviate some of the strain and the danger." Anything to protect Rus was a good idea in Azure's book. "Anything else?"

There was another long moment as Rus thought. She was a clever woman, always had been, but Azure knew she'd hardly ever turned her thoughts to her own safety. "I'll take Darcy this time. He can act as my tether, since he won't draw on the magic of Moondale directly either."

"Lizzie can come as well. I know she can't act as a tether, but it's always better to have two familiars than just one." Azure smoothed her fingers over the fabric at Rus's back. They were all still in their ceremonial attire, and the velvet felt good against her skin. "Do we need the others there?"

"No. I think they'll just pose more of a distraction." Rus shook her head, her hair tickling Azure's bare neck. "But we will need to ward the area with our own wards."

Azure pulled away from the embrace to wrinkle her brow at Rus in confusion. "The Heart already has wards."

"They're not enough." Rus sighed, scrubbing at her nose again, nervous now. "There was something in the clearing with us tonight. Something I couldn't see, but I felt it there. It might have been harmless, but I don't want to take any chances with the soul jumper coming home to roost."

"Do you think that's what it was?" Worry dragged Azure's stomach to her feet, everything she'd eaten and drank souring. She knew the soul jumper returning was always a possibility, an inevitability, but she'd thought it wouldn't be right away. She'd thought they'd have more than just a couple of months reprieve.

"I don't know. Soul jumpers don't like to remain bodiless for long, so my best guess is no, it wasn't the soul jumper." Rus's fingers tapped a rhythm against Azure's shoulders, her jaw working as she chewed on the inside of her cheek. "We should probably determine what it was, if it's still there, too. I'll get everything together to hold a séance as well."

"I don't like this."

"I don't either, but we're working with what we've got right now." Rus smiled at her, that soft, sweet smile that made Azure's knees weak. "And like you said, I'm not doing this alone anymore."

Azure inhaled deeply and bent to press her lips to Rus's forehead. "I'll go get some crystals."

"Perfect, I'll explain what we need from our coven."

They separated and went to work. It was going to be a long couple of days.

Chapter 5

Things should have been harder for Azure without Taryn to help her along through the last-minute things that came the day before the centennial celebration officially started. Without someone else in charge, another set of hands, most would assume that Azure would be spread thinner than usual. But the thing was this: Without Taryn there to question her every move and make her explain herself, everything was actually going smoothly.

Until it wasn't.

"What do you mean, the tables were never delivered?" Azure asked.

There was a headache building along the bridge of her nose, all her stress settling there like a band that would eventually wrap the entire way around her skull and leave her in agony. She just wanted to go home and lie down. To press her face into Rus's lap while her girlfriend brushed her fingers through her hair and massaged her scalp. But no. She was here. Before dawn. After a long night with the coven, preparing for their return to the Heart this evening. Not even Nando's magically augmented tea could mitigate the effects of four nights in a row of not enough sleep.

"They didn't show up." Jennifer shrugged. She was one of the younger members of the Crimson Tide, and she didn't seem overly interested in what they were doing here. Which was just silly, considering it was the Coven of the Crimson Tide that kept the wards maintained, constantly on watch for holes and patching cracks when they appeared. Azure would assume that someone who was that intimate with the protections of Moondale would understand the necessity of charging the Heart of Moondale correctly. But she was young, early twenties at the oldest, and Azure was finding that many of the folk that age just didn't understand the full ramifications of the centennial.

"They were signed for." Azure flipped through her email to pull up the notification she'd received that the tables had, indeed, been delivered. She clicked the PDF to open it, as she had that morning over the breakfast table when the email came in, to check the signature on the document. Signatures were notoriously hard to read, but she remembered this one being clear enough that she could make out the first few letters, although at this point she couldn't remember what they were.

Her phone didn't do anything.

Where that morning the PDF had popped right up and allowed her to check it, now nothing happened. She tried again, holding her thumb over the document for a half second longer in case she just hadn't hit it hard enough. Honestly, she didn't understand technology well enough to know. That was Rus's department. But again, nothing.

With a scoff, Azure clicked and held the PDF until something happened. Unfortunately, the thing that happened was a notification that the file had been corrupted somehow. Which didn't make any sense. She'd glanced at it only an hour ago before leaving the house!

"What do you want from me?" Jennifer asked, defensive. "I didn't sign for them, and they're not here."

"Okay." Azure took a breath, pinching the bridge of her

nose where the throb of her headache was only growing more intense.

Fuck. She still had the visit with Phyre and classes to get through today. And even then, her day wouldn't be over. Because she couldn't let Rus go back to the Heart of Moondale alone. Why did everything have to hit the fan at the exact same moment?

"Okay," she repeated. "I'm going to call around and see if I can get us some tables. In the meantime, I want you and the others to see if we can't figure out where they ended up. If we can't find them, we won't get our deposit back."

"Sure." Jennifer nodded, but she didn't look overly enthused about the idea of having to run around and search for the literal hundreds of tables they'd ordered for this event.

Fuck. Maybe it would have been easier with someone like Taryn on her side. At least then she'd have someone to stay on top of everyone. As it was, she'd become the de facto leader and had no one else to help share the responsibility. She should have asked Violet for help, but her relationship with Violet was... still strained, at best. Not that Azure could blame her. Azure did help Rus essentially run Violet's wife out of town. The fact that Violet's wife had been possessed by a soul jumper didn't matter when it came to feelings. There was no rationalizing with heartbreak. Azure knew that.

With Jennifer off searching for the tables, Azure clicked Ava's number in her contacts. If she couldn't count on her board-mandated group to get this done, at least she was sure she could count on her coven. They had already proven themselves willing to do anything they could to help.

"What's up?" Ava asked when she picked up, her clothes shuffling near the speaker, which meant she'd probably put the phone on her shoulder as she worked on something else. Maybe stocking at her small yarn shop over in Ironport.

"Do you think the university has any fold-up tables I could borrow for our event?" Probably not enough, but between the university and asking the citizens of Moondale themselves to contribute, she might be able to hobble together the numbers.

"Probably. Do you need Nessy's number?"

"If you wouldn't mind. I could call the dean's office, but there's no guarantee that she's there, and this is an emergency."

If they didn't have the tables there and set up by the following morning, the centennial couldn't go along as planned. All the vendors would be without vendor spaces to sell their wares. Which would disgruntle them, along with those who had already planned to come to the event. That negativity would feed into the ley lines of Moondale. Azure didn't want to think of the danger that posed to the Heart itself. Everyone who lived here was tied to the Heart of Moondale, whether they were folk or not. Even those without magic ate the food, drank the water, lived on the soil. What they needed, Moondale provided. And any potentially ill effects from the centennial not going according to plan would be catastrophic for all of them.

"Yeah, just hang on." There was more shifting on the other end of the line, then Azure's phone buzzed against her ear. She didn't have to pull it away to know that Ava had forwarded her Vanessa Cochburn's contact information. "I have a couple of tables in the back of my shop for when I do sidewalk sales," Ava continued once the phone was back against her ear. "If you need me to, I can bring them down."

"That would be wonderful. Thank you." Azure couldn't

help but smile. She had known, always, this was what a coven was meant to be like. That they were meant to be able to call on one another in times of trouble, to support one another. But there was always this dissonance between knowing that and feeling it with the Circle of Jade Waters, which was so large that it felt hard to reach out to anyone.

"Of course." Ava clicked her tongue. "Anything else you need?"

"Not currently."

"I'll check in and see if any other businesses in my area have tables you can borrow too," Ava offered, unprompted.

"You really don't have to. I'm sure—"

"Did I say I had to?" There was a gruffness to Ava's tone that Azure found she appreciated. She was used to kindness coming from the people most would think least likely to give it. From the necromancer. From the gruff blacksmith. From the eldritch horror that was an elder on the board. It just... It made sense to her somehow. Kindness and niceness were different, after all.

"No. I suppose not." Azure's grin stretched further, unstoppable. They had made the right choice in adding Ava and Hunter to their ranks, in finding a way to work around their need to live outside of Moondale. Even if she'd been unsure of it at first. "Let me know what numbers you've got by end of day, if you could? I need them here tomorrow morning so the vendors can set up."

"Will do." Then Ava hung up.

THE ISSUE of tables settled as if by magic, Azure moved on to her next task for the day: a semi-awkward meeting with Phyre. Rus had forgiven Phyre easily for ratting them out to Brant Ironwood some months ago, but Azure had no such ability. She tended to hold a grudge, be petty and vindictive, and make people pay for the choices they made. It was just a little harder to do when those people happened to be those that Rus considered family. So here they were.

"Would you like some tea?" Phyre asked, fidgeting where she sat across from Azure on the couch in the small back room off the jewelry store the Ironwoods ran to keep their blacksmith business afloat. It was a comfortable space to speak to clients. Azure could see how it would work well when discussing changes in designs and the necessary functionality of one's athame—a witch's most important tool. None of that meant she had to feel comfortable in Phyre's presence.

"No, thank you." It was said with perhaps a little more bite than necessary. Azure sighed. She promised Rus she would at least try. The problem was that she'd never really had much of a relationship with Phyre to begin with. They were friendly when they saw each other at functions or on the street, sure. But she'd never gone out of her way to sit down with Phyre and actually talk. Their sole connection was Rus, and when Phyre betrayed her, she'd kind of fucked that all up.

"Right." Phyre shifted uncomfortably on the couch. It groaned under her movement, as if unused to accommodating such awkwardness. "I've apologized to Rus about what I did. And I'm doing my best to..." She paused, her gaze flicking about the room as if checking to be sure they were alone. "To mitigate some of Brant's influence."

"I know." That didn't mean Azure had to forgive her. Just like Violet didn't have to forgive Azure simply because she'd been proven right that Taryn was awful. People were allowed to have their feelings about things. "Can we get started?"

"Right. Of course." The couch groaned again as Phyre grabbed a pad from the coffee table, and a pen. "You'll need two athames for your new coven members. I assume they'll be by at some point to choose their ore."

Azure licked her lips, the box in her pocket jamming into her thigh as if to remind her it was there. Could she trust Phyre with that as well? She'd trusted her to make Rus's pendant, to ward her against the After. Why was this so different? Well, the difference was Phyre had already proven she couldn't keep secrets. "Yes," Azure said after a moment. "They should be by this afternoon. They're bringing some tables to Moondale for the centennial since my order has gone missing."

Phyre nodded. "Do we want the design more akin to yours, or to Rus's? I made Nando's more like Rus's so it would be consistent. But I was thinking, what if we combined the styles of the Elwood athame and the ones we generally make for the covenless to create something... new?"

"We would all need new daggers then." But Azure didn't hate the idea. It would unify them. It would bring them even closer. It would start a new tradition, one that they could all build together. It was... it was a good idea. "Would we be able to reuse the same ore Rus and I chose for our first athame? Or would we need to choose new?"

"I could reuse the same ore." Phyre offered a soft, understanding smile. She knew as well as Azure did how deeply personal that part of their tradition in Moondale was, and she would treat it with respect. It was why the witches of Moondale had always had their own blacksmith family. Why they didn't farm the production of their athame out.

"Then yes, we would like that." She knew without even discussing it with Rus what she'd choose. They wanted unity. They wanted to build something. Rus would understand that the best way forward was to utilize the foundation she and Azure had started to create something new. "We should likely work better wards against spirits into them, too, especially considering what Rus usually uses hers for."

Phyre nodded, scribbling notes onto the pad in her lap. "Any specific design aspects you think you'd like to see?"

Azure pressed her lips together for a moment, thinking. "A spider lily."

Phyre looked up with a smile. "I can make that work."

"How long would production take? Rus needs her athame this evening."

"A couple of weeks total. I could start after the centennial, though, just so no one is left without."

"Waiting would probably be for the best." Azure nodded. She didn't like the thought of Rus not having every tool at her disposal, should the worst come to pass.

"Good." Phyre's smile bloomed pleasantly, like she approved of Azure's decisions. She likely did. She was Rus's elder sister in everything but name. It was what was going to make the next part of this conversation so awkward. "I'll start on some sketches right away."

"In the meantime," Azure said, her fingers trembling as she reached into her pocket to pull out the velvet box, "I assume you know how to magically size rings?"

Phyre's head jerked up. Her smile fell for a moment, then came back twice as large with a hint of mischief.

Goddess, was Azure really so transparent? "I do. It's one of my specialties. What do you need sized?"

"I have this—" Azure swallowed around a dry tongue and opened the box. The hinge creaked, but the gemstones sparkled in the warm lights of the room. She'd been sure to keep it on the off chance that she needed it, and now it'd seem she finally did. In the center of an intricately engraved white gold band sat two stones. One salt and pepper, the other a pale sapphire. They curved around each other like yin and yang, set so close together they looked like they might be a single stone.

The design felt even more symbolic now. A true representation of Azure's love for Rus.

"Oh Azure," Phyre gasped. "She's going to love that."

Azure nodded. It was a relief to hear that from someone who knew Rus as well as Phyre did. It meant maybe it was true. "I bought it when we were together... before..."

"And you want to use it to propose finally?"

"I already have." Azure huffed a laugh that was equal parts fond and annoyed. "But she hasn't said yes yet. Her last argument was I didn't have a ring."

Phyre tilted her head for a moment, then chuckled softly. "I see. Well, I should be able to have this ready by this afternoon. If you want to leave it with me and come back after your classes?"

"That is satisfactory." Azure nodded, shut the lid, and passed it to Phyre before her mind could catch up with the fact that she was handing something so *very* precious over to someone she didn't entirely trust. Rus trusted Phyre. That would have to be enough.

"I'll take good care of it," Phyre promised, seeming to read Azure's hesitance.

Azure nodded. "Thank you."

Chapter 6

"I don't see why I have to do this," Meiling grumbled, shifting where she sat on the floor of the back porch to the coven house at 155 Mourning Moore. It was after school, and Rus had decided now more than ever was a good time to get some medium practice. They could have done this back at 157, but Rus didn't want to draw anything into their home that she couldn't combat easily. She'd learned her lesson about that, finally.

"Because, A'Ling, you're fourteen. I understand that you're afraid of the spirits, and they make you uncomfortable, but they aren't going anywhere. You can't spend your entire life turning your head to avoid eye contact." Although Rus kind of wished she could. If she could make it easier for Meiling and take this part of her away, she would. She would give Meiling some other ability. Allow her to slip through the present the way Az did. Or touch an object and understand its history as Indigo did. Anything was better than her having inherited Rus's cursed power.

But Meiling had something Rus never did. She had people who understood her ability and wanted to help her learn to use it in a way that was safe. Meiling wouldn't be throwing herself headfirst into a graveyard, hoping for a glimpse of the After without a lifeline to guide her home. Rus would make sure of that.

"Why not?" Meiling's dark eyes flicked about the porch,

as if she might catch a glimpse of the ghosts they had yet to summon.

"Because that's no way to live, sweetheart." Rus leaned forward to take Meiling's hand and give it a firm squeeze. If her parents were here, they'd probably go about this differently. But if they were here, maybe Meiling wouldn't have become a medium at all. There was some superstition about orphans that—

"All right." Meiling's shoulders drooped under the weight of the knowledge that there was no escaping this.

"We'll start small," Rus promised. "We won't call anything that could possibly hurt you. Although I can't promise that they won't be scary. Many spirits don't recognize that they've become something humans might fear. They're not trying to scare you, they're simply existing as they do."

"I know that." Meiling huffed, rolling her eyes.

She knew because Rus had told her over and over again. She'd tried to help with Meiling's fear of the spirits any way she possibly could. But Meiling was getting close to the age where she'd have to fully embrace her power and make choices about where she was heading with it. She couldn't continue to turn a blind eye to what she was capable of. Not just because it wasn't right, but because it was dangerous. A cruel spirit could take issue with her neglect and react badly. A malevolent shade could slip past the barriers she hadn't built up enough and possess her. Rus wasn't going to let Meiling take that kind of chance.

"I know you know." Rus nudged Meiling's knee lightly with her own where they were touching as they faced each other, legs folded in careful lotus poses. "But a reminder is never a bad thing."

Meiling nodded. She still looked afraid, but some of the

tension had eased away from her pinched brow. The reminder that Rus was right in front of her, unwilling to let anything happen to her, even if it was unspoken, seemed to relax her.

"Okay," Meiling said, her fingers flexing around Rus's hand. "Let's get this over with."

"Love the attitude." Rus snorted softly, but she didn't let go of Meiling's hand. She would not let Meiling drift along alone in this world the way she often had. She wouldn't let either of her girls do that. Neither of them would ever have to feel like they had to face the world, and the After, without her. "All right. Close your eyes."

Meiling blinked at her, annoyed, then did as she was instructed.

It would have been easier with some summoning aids, but those things tended to signal too loudly that someone was looking to chat. They drew in every shade for miles with any kind of grievance, but most importantly, they got the attention of those looking for a vulnerable person to take advantage of. It's why Rus had forbidden spirit boards and other such things in their home. It was too dangerous to the girls, who were already compromised by their nature as mediums.

"Good," Rus encouraged gently as she watched Meiling's magic lift slowly from her skin like fog. It hadn't settled on a color yet—she was still too young for that, even if Aihuan's had—but it leaned toward a seafoam blue-green. A mix of Rus's and Az's colors in a way that had Rus's heart jolting in her chest whenever she saw it. She could examine that emotion later. For now, she turned her focus toward letting her own magic gather beneath her skin, should they need it. "Now, this next part is a little harder to explain."

One day Rus was going to have to write some actual

instructions on how this worked. She'd managed to start a blog a bit ago about how to protect oneself from ghosts. But wards and talismans were easy enough to explain. They were something tangible that all living things could feel, even if they weren't folk.

Reaching out to spirits was not.

"It's a feeling," she offered, struggling to find the words. She'd been giving this some thought for weeks and still didn't really have the language to accurately convey to Meiling what she needed to do to open her senses and listen for the whispers. Probably because she'd been hearing them all her life. Ever since she was a child. But she imagined it was similar to how she sometimes called them in. "Like popping your ears, but not literally."

Meiling exhaled, annoyed, and shifted again. "I don't understand."

"You will." Rus knew that without a doubt, because Meiling was a smart, capable young woman. She would grow into her power easily, even if she'd spent years denying it because she was afraid. "Imagine," Rus tried, knowing it sounded ridiculous, "you have headphones in your ears, and you're removing them."

"Won't that open me up to *everything*?" Meiling opened her eyes and fixed Rus with a terrified expression. "And how do I put them back when I'm done?"

"Az had a talisman made a bit ago for you, remember? It'll help muffle them, when you're without supervision. I don't want you listening without me there, at least not yet. Am I clear?"

"Right. Yeah."

"And why do you need supervision?" Rus pressed, because she knew Meiling needed the reminder.

Meiling rolled her eyes in typical teenager fashion but

recited what Rus had told her near verbatim, and it seemed to ease her. "So you can monitor whatever answers my call. So you can keep me safe."

"Exactly. I'm here. I've dealt with a lot of ghosts over the years. Whatever answers your call will not harm you so long as I'm here. I won't let it."

She'd done the work to clear the area of malevolent spirits over the last year, to make sure of that. All it took was a little work on the graveyard that surrounded the two homes now belonging to her and Az. Planting flowers. Cleaning headstones. Listening to the shades who needed an ear. It was the simplest way to protect her girls. To ingratiate herself to the dead of Moondale so they would answer her call when she needed them and circle her grounds to make sure they were all safe. She hadn't had to tear anyone out of their graves in a while; the spirits had been enough. But still.

"Now. Close your eyes. Try again. Breathe deep. Remember that I'm here. And remember that oftentimes, all they want is someone to listen." The dead were much simpler than the living that way. Vengeance was usually off the list of their desires. They just wanted peace, one way or another.

Meiling inhaled deeply and nodded, then did as she was told. It took a few minutes of concentration, but Rus saw it when Meiling's magic shifted, glowing brighter. The whispers began a moment later. They were gentle, unhurried, unlike the ones Rus usually called upon herself to do what she needed.

"Good." Rus kept her tone gentle, encouraging, even as excitement buzzed through her veins. She knew Meiling could do this. She knew she could call upon the ghosts living in the area and speak to them. It was just a matter of teaching her not to be afraid of them. To see them as people instead of monsters. No easy task, but Rus wouldn't quit. "I want you to pluck a voice from the whispers."

"How do I choose?"

"I can't tell you that." Which was unfortunate. This would all be so much easier if Rus could make choices for her girls. If she could tell them what to do and how to act when it came to the dead. But that's not how magic worked, even if the Board of Magic liked to think differently. It couldn't be shoehorned by convention, and Rus had no interest in trying to make it so. "How you decide to interact with the spirits you speak to is up to you. Just remember that they're people, A'Ling. They might not even remember that, but *you* have to. *You* have to treat them with humanity."

Meiling swallowed loudly and nodded. She wasn't straining against the magic, though, and that was an improvement, even for all she was nervous. She was accepting what came. How long that would last, Rus wasn't sure. She only hoped whatever shade Meiling chose to speak to didn't scare her further.

"There's a younger one here. Someone who's— I don't think he's much older than me."

Rus sat up straighter and let her magic flow from her. Just in case. She knew that her girls could repeat her mantra backward and forward—sometimes, like the living, the dead lied—but that didn't mean they'd be able to spot an obvious fib right away. And Rus had a particular mistrust for ghosts who presented themselves as either more vulnerable or close in age to the medium in question. Especially when the spirit was reaching out and it wasn't Rus going off to hunt them down. She'd known too many malevolent creatures that had found ways to shapeshift into forms that would tug on someone's heart-strings.

With a little push that Meiling didn't even seem to notice because she was concentrating instead on the spirit, Rus tapped into the conversation.

"What does he want?" she asked out loud.

Lost. Lost. Lost. The word echoed through her mind like a bell.

"He says he can't find his way into the After. He wants to go, but the way is... confusing." Meiling wrinkled her nose. It was impressive how calm she was now that she wasn't letting her fear get in the way. It likely helped that she wasn't being forced to see the boy hanging over her shoulder. His neck was twisted the wrong way, his face a mottled mess, his eyes hollow voids of darkness. Likely the victim of some "harmless" prank. Rus had seen enough of those in her time.

"All right then. Next steps, I need his name."

"He—" Meling shifted again, her mouth twitching into a sad little moue. "He doesn't remember."

"Okay. That's really common. If he doesn't remember, help him pick one." Rus kept her eyes on the boy. He hadn't shifted or flickered at all. And although he was *looming* in a way that would likely terrify Meiling should she turn around and see him there, he wasn't touching her, not even trying to. His hands were at his sides, peaceable and calm. No trace in his face that he was lying about who he was to trick Meiling.

Meiling sighed a little, as if in relief. "Cecil."

"Cecil is a good name." Rus fixed the boy with a grin and tilted her head when he met her eyes, his own hollow sockets of darkness. "I'll take it from here, Meiling. You did very well for your first séance."

"I did?" Meiling opened her eyes to blink at Rus.

"You did. But I don't think we're going to have you touch the After. Not yet. Not until you're in better control. Okay?"

Meiling jolted when the boy moved around her to stand next to Rus instead. She looked scared, her face paler, but also intolerably sad to see the signs of what had happened to Cecil before he'd died.

Rus held up her free hand, the green of her magic glowing eerie and neon across her skin. "Touch my hand, and I'll help you along, Cecil. If you ever want to come back, ask for Icarus, and you can come back for a visit. Maybe check in with Meiling here, to make sure she's doing okay?" Rus tilted her head in question.

Friend.

"Yes. Meiling and I are your friends. We'll make sure you get where you were supposed to go."

Cecil looked from Rus to Meiling, likely for the reassurance so many spirits sought when they were about to go over. Especially from the witch they'd first been in contact with.

Meiling nodded, offering him a shaky smile. "My mom will take care of you. She's good like that."

Her *mom.* Rus's heart leapt into her throat, her eyes burned with tears, and her magic blazed out of control. She was... she was Meiling's *mom?* Since when? Since... She swallowed. There were other things to worry about right now.

"I've got you," Rus encouraged, her throat tight.

Cecil floated forward and reached for her hand. A tingle ran up her arm, and he smiled, peaceful and content, then he was gone.

Meiling slumped forward, her arms curling tightly around herself.

"Mom, huh?" Rus teased and nudged her knee again.

"Don't get used to it. I was freaked out," Meiling groused, but her neck was hot with embarrassment. "There was someone else who wanted to talk to you in there. But I prioritized Cecil."

"To me?"

"One of your spies, I think," she said, leaning back on her hands and brushing a hand over her face. She looked tired to Rus, but that made sense. After so many years of denying who and what she was, of course it would take a lot out of Meiling to get in touch with that part of herself again. It hadn't ever happened with Rus, because she'd never denied her ability like that.

"All right. I'm going to deal with that. You go into the kitchen and grab a snack. Maybe 155 will make you some cocoa?"

The house responded with a cheerful flickering of the lights, and Meiling rose to leave Rus to it. With her gone, Rus turned her attention to the shadowed corner that had been writhing slightly throughout all of this.

"What did you find?" she asked, making herself more comfortable by leaning against the wicker chair behind her and propping one of her legs up while the other fell straight.

"We lost track of him at the border between Moondale and Ironport," the older woman said. She had a clever face, like a fox. And if Rus didn't know better, she might consider that she hadn't been entirely human nor folk, but Rus had vetted all her spies thoroughly.

"Surely that's not all."

"The souls of Ironport were willing to cooperate. There

is unrest on their land as well. Its root is very likely the soul jumper."

"And what did they tell you?"

"Brant Ironwood met with Taryn Addington. They could not get close enough to hear what was said. The soul jumper is still very much active."

Great. So it was out there terrorizing the spirits of Ironport as well. Rus wondered if maybe she'd need to train Hunter to deal with the dead soon. If the soul jumper continued to stir the pot, he might not get a choice in what specialty he leaned toward. Ironport might choose for him. That happened sometimes.

"And?" That wasn't enough, not to take to the board.

"We think the soul jumper is also interfering in Ironport beyond just the spirit realm."

"Of course." Rus rubbed at the back of her neck where an ache had settled. The beginnings of a migraine. "It couldn't turn Moondale's board against me, so it'll try to turn Ironport's against my coven." Fuck. What was she going to do about this? She didn't have any pull in Ironport. And as far as she knew, neither did Hunter and Ava or their little family unit of vampire hunters.

All that was left to her was to lure the soul jumper back to Moondale and force it into the After. This was going to *suck*.

Chapter 7

"I don't like it." Which shouldn't have been terribly surprising to Rus. There was a lot to not like about her plan. Azure was just being the levelheaded one of the two of them, as per usual. Not that she minded. But she had hoped that maybe when Rus said they'd do this together, she'd also include the rest of Moondale. Apparently not.

"I don't either. Trust me." Rus exhaled slowly as she focused on tacking talismans to the trees in the clearing to create a double layer of protection around the Heart of Moondale. A task that didn't take near as much effort as she was putting into it, since Azure had created the talismans before they'd come up the mountain.

"We should take this before the board. Or at least to Nixie." Even as she said it, Azure knew what Rus's arguments against such actions would be. It was obvious. And Azure couldn't say she blamed Rus for them, not really. The Board of Magic had let her down time and again.

"And tip our hand so Brant can corrupt the other elders against us? No." Rus shook her head, an incredulous fury building under her words. "Besides, I still haven't forgotten how he helped push me out of Moondale once and probably would have done it again this time if he could. No. I'm not playing fair with someone like that. He doesn't deserve it."

Azure could agree with that. Brant didn't deserve the kindness of them coming at him directly. It would make it too easy for him to attempt to slip through their fingers the way the soul jumper had. But still, she couldn't help but point out that "I'm an elder now too, Rus. We're officially a coven by board standards, and we have a voice on the board. Not just a voice, we have allies."

Not many allies. Likely not enough to overthrow the stranglehold Brant had on the Board of Magic after decades of being there. Azure would need to work on that. She'd never seen a coven or clan decision be overthrown and the coven disbanded, but something like that was always within the realm of possibility, especially when that coven was host to a witch many of the elders deemed "bad" to some degree. It was written into the laws of Moondale that should a coven or clan not act appropriately, they could be pushed from the town.

With a sigh, Azure asked, "What do you suggest instead?"

"I suggest we use the allies we do have to our best advantage." Rus still wouldn't look at her, but she had at least stopped moving around the clearing. It was like she thought Azure would fight her on this. That Azure would call her amoral and demand she do things the way Azure thought they ought to. Maybe once upon a time, she would have. Maybe before Rus left, she'd have told Rus that she was wrong and that everything was black and white. But the fact of the matter was, it wasn't. Everything was gray. And even almost a year later, she and Rus were still getting used to the new them.

"Which ones?" Azure was genuinely curious. Rus wasn't a fool. She wouldn't do something that put the girls and the coven in danger. Azure trusted her.

Whirling around, Rus fixed her with widened eyes. It still amazed Azure how Rus hadn't caught on to the complete shift in their dynamic. Or at least, not wholly. A lot could change in eleven years, and a lot had. Azure had grown into an entirely different witch. One who, quite frankly, didn't give a flying fuck about what the Board of Magic thought about her or her coven, so long as they were safe and doing the right thing. One who was willing to fight for the things and people she loved.

While Rus had changed, too, and had many things she needed to tell Azure before she'd agree to getting married, Azure knew at her core, she was the same. And Azure loved her still.

Rus tilted her head, her gaze flicking over Azure, assessing. Whatever she saw on Azure's face seemed to indicate to Rus that she could trust Azure not to completely lose her shit at what she was about to propose. "Phyre and Brenton."

"You want us to utilize Brant's own niece and nephew against him?" It wasn't terribly ethical, but then Azure supposed that Brant had set them up in a way that there wasn't a lot of options available to them. "To what end?"

"To prove he's not fit to be elder." A smile tugged at the corners of Rus's lips that was cold and a little cruel. It sent a chill down Azure's spine. "Why should we play fair when he and Taryn funded a smear campaign against us?"

"You think this will lure the soul jumper back to Moondale so that it can be pushed into the After where it belongs?" It sounded like a decent enough plan. And really, they didn't have any others currently. Azure didn't like the idea of letting the soul jumper run around Ironport doing whatever it pleased, especially if it was still influencing things in Moondale.

"If it doesn't come back for the centennial first. It can't hurt to try." Rus shrugged, tilting back onto her heels. "Plus, is it incorrect to say that he isn't fit? He's proven that. He was bribed by a soul jumper, nearly put that creature in power, and is still in contact with it even after its nature was exposed. Honestly, the fact that no one has questioned whether he should remain an elder is more suspicious than anything else."

Azure hummed her agreement. Rus was right. Brant was inherently problematic, had been for decades now, and the other elders had allowed him to run around unchecked. Maybe it was time he saw the consequences of his actions. Maybe it was time they all did. Now that there was a new generation of folk willing to take their spots on the board. Azure could think of a few others who she would be very happy to see the back of. "Very well."

"Right then, we'll just— Wait, really?" Rus blinked at her in awe, her jaw hanging open.

"Yes. Really." Azure thought maybe she liked that look on Rus's face, so long as it was directed at her and no one else. "You're right in your assessment. The board has been left to its own devices too long. It's time for a—a shake-up."

"Do you think Nixie will approve?"

"Maybe not. But that matters little to me. It was her idea to bring me in as an elder, her idea to give me free rein to do what I needed to change things. If she didn't mean for me to do this, then she should have been more specific with her instructions."

Rus laughed, and Azure couldn't hide the way her lips ticked up in a grin. It was good to be wholly on the same side as Rus. To be a rebel.

IF RUS WERE BEING HONEST, she didn't think she'd ever be able to shake Az's rebellious grin from her mind. Nor would she ever be able to come fully to terms with how Az had changed so wholly. She was a rule follower. Strict and stanch. For years. And now here she was, standing by Rus's side while Rus plotted to get another clan elder thrown out and reaching toward the Heart of Moondale when she very much shouldn't even be in the clearing at all.

Rus wanted to tell Az that she'd changed. She wanted to drop to her knees and beg Az to marry her. She couldn't do either of those things, and not just because they still had work to do and the right was quickly slipping away from them. But also because she still had plenty she needed to tell Az about herself, to show all the ways in which she herself was different.

"Let's get this done," Rus said, the grass crunching under her butt as she dropped down to sit beside the Heart of Moondale, her back pressed into the stone. "Then I'm taking you home and mauling you."

"Is that a promise?" Az sounded like she was laughing.

"It definitely is." Rus tilted her head back so she could wink at Az just to see her blush, then held her hand out. "Athame."

Az dropped the dagger into her hand without a word before falling to her knees in front of Rus, heedless of the way the ground would dirty her long pale skirt. It was good. It was so good. Rus wanted her close. Within arm's reach. And Az seemed to want the same thing. Rus wondered if maybe they always *had* wanted the same things but had never been able to put them into words before.

She leaned forward and pressed a kiss to the soft moue of Az's lips, her thumb brushing over the worry line that formed between her brows. "I'm all right, Az. It'll just take a minute."

Az nodded, momentarily mollified, and left Rus to her work, although she didn't move away. Which was a relief.

The dagger bit into her arm, drawing a thin line of blood. Not enough to even leave a scar if Rus didn't pick at the scab as she'd been wont to do for most of her life. Swiping her thumb through the blood, she reached over her shoulder and pressed it into the stone. It wouldn't take much, she knew that. The Heart wanted to talk to her. It was begging for someone to listen to it, as if it had a spirit of its own. And so far, Rus seemed to be the only one who could understand its language or had even tried.

It took a second for the magic to take. Like the Heart had been sleeping. Which made sense, Rus supposed, with how close they were to the centennial. It was likely trying to reserve its energy stores in case of an emergency. All they could hope was that there wouldn't be one.

Then Rus tipped forward—spiritually—again into the warm, deep darkness.

Wherever she was, it echoed with a silence Rus found unsettling instead of peaceful.

And then it wasn't quiet anymore.

The darkness remained, but screams echoed through the void.

Chaos and panic.

Rus jerked, twisting, trying to see where they were coming from and what was causing them.

But it was too dark. Like the Heart didn't have what it needed to give anything more than this. To show her more. Nothing about it made sense. Why would the Heart bring her here? Why would it leave her with just this impression of disaster?

"What does it mean?" Rus tried to ask it, her voice shaking with anxiety.

She is coming.

Vague. But Rus could make an assumption about that statement.

"When?"

The centennial.

That gave them a total of two days, officially, before the shit hit the fan. The celebrations started the next day, but the official date of the centennial, the anniversary of Moondale was just two nights away. It wasn't much time to prepare. Not near enough to overthrow Brant either. But they could start putting in the work. They could sow doubt. Maybe it would be enough. It would have to be.

She is coming.

"Yeah, I got that bit. But why? She has to know coming back here will only get her sent into the After." It seemed foolish to Rus that the soul jumper would put herself right where Rus wanted her. She'd barely survived last time they'd fought, and Rus had a larger coven on her side now. The soul jumper didn't stand a chance.

She will have vengeance. There is no stopping her.

Okay, well that sounded ominous as fuck.

"Right. Then what do we do?"

She will make them pay. They will pay for what they did to her. There is no stopping her. There is no stopping her. There is no—

Rus fell again, backward through the warmth and the dark, landing on her ass on the ground, her head jolting back hard enough that she cracked it against the Heart.

"Fuck me, that hurt." Rus rubbed the back of her head, hissing when she pulled her hand away to find blood on her fingers.

"What happened?" Az asked worriedly. She reached for Rus to pull her in close and check her over. It was sweet.

"The Heart says the soul jumper is coming back. She'll be here in time for the centennial. And we can't stop her. She's going to have vengeance." Normally, maybe Rus would have tried to keep that to herself. To hide it away and do something about it alone. But Az said they were in this together. Az was willing to hear her plans for Brant. Az had even agreed with her. They were a team.

"On whom?"

"The Heart didn't say." Rus rubbed her ears. They were starting to ring, likely from the strain. "We've got two days until the official centennial to figure out who the fuck she's going after and stop her."

Az let out a slow breath and nodded. "Tonight, we will rest. Tomorrow, we will talk through our next move."

"I really think we should—"

"We are no good to anyone so long as we're exhausted. Which you *are*. We're going home." Az lifted Rus by her underarms, not giving her a moment of rest. She turned to splash water on the blood left behind by Rus's spell, then started them toward their car, with their familiars at their sides.

She was probably right. They had a lot to do and not near enough time to do it in. Rus needed to sleep, then they could regroup.

Chapter 8

"I want to climb you like a tree," Rus purred low in her throat in a way that Azure was sure was meant to be sexy. But it slurred at the end. Her eyes were lidded with exhaustion instead of the lowered-through-her-lashes way she liked to look at Azure when she was flirting. It was kind of cute, actually.

"That's very sweet, but you can hardly climb the stairs." It wasn't that Azure didn't want to, but she was bearing much of Rus's weight as they trudged up the back steps from the kitchen to the second floor. The other residents of 157 Mourning Moore were already asleep, and the house itself was muffling their movements so as not to wake them.

"Aaaaz," Rus whined, bumping her head against Azure's.

Azure couldn't tell if it was by accident or on purpose, especially as it hurt a little more than it likely should have if Rus were doing it intentionally. "It has been a long couple of days."

And it would be a long few more. Two days. They only had two days to prepare some kind of defense against the soul jumper and absolutely no idea how to convince the rest of the town that she was coming. The rest of the town, which the Board of Magic had spent the last few weeks putting at ease.

"We won't have time later." Rus pouted.

A valid argument. Classes were on hiatus during the centennial, so all students and faculty could attend the celebrations, but that didn't mean she or Rus would have time to spend together. Rus still had the girls, the booth, and the coffee shop to look after while Azure was in charge of overseeing all the vendors throughout the event—not just tomorrow during setup. She needed to make regular rounds to make sure people were comporting themselves properly and not selling anything that hadn't been pre-approved. They would be lucky if they saw each other more than a couple hours during the day.

When this didn't get the response Rus wanted, she went with a different tack. "C'mon, Magpie, I'll be good for you."

A shiver raced down Azure's spine. Rus's want for that form of intimacy waxed and waned like the moon, and generally speaking, Azure was more than happy to take advantage of it when it was there. Especially when Rus said things like that, entirely handing over the reins to her and trusting her to take care of them both. It was a small thing, a shift in their dynamic. A way for Rus to prove to Azure, and herself, that it was okay to be vulnerable, that Azure would always be there.

There was hardly any saying no after that.

"Mark your words." Azure sighed softly and tugged Rus through the doorway to their attic bedroom. "But if you start acting like a brat, we're going to bed."

"Acting like a brat. When am I ever a brat?" Rus nuzzled her cold nose against the hinge of Azure's jaw, raising gooseflesh in her wake.

"About 80 percent of the time." Azure dropped her to sit on her side of the bed and went to their wardrobe to retrieve pajamas for them both.

"Did you do the math on that? Or are you just guessing?"

Azure glanced at Rus over her shoulder and found her lazing back on her hands, a smirk dimpling her cheek on one side. She could be such a nuisance when she wanted to be. Why did Azure find that so unbearably attractive?

"I ran the numbers," Azure lied, just to see the brief look of shock cross Rus's face right before she started laughing. Eyes squinted in joy. "Shorts or pants?"

"Can't we just sleep naked?" Rus rubbed her eyes, which glistened with unshed tears, likely a combination of her laughter and the bone-deep tiredness Azure could see weighing her down.

"The last time we did that, Huaner woke up in the middle of the night with a nightmare, and we had to rush to put on clothes to check in with her." Which really wasn't that big a deal. What was a big deal to Azure was that Aihuan was having nightmares at all. She wasn't afraid of the ghosts that tended to float around her and Rus like ducks following their mother. And they had never really gotten out of her what frightened her so badly that she'd woken up crying.

"So?"

"So. You couldn't find pants and wound up tripping down the stairs trying to put on mine."

Rus grumbled, flopping back down against the comforter. "You're no fun."

"We don't have to wear them, but if we have them out, then we can grab them in a hurry." A compromise. Still not ideal, but better than the way Rus tended to throw her clothes all over the room, then not be able to find them when she was in a rush. "Now, shorts or pants?"

"Pants," Rus huffed. "The thick ones, it's kind of cold in here."

"I'll turn on the heater too." Azure didn't find it chilly, but she'd come to realize that Rus got cold after using magic. She didn't know if it had always been that way or if this was a new thing, but whatever it was, she was happy to accommodate. Even if that meant she had to sleep with just the sheet over herself.

"You don't have to."

Azure ignored her, and the heater kicked on as she came back to the bed, dropping their clothes at the foot of it, where they would hopefully not get kicked off and disappear underneath. No guarantees, though. 157 was shameless in its sense of humor and lack of willingness to be helpful when it didn't want to be. Azure wondered if that was a consequence of the previous owners or if it was just the soul of the house itself. Nesta would know.

"There, now we've got everything we need," Rus declared, holding her hands out toward Azure, although she hadn't moved to sit up. She opened and closed her fingers. "Please?"

Azure's smile settled onto her face as she stepped between Rus's spread thighs. "Before we do that, I think I'd like to ask you a question."

"What?" Rus lifted her head to look at her and groaned when she saw Azure pull the ring box from her pocket. "Come on, Az, I'm too bloody tired for that."

"Attempt number three," Azure said, counting it off to herself, unable to help when her voice shook with laughter. "Will you marry me?"

Rus kicked her shin lightly, not even letting her open the box before she swatted it away and said, "Poor timing. Put that ring away and kiss me."

It wasn't the timing, Azure knew that. Rus would love to be proposed to in bed. Comfortable and cuddled close. It was the looming fear. The insecurity that still held her back from telling Azure everything.

"I'll try again later," Azure promised, setting the box on Rus's nightstand before she leaned over her, fingers brushing hair back from Rus's face as she settled between her legs and pressed a kiss to her lips. Long and lingering. It tasted of the salt of sweat, and a little bit of worry, but it was still Rus under all the layers. Her magic. Her heart. It was enough. It would always be enough.

She bit down on Rus's lower lip, and Rus keened, her hips lifting to rub against Azure's in a siren's call of longing that Azure swallowed whole. There was a lazy, greedy desperateness to her movements. Rus's fingers fisted in Azure's skirt, wrinkling the fabric and tugging it up so the cool air caught on her bare ankles.

"Be still," Azure murmured, nipping a trail of little bites from Rus's chin up to her jaw. Rubbing the tip of her nose along the skin beneath Rus's ear, Azure hummed happily, low in her chest.

"Make me," Rus challenged, but it was halfhearted. She was too tired to be much of a brat, to test Azure's patience too much. There was a softness to her like this, and Azure adored it. She didn't like the reason behind it, of course. It was worrisome that Rus's magic drained her sometimes. But she liked the end result—being able to take care of Rus.

Normally, Azure would use magic to restrain Rus when she got like this. Tangle her up in ropes made of soothing, cool power. But neither of them had the energy for that, and Azure could tell that Rus needed something else. More contact.

With a soft grunt, Azure nipped the skin below Rus's

ear and reached down to grab her by the wrists, wrestling them above her head with little resistance. "You said you'd be good."

"You like it." Rus fell still, her chest heaving with want through lips swollen and spit slick. She was beautiful like this. Her gray eyes hazed over, her body pliant.

"I do." There was no denying it. The push-pull of them had always been the draw for Azure. The way they were so different and yet at their core so very much the same. Their opinions on things varied greatly, but in the end, they just wanted to do what was right—to be good witches who protected the people they loved and the town that loved them. Moondale approved. Azure wasn't sure how she knew that for certain, but it was something she knew down to her bones.

"C'mon, Magpie, enough foreplay." Rus lifted her hips off the bed again, the seams of her black jeans scraping uncomfortably through Azure's skirt where they touched. But it didn't dowse the flame. Nothing ever could.

Azure scoffed an annoyed laugh. "Leave them here, or I stop," she threatened, giving Rus's wrists a squeeze.

Rus nodded vaguely as she licked her lips. "Sure. Sure."

It wasn't terribly convincing, but the way Rus tilted her head to the side, exposing the red mark Azure left behind with her teeth, was. She could mask how tired she was with her words, but her body language would always give her away. It made Azure second-guess this. Rus was clearly exhausted, burned out, and needed to go to sleep. But whatever she'd seen at the Heart, it scared her, down to her core. Azure could understand needing the reminder through physicality that she was all right, safe, in Azure's hands.

Azure would give her that. Then she'd put Rus to bed

and turn on their alarms so they could be up in a few hours for the start of the centennial celebration.

Azure patted Rus's knee lightly, a subtle signal for her to loosen the way she'd wrapped her legs around Azure's hips, and Rus did as instructed, letting them flop back down onto the bed. Her fingers twitched where one hand held her opposite wrist above her head, but otherwise she made no other movement, leaving Azure to her task.

The jeans were a pain to get down. She had to roll them off because Rus preferred skinny jeans, even if they were rapidly going out of fashion. She took the underwear with them and pressed a warning kiss to Rus's hip bone when she jerked from the cold. Rubbing soothing circles into Rus's skin, she tossed the clothes over her shoulder and trusted 157 to help them into the laundry basket in the corner. The one Azure demanded they get when she moved in because she was tired of seeing their clothes in a mountain.

Then she dropped to her knees between Rus's spread thighs, and Rus's breath came in a choked-off sob. She wanted to move. Wanted to reach for Azure. Azure could tell. But she stayed still, as she'd been told.

"Good girl," Azure murmured approvingly, pressing a kiss to the inside of Rus's thigh that had her twitching involuntarily, a whimpered cry ripped from her throat. So she liked that—Azure would store that knowledge for later. Right now, she had a task to see to.

It was almost too easy to fall back into what she knew Rus liked from before. To press her face in close and run her tongue over Rus's folds. To nip at her clit lightly with her teeth. Her finger slipped easily into Rus's entrance, working her slow and careful until Rus was squirming on the bed while Azure rolled her tongue over her again and again.

"Magpie, please," Rus begged, although it didn't sound

like she particularly knew what she was begging for anymore. Release, likely.

Azure hummed an agreement and pressed a second finger into her, hooking them slightly as her thumb moved to come down hard on her clit. Grinding against it in a motion that was almost brutal, sure to leave Rus sensitive come morning. Merciless. Azure pressed her face lovingly into the crook of Rus's thigh, worrying the skin with her teeth.

It didn't take long at all. Rus was tired, spent, and when she got like that, it was almost too easy to get her off. Not that it made the noises she made, the choked-off sobs and whimpered *Magpies*, any less beautiful. Azure loved wringing those sounds from her.

When Rus finally came, it was with a whimper instead of a shout, her whole body falling lax against the bed. A spring that had wound itself too tight and been released.

"Fuck, I love you," Rus whispered.

"So you'll marry me?" Azure asked, only half joking.

"Shut the fuck up and come here and cuddle me, you asshole." Rus laughed, swatting her shoulder, then pulling her up to press her lips to Azure's, soft and lazy.

"Pajamas first," Azure chided softly, feeling a little spent herself. The clothes were far away at the end of the bed, and Rus's body was warm and pliant.

"Fuck the pajamas," Rus hissed. "Just take off your starchy-ass clothes and come to bed."

Then she wiggled out of her own long-sleeved T-shirt with minimal struggle. Azure laughed softly to herself, shaking her head as she pulled back to get undressed, then help Rus beneath the covers before she climbed in with her. Rus pressed her entire body into Azure's like a cat, long and languid. Her nose brushed Azure's collarbone, even though she was the taller of the two.

"There are other things we need to talk about," Rus said, her voice so low Azure almost didn't hear it over her slowly regulating heartbeat. "Other reasons."

She didn't have to say what she meant. Azure understood. More things standing in the way of them being together the way Azure wanted them to be. It was all right; Azure could be patient. What was a couple more weeks or months when she'd been waiting all her life to marry Rus? Even if she hadn't known it was Rus she was looking for in the beginning.

"Not tonight. You're tired."

"Okay. But soon."

"Yes. Soon." If they kept Moondale from fucking imploding. "We have to be up early tomorrow to set up the booth before the ribbon cutting ceremony."

Rus groaned loudly. "Don't remind me."

"It can't be helped."

There was a huff, good-natured and fond, as Rus tangled her cold feet around Azure's ankles. "I'm glad you're here, Az."

"I'm glad I'm here too." And then she took to stroking Rus's hair, slow and steady, working out the tangles until Rus's breaths had evened out entirely in sleep.

Chapter 9

The scissors were missing. The huge fucking ceremonial scissors that had been used for every event in Moondale for as long as Azure was alive, and definitely before. They were missing. Scissors that were was as long as her fucking *arm*. Had just up and disappeared.

Was it the end of the world? No. But it was a nuisance.

"What are we going to do?" Seok asked, shifting from foot to foot. He was young still, new to Moondale and her ways. The nervous sort, likely worried he would be kicked out of the Clan of the Unseen Moon—the fae faction in Moondale—should he do anything wrong.

"We'll just have to use regular scissors."

It wasn't like the ceremonial scissors were magic. They didn't have ancient runes carved into their blades to ensure luck for the coming years. They weren't crafted in magical fires, forged by gnomes. They were just a really big pair of antique scissors someone had picked up along the way and decided to use for every ceremony in Moondale. They'd seen the openings of new businesses, other town celebrations, the anointing of the new fairgrounds, and even the building of a new neighborhood a time or two. They were special, yes. They had a certain kind of power, but it was rather limited by comparison to other magical objects.

They were also *missing*. But Azure understood thoroughly the cost of delaying this ceremony just because she couldn't find the bloody things.

"But then the—"

"If we do not get started on time, the people who have bought tickets and are waiting to come in will become disgruntled. That disgruntlement will color their entire experience and make it less than what we need for the event. The Heart's power is already running dangerously low. We cannot risk the negativity a late start would cause." Azure would just have to take the heat for it when the rest of the elders found out and were inevitably pissed at her for losing the blasted things.

Seok sighed heavily, his shoulders drooping in what could only be defeat. "I'll go let the others know."

Azure nodded and began to mentally prepare herself to face Nixie Vernan, who was no doubt going to be supremely annoyed with Azure for this. They had a half hour till the ribbon cutting ceremony. Not near enough time to scour the town for the scissors. Just enough time to find a suitable replacement.

NOT SUITABLE ENOUGH, apparently, as Nixie was holding the regular pair of scissors that Sunila pulled from the drawer of Elwood & Co's counter like they had personally offended her entire lineage.

"What are these?" Nixie asked, turning the scissors over in her hands. They had exactly five minutes to get to the stage, where the big red ribbon was strung across Main Street.

"I cannot find the ceremonial scissors. When I went to

retrieve them from the storeroom this morning, they weren't in their box." Which made absolutely no sense, because they'd been there when Azure had gone looking for them the day before to pull them from the drawer and stack them on top of the box of other things she'd need. So they'd been put back correctly after their last use. And the box remained. That meant someone had taken them. Someone with a key.

"I see." Nixie opened and closed the scissors. They screeched a little from years and years of use. They were all metal, with a golden handle. Similar to the giant ones, only smaller. Azure wouldn't doubt that they were just as old; things didn't tend to get thrown away at Elwood & Co. "We'll just have to make do."

"We will." This was the best of a bad situation. That didn't mean Azure wasn't nervous about it. It was the only logical choice, but what if it was the wrong one? "The ceremony begins in three minutes."

"Let's get to the stage then." Nixie nodded and motioned for Azure to take the lead out of Elwood & Co. and up the street toward the stage where everyone waited.

The crowd was already growing restless.

THE FIRST COUPLE of hours were a mad rush of activity with setup and everything, and a haze of Rus being too fucking tired to really function. She had slept amazingly after she and Az got back to the house, but that didn't change the fact that it had been late as fuck, and she wasn't in her twenties anymore. She couldn't do all-nighters, not like she used to. Getting older fucking sucked.

A reusable tumbler appeared beneath her nose, and Rus jerked her head up to see Nando standing there, a small smile on his face. "You look like you could use the pick-me-up."

"I thought I wasn't allowed to have the hard stuff anymore."

Nando shrugged. "This is a special case. Don't get used to it."

Rus nodded and snatched the cup from him to take a grateful sip. She didn't know why Az had told her she needed to cut back on the espresso. Other than the fact that it literally contributed to her insomnia and made her jittery. But that was just an interesting side effect. It didn't mean she had to stop drinking it, right?

"How's it going over here?" Nando's eyes flicked around the little booth they'd set up for the Coven of the Forgotten. It didn't say that's what it was for, of course. To keep the normies at ease, they were selling cute little ghosts that Indigo, Az, and Ava had crocheted. Which, so far, no one had bought because they were too busy trying to load up on carbs and caffeine in Necromancer's at Rus's back. But that was okay.

"I haven't talked to anyone yet, but it's still early." Rus shrugged. She wasn't worried about it. She didn't actually think they'd get any new coven members this way, especially since she'd said she wasn't willing to poach from the big families. But Az had insisted on the table, said it was part of the tradition for covens and clans to set up tables during these events and sell handmade items to normies while dispelling information on their groups to folk on the sly. So here she was.

"Well, Ava and Hunter will be here this afternoon. Hopefully more people will make things pick up a bit."

Nando glanced over her shoulder through the window into Necromancer's, where Indigo and Meiling were helping out, at least for the morning rush. They should probably look into hiring a part-timer for the holidays, but Rus wasn't willing to take that financial risk. Not yet.

"You should get back in there. The last time Meiling tried to use the steamer, she nearly melted the spoons."

"She's fine."

"The spoons are metal, Nando."

Nando shook his head, amusement clear on his face. "Right. I was just checking in with you. You're not too sore, are you? I could bring the cushioned mat out here, or a chair."

"I'll be fine." She was, in fact, sore. Her hip and lower back were twinging, and she felt herself favoring her cane more and more. But she wasn't going to let it stop her. She'd just have to have one of Az's healing baths and massages when they got home.

Nando squinted at her, clearly not believing her lie.

"Bring her the cushioned pad and the chair," Az said from over Nando's shoulder as she approached.

"Az, I'm fine. Really." Rus groaned, and stood up straighter to hide her pain.

"I'm sure you are." But it didn't sound like she was buying it, which wasn't helpful. Since when had Az and Nando decided to gang up on her like this? "But this is going to be a long weekend, and you still need to be in top form for when the soul jumper makes her appearance."

Nando stiffened, his head whipping to look around to make sure no one else was nearby to hear them talking. Az didn't seem at all worried that someone might be listening to them. Rus had to say she agreed. Let them hear. Let the other folk of Moondale realize something was coming.

Maybe this was the best way for them to prepare. All they could hope was that it wouldn't sow fear among them and ruin the whole point of the centennial celebration.

"Fine." Rus grumbled, her arms crossed over her chest. "Get the pad and the chair, but don't expect this to slow me down."

"I'd never." Az lifted her chin toward Nando and waited until he hurried into Necromancer's to return her attention to Rus. "I couldn't find the scissors this morning."

"The scissors?" Rus cocked her head, confused.

"The big ceremonial ones we use for ribbon cuttings. Someone took them out of their box in the storeroom. My best guess is Brant, but there's no evidence."

Rus's gut twisted. That was two minor inconveniences that could have thrown this event into a tailspin in a row. Was Brant deliberately trying to sabotage the celebration, or was it a distraction? "Well, we'll have to keep an eye on things, make sure he doesn't do anything else to mess this up."

"Right." Az leaned over the table to brush a piece of hair back behind Rus's ear, the gesture soothing enough that Rus practically turned to liquid under it. "I have spoken to Phyre. We're going to meet at the house this evening to discuss our other plan."

"All right." Rus still wasn't sure how they were going to overthrow Brant, but it was worth talking to Phyre and getting her on their side. She might know some other Ironwoods who were tired of Brant and the way he did things. Which would be a good start to their little mutiny. "Do you think this is the end of his interference?"

"No." There was a bone-deep certainty in Az's tone that Rus felt down to her core. And unfortunately, she was likely right.

"Is there any way we can get ahead of some of it?"

"I don't think so." Az sighed. She brushed her hands over her neatly pleated pale-turquoise skirt and the white button-down she had tucked into it. A nervous gesture. "We will just have to deal with the issues as they arise."

That was great. Just *great*. Fuck. She could see the way this thought bothered Az just as much as it did Rus. And Rus wasn't a planner. She didn't think ahead. She lived on instinct. But Az had always been the type to look to the future and try to mitigate the worst. "Well, good thing we've got our friends, right?"

"Yes." Az looked relieved at the thought, her shoulders dropping from where they had been hitched up around her ears. "We are not in this alone."

"No. We never were." Rus had to remind herself of that constantly. She'd felt like she'd been fighting by herself for so long, but she never really had been, had she? She'd always had Az, whether she knew it or not. And Phyre, and Cagney, and Nesta. And now she had a whole host of others to help.

"I've got to return to overseeing things." But it didn't look like Az actually wanted to go. Her hands twitched at her sides, the desire to reach for Rus obvious.

Rus could understand that. She felt it too. Something lingered in the air of Moondale now. Something sinister. A ticking clock. And all Rus wanted to do was pull the people she loved close to her and shield them as best she could.

"We can have lunch?" she offered as a way to ease some of the strain on Az's face. "You, me, and the girls?"

"The table—"

"Will be fine for a bit without me sitting here, manning it." Rus reached across the table for her, taking her hands and giving them a fond squeeze. "You deserve a break, too, I think. This whole thing is going to give you gray hairs."

"The women in my family don't go gray till they're at least a hundred." Az grumbled, poking out her lower lip. *Cute.*

"Mm-hmm." Rus smiled more broadly at the pout and lifted one of Az's hands to her lips to press a kiss to her knuckles. "Plus, the girls have never had crabs before. You'll teach them how to pick, right?"

"Only because you're hopeless at it." Az rolled her eyes fondly.

"I am hopeless at a lot of things. Good thing I have you."

Heat flared in Az's cheeks, but she looked impossibly smug at the admission. "Good thing."

Nando returned a moment later with the rolled-up cushioned mat under one arm and a chair slung over the other shoulder. "I have the pad and the chair."

"Perfect!" Rus laughed, letting Az pull her hands away. She didn't want to sit down. It would make her feel like she wasn't being active in the celebration. But there were other things she needed to turn her attention to, like how the fuck she was going to separate a soul jumper from a host that had invited it in willingly. And being in pain would only make thinking harder. "See you later, Az."

"Yes, later." Az leaned over to steal a quick kiss, then turned on her heel and disappeared in the swell of people while Rus sat dumbfounded, brushing her fingers over her tingling lips. Goddess, she loved that woman.

Chapter 10

With Ava and Hunter finally there to help look after the booth, Rus could focus on the things she needed to focus on. Namely, what the fuck to do with the soul jumper when it finally showed up again. Because it was going to. And at this point she had about a day and a half. Maybe a little less. The word "day" was rather vague when used in this sense, and Rus supposed she should have pushed the Heart to be more specific about her deadline. But then, it'd been vague about absolutely *everything*.

Like whom the soul jumper was going to try to seek vengeance on. Was it Rus? Was it Az? Was it the entire Elwood family for whatever they'd done to it? Or was it Moondale as a whole? Knowing in advance would definitely help her keep whoever the soul jumper was after safe, but the Heart hadn't been willing to specify. And then there had been the screams. So many. Rus shivered at the memory.

Maybe it *was* the entire town.

"What're you working on?" Hunter asked, peering over the top of the legal pad she'd pulled out of her bag. It was definitely worse for wear. Several of the pages had been bent back or torn. And she'd spent so much time scribbling along the top binding while working thinking that it was now entirely black.

"I'm trying to come up with a way to contain the soul

jumper when it comes for us." When. Not if. Because it was coming, whether she liked it or not. And if she was going to do anything about it, the first act would be to contain it. Which—at least she thought—should be the easiest thing to do. After all, there were containment circles, and salt, and any number of other ways to keep a creature of the dead in one place. But salt hadn't held the last time they were up against it. And Rus didn't know exactly how strong the soul jumper was, whether it could break through her normal method of containment or not. There wasn't enough time to experiment, and she couldn't leave something like this to chance.

"So no on salt? I thought that was meant to be the best thing for ghosts." Hunter frowned at where Rus had scribbled through the word "salt" viciously enough she'd almost torn through the paper.

"The last time we were against it, the wind picked up because it was fu—" She glanced over at where Aihuan was happily sitting next to Ava, learning to crochet. "Ripping so many bodies out of the ground. I've never seen anything like it."

That wasn't entirely true. She *had* seen something like it, when she'd done it herself in the past. She was a necromancer, after all, and her first instinct would always be to lean on the dead. To pull bodies out of the earth when she needed them, to beg the dead to let her puppeteer them in search of peace. She always asked first, though. It was easier to use a body and a spirit if they were willing to work with her. Plus, there was something morally wrong, to her mind, in using a dead body that didn't consent to it.

"What about iron?" Hunter asked. If he noticed the way Rus's mind had drifted off, he didn't say so. He was good like that, Rus was starting to realize. Maybe because he spent so much time in his own head that he understood what it was like for others. She should probably ask him how he and his boyfriends were fairing now that Eric was back, but she didn't think she had the mental bandwidth to deal with their problems on top of her own. Not yet, anyway.

"What about it?" Rus brushed her pink hair back from her face.

"It worked against a really old vampire." Hunter shrugged.

Rus tilted her head. She hadn't thought of that. Salt was kind of her go-to, because she always had it on hand. It was in her pantry. She could grab a packet of it from any fast-food chain. Iron would be harder to come by, but she was meeting with Phyre later. "What would you suggest?"

"We created a net of sorts that Eric could lay out on the ground and—" He cut himself off, his deep-brown skin growing a little pale, clearly upset by something. Rus wanted to ask if it was in relation to what happened to Eric, but it still seemed too soon, too fresh. She'd wait. "Anyway, it worked for the vampire."

"I don't think I could trick this thing into a net." Well, she might be able to, but it was too risky, in her opinion. Using a net meant she had to stay in one place. It meant she couldn't be flexible, which was half her tactic when dealing with creatures like a soul jumper—being able to spin on a dime. "But maybe if I had a way to set up a barrier without it being so static."

Hunter snapped, his eyes widening behind his glasses in excitement. "Iron nails. With wards etched into the tops."

Rus thought over the words for a moment, then she understood. It was strange how she and this witch she hardly knew could be so on the same wavelength sometimes. "And a nail gun. Yes. That would work. It would give me the mobility I need."

Az was definitely onto something about including witches like Hunter and Ava in their coven. They fit in so well. And so far, they'd done nothing but prove their willingness to help with any problem that arose. They were brave, too, far more than Rus would have thought they'd be, considering they'd never faced things like soul jumpers and spirit eaters the way that Rus had. Everyone, it seemed, was full of surprises.

"I'll just need to go to the..." Her words trailed off as her eyes caught on the back of a head in the crowd. It wasn't a terribly out-of-the-ordinary occurrence to see someone with long, dark hair. What was out of the ordinary was the floor-length dress and the way Rus could almost see *through* the woman. A ghost.

What was a ghost doing, wandering through a crowd of the living? At midday, no less? They tended to keep to the outskirts. To avoid reminders of what they had been and what they had lost. But this ghost was acting as if she belonged there. As if she were just another who'd come from far and wide to experience the celebration. There was no excuse for her not knowing she didn't belong among these people, not realizing she was dead. She was too put together for that, and her clothing too old. No. This ghost knew what she was doing.

"I'll be right back," Rus said, shoving her notepad into Hunter's hands. "You two watch the girls."

"Sure." Ava narrowed her gaze, then turned her head to try to see what Rus saw.

But that was the thing about being a medium: No one else was going to see what she did, except another medium.

"Who was that, Auntie Rus?" Aihuan asked, her own

eyes fixed on the transparent head that was rapidly being eaten up by the crowd around the woman.

Rus had to catch up to her, before she lost her. "Don't know yet. Stay with Hunter and Ava. Auntie Az should be by soon." Rus bent to press a kiss to the top of Aihuan's head, then scooted around the table to follow the woman through the crowd.

It was a struggle to catch up to her, especially with Rus hobbling a little on her cane. And the ghost didn't have to bob and weave through the living the way that Rus did. But Rus was also determined and well acquainted with the technique of saying "excuse me!" very loudly then pushing her way through if she had to.

The ghost disappeared for a moment, blocked by all the people, but Rus caught her ducking down an alley. Which meant the ghost knew she was being followed. That wasn't ideal. Especially when Rus didn't have any of her tools on her to help her deal with a confrontational spirit...

Fuck it. She didn't have time to head back to the table. There would be too many questions.

Rus turned down the alley after the spirit, grateful for the way the space muffled the sound of the crowd on Main Street, and came face-to-face with a woman who looked way too much like Az. It wasn't Az, though, Rus knew that. Her skin was a shade too light, her nose too slim. But there was the air about her, the way her chin tilted back. It could only be one person, then.

"Mazarin Elwood," Rus said, stepping closer but making sure she kept her distance, should the shade try anything. From what Rus'd learned of Mazarin a few weeks ago, she was the last necromancer of the Elwood family, and she'd been been shunned for it. Cast out. Scrubbed from the records and set adrift. It was why she wasn't buried with the other Elwoods. Why her spirit hadn't entered the cycle of reincarnation.

What it didn't explain was why they hadn't seen anything of her since the soul jumper disappeared. One would think that without the soul jumper there to block her way, she'd be more willing to come to Az and Rus and tell her story, but she hadn't.

"I find I am at a disadvantage," Mazarin said, her voice echoey and haunting. "You are Azure's necromancer, and you know my name, but I do not know yours."

"Rus Ashthorne." Rus tilted her head in question. There was something strange about Mazarin, something that didn't sit quite right with Rus, but she couldn't put her finger on it. Her features were sharper than they'd been before, less blurred by the magic the soul jumper had been using to keep her out of Moondale. And Rus could finally see her face enough to note the differences between Mazarin and her kin. Maybe it was in the way she moved? "Did you just come to give me a shovel talk now that Az has proposed?"

"I am unclear on what a shovel talk is." Mazarin frowned, the lines on her face shallow, as if she were faking the emotion somehow. "But it is wonderful to hear that my kin has found someone to love her as such. She is very lucky. As are you, Rus Ashthorne."

Something crawled along Rus's nerves at the way Mazarin said her name, and suddenly she was very glad she hadn't given away her full one. "Yes. I am," Rus agreed readily, because she was, and she recognized that. Az was everything she'd ever wanted, ever needed, and she'd been lucky enough to get a second chance with her. "But that's not why you're here, is it?"

Mazarin smiled. The expression didn't reach her eyes.

First rule of necromancy: The dead lie.

"No. That is not why I'm here," Mazarin conceded, her tone light, amused. "I come to tell you more about the soul jumper, as you are calling her. I understand that you are the reason she was driven out of Moondale some time ago, and I wish to help you in defeating her once and for all."

There was a catch, Rus could feel it hanging in the air between them. But she didn't think Mazarin would tell her what it was. "Then by all means"—Rus flapped her wrist—"let's hear it."

"Once, the soul jumper was a witch named—" Mazarin said a name, but Rus couldn't hear it. She saw Mazarin's lips move but couldn't make out what she had been trying to say. A pity, because the name would have made things easier. Still, it was no real surprise that the soul jumper had found a way to block her name from being heard. Mazarin scowled and tried to say it again, but it came out a blur of noise.

"You can't tell me her name because she's hexed it." Which was going to be a problem, but it was one she'd have to deal with later. Though it did provide a hint. Why would the soul jumper hex her own name if it weren't something powerful that could be used against her? "Just get on with your story."

"Very well." Mazarin exhaled a petulant breath and continued. "We were in love, once upon a time. So in love that when she died, I did the unthinkable. I brought her back." Mazarin paused, whether for effect or because she expected some kind of response, Rus didn't know.

"Okay?" Rus raised a brow in curiosity.

"You are not..." Mazarin's eyes flicked about, searching for the right word, it seemed. "You are not disgusted by this?"

Rus shrugged. "Can't really blame you for doing something I'd do myself."

"I see." Mazarin's shade flickered a little, as if unsettled.

"But that doesn't explain how the soul jumper was forged." Rus leaned forward on her toes. She was getting somewhere with this, she could feel it. "I've brought people back before, and they haven't turned into monsters."

"I suppose it had more to do with the method in which I brought her back than the bringing her back itself." Mazarin's head tilted downward, her eyes flitting about the ground as if searching for something. Thinking.

"You didn't keep the balance in mind," Rus said, not even having to question it.

It was one thing she'd learned early on in her own journey as a necromancer, one rule she set for herself that was never to be broken. There was a balance, a cosmic equation, that always had to be taken into consideration when doing something of this magnitude. The first thing she'd ever brought back had been a mouse, and when she didn't sacrifice something else to do it, the mouse had turned into something twisted. Wrong. Rus was all for experimentation, but it didn't take her more than once to learn that lesson, even if it took her a bit longer to figure out how the balance itself worked. To feel it in the world around her. The ebb and flow of a changing tide. For Darcy, it had been the life of another bird of his size. For Sage, it had been another fae heir. For Aihuan, it had been the life of all the unborn children Rus harbored in her own body. And for Eric, it had been a calf, although that would only buy him so much time.

"I did not know I needed to. It was the first time I had —" Mazarin cut herself off, pressing her lips firmly together. "Be that as it may, what I did created something hungry.

Something that would never be satiated. That would have to subsist on other life in a way no living creature ever should."

"Yeah. That tracks." That had been what happened with the mouse, after all.

Mazarin looked up at her, her eyes narrowing as if she were seeing Rus for the first time. It was a shrewd expression. Not one of thoughtfulness and longing to be understood. One of someone who was trying to find the best angle to work to get what she wanted.

First rule of necromancy.

"She stayed, jumping from body to body when the one she was living inside of began to fail," Mazarin said, continuing her story. "For a while, I lost track of her. She did not seem interested in me or mine, and I fear I was all too happy to let her continue as she was without too much of a fight. I was... a coward."

If she thought Rus was going to argue that point, she was sorely fucking mistaken.

"So then what?" Rus asked instead.

"This generation, my eldest sister reentered the reincarnation cycle."

Rus started, her shoulders jerking up. "Vi."

"Yes." Mazarin nodded. "She was known to me as Hyacinth, when we were sisters. I fear the soul jumper thinks that she will be an easier target."

"Or, as your former lover, she's looking to get revenge for you on the sister who forced you out of your coven."

"That is very likely."

"Can you tell me anything else about her?"

"I am afraid I cannot. However, I would recommend you search for her name. Names have power, after all. Do they not?"

Rus nodded, brushing a hand through her hair. She had her work cut out for her. But at least now she had a direction to head in. "They do."

Although if the soul jumper hexed her name, Rus would be unable to find it in any records...

"Good." Just as Rus looked up, she thought she caught a twist of Mazarin's mouth. A vicious, dark slash of a smile. Although Rus was unable to tell if the hatred that resided there was for the soul jumper or someone else. A shiver raced down Rus's spine.

And a second later, Mazarin disappeared.

Had she imagined it? Was the cruelty really there, or was Rus being paranoid and suspicious? There was no way to tell, and besides, she had other brooms to fly, so to speak.

Chapter 11

R us was a jittery mess—her leg bouncing where it brushed against Azure's thigh, her hands never once still as she rearranged the plate in front of her—but she wouldn't tell Azure why. Which was making Azure feel unbalanced. A fact that wasn't helped at all by the amount of shit that had gone wrong since Azure left Rus's side that morning.

Water-damaged ride tickets at the carnival.

Entire bushels of crabs rendered unusable because they'd died before they could be cooked.

The cell phone signal needed for vendors to take credit cards going in and out for no reason at all.

And on and on.

Nothing supernatural had happened. Yet. But Azure knew it was only a matter of time. These minor inconveniences were just the prelude to a much bigger problem. And Rus's anxiety was not making Azure feel any calmer about the absolute shit show this day was turning out to be.

"I'm sorry," Rus said, as if she'd read Azure's thoughts. Or maybe Azure had said that last bit out loud? She hoped she hadn't cursed, not with Aihuan and Meiling sitting across from them at their little picnic table. The only good thing about her sour mood was that it seemed to be visible enough that no one else dared crowd into their space.

Which was nice. It meant Azure got some time to spend with Rus and their girls.

Azure looked up from where she'd been carefully lifting crabs from the pile in front of her to frown at Rus. She'd been trying to find one that felt heavy, so it would be easy for the girls to see the process of picking. "What for?"

Rus shook her head, a clear indication that she didn't want to talk about this with so many listening. Maybe she didn't want to say it in front of the girls, either. That set off alarm bells in Azure's mind. Something had happened. Something that might change everything.

"How about this one, Auntie Az?" Aihuan asked, holding up perhaps the smallest of the bunch and waving its claws at Azure.

Auntie Az. It still hit Azure like a gut punch every time one of the girls said it. It meant she was theirs as much as they were hers. Which, admittedly, she knew. But that didn't change the way it left her reeling and smiling all at the same time to hear it said out loud.

"Let me see it." Azure held out her hand. Being born and raised in Maryland meant that crabs were a part of her culture, a part of her history, even if she didn't eat them anymore. So she'd long since acquired the ability to tell what a crab would be like on the inside by just holding it. She'd also developed the skill of picking. Fast. Because when one grew up in a family with several cousins, they learned that the only way to get their fill for the summer was to race through the process.

Aihuan dropped the crab into her hand, and Azure tested the weight before nodding. "This one will do."

She then began the process of pulling the legs out, wedging a knife below the bib, and peeling back the top shell.

"Gnarly," Meiling said, as if impressed, as Azure set about opening the crab for them so that they could see how it was done. She'd probably still have to cut them for Aihuan—she was too small to use the knives laid out on the table—but she should be able to pick on her own once she'd been shown how. Rus, on the other hand...

"Am I picking this one for you or the girls?" Azure asked, tilting her head down to look at how Rus had rearranged the vegetables on the plate. She'd separated them into neat little piles by type, and then again by some other method which was unknown to Azure. There were potatoes and carrots clearly from one of the boil pots, but also kale, collard greens, and green beans. She'd even snagged a little cup of vinegar from somewhere.

"If you pick for me, I'll pick for you." Rus smiled with too many teeth, her eyes squinting in her joy. Goddess, she was such a dork sometimes. Azure loved her so much, it ached in her bones.

"Is that what that is?" Azure tilted her chin toward the neatly organized plate before returning her focus to the crab in front of her, showing the girls how to clean it, what parts were safe to eat, and which were not by what she put in the little bowl to her right and what she dropped into the trash pile to her left.

"Some of them were mushy," Rus said by way of explanation but didn't elaborate. Not that she needed to. Azure could read between the lines. Rus knew how much she didn't like overcooked vegetables, especially the broiled kind.

"What are those?" Meiling picked up something from the trash pile and squished it between her fingers.

"Dead fingers. You can't eat those." She slid the little bowl with the meat across the table to the girls. "Try it. If you don't like it, we can find you something else to eat. There's plenty of other food."

Rus held up a fork toward her, a piece of seasoned potato on the end. Azure could see the red flecks from where someone had scattered Old Bay on it. She wondered if that had been Rus or whoever was in charge of cooking. Rus's smile spread wider, a dimple appearing in her cheek as mischief sparkled in her eyes, a clear sign that it had been Rus.

The smile that took over her own face was inescapable. There was something nostalgic, sweet, about this setup. Azure picking crabs for Rus while Rus weeded through whatever vegetarian options were on offer to pick out what she knew Azure would actually eat. It had happened every summer, since Azure chose to become a vegetarian at fourteen. It made her unreasonably pleased as she tilted forward to take the potato, then chewed happily.

The girls were still chewing on the crab meat on the other side of the table, debating if they liked it or not. Which was a reasonable response to this sort of thing. Maryland crabs weren't for everyone, and they had a distinct texture and taste that people who hadn't grown up on them maybe wouldn't like.

Meiling curled her nose after a few seconds of thoughtful chewing. "I'm going to go get a burger."

"That's fair." Rus mumbled around the potato she'd popped into her own mouth. Azure noted it was from a different pile than the one Rus had given her. Maybe those were the mushy ones. "What about you, Huaner? How's the crab treating you?"

Aihuan looked up from where she was stuffing another lump into her mouth. "I like it!"

Rus laughed softly, shaking her head. "Oh no, Az, we've created a monster."

"I believe you mean we've created a Marylander." Azure snorted and reached for another crab to set to work opening it up for Aihuan. "I'll open them for you. Do you think you can pick them, then?"

"Yeah." Aihuan nodded firmly and handed the bowl back so that Azure could begin filling it for Rus.

"Just be careful not to cut your little fingers," Rus advised, passing over the extra fork she'd tucked under her plate of vegetables. "Use this to scoop it out if the space is too tight."

"Okay!" Aihuan grinned at her. She tapped the fork on the table impatiently.

"Eat some veggies while you wait. Here, try some of this." Rus scooped up some of the collard greens and held them up for Aihuan while Azure finished cutting the crab in half so she'd have an easier time working around the inner cartilage.

Aihuan took the bite, her eyes wide and trusting, but the look fell the moment the greens touched her tongue. She pressed her lips together, disgust clear on her face.

"You can spit it out if you don't like it," Azure told her gently. It really was an acquired taste. She hadn't liked them for the longest time either.

Aihuan snatched the napkin Rus offered, then spit the half-chewed bite into it, scowling at Rus's laughing face. "You're mean, Auntie Rus."

"No, I'm not." Rus's cheeks puffed out. "Auntie Az likes them, don't you, Az?"

Azure leaned over and pressed a kiss to Rus's temple. "Stop teasing the toddler. Eat."

Rus grumbled but turned back to munching on the

vegetables she'd set aside to not give to Azure while Azure opened a few crabs for Aihuan and then set to work picking for Rus. They settled into something quiet and relaxed, something that felt undeniably good. This felt like family in a way Azure couldn't put into words. It was everything she'd ever wanted when she and Rus were younger, and the ring in her pocket weighed heavy on her mind. But she wouldn't propose in front of the girls. She wouldn't put Rus in a position to feel pressured to accept, not when there were still things they hadn't discussed. It wouldn't be right.

"Auntie Rus," Aihuan said after a long silence stretched between them. "Who was that lady?"

"What lady, little monster?" Rus tilted her head, dipping some of the greens in vinegar before offering them to Azure.

"The one from earlier, near the table." Aihuan wrinkled her nose in thought, her brow creasing as if she was trying to figure out how exactly to describe the person she was thinking of. "The... the see-through one."

Azure stopped what she was doing, her hands itching with the spices on her skin, and lifted her head to look at Aihuan. The see-through— "There was a ghost in town today?" she whispered, her gaze flicking about to make sure no one was close enough to overhear. It would start a panic if people were to realize there were ghosts wandering around during the day, and she didn't need that. There was already enough going wrong with this event.

Aihuan nodded.

Rus went still beside her, finally able to control whatever need she had to move around so much. This had been what she hadn't told Azure. Likely because she didn't want to add to Azure's list of worries. It would be sweet if it weren't so fucking frustrating. "Mazarin, actually," Rus said softly.

"Mazarin *Elwood?*" Azure's nerves were alight with foreboding. They hadn't heard from her in weeks, and some part of Azure thought maybe that was because without the soul jumper in town, her ancestor finally found a way to rest in peace. Apparently not.

Rus sighed, pushing the kale around her plate. "Yeah. That one."

"What did she want?" Because all spirits wanted something. They didn't appear to Rus just because they were popping in to say hi. There was always a reason.

"Can we not talk about this now?" Rus shifted on the bench, the wood dipping beneath her. There was something drawn about her expression all the sudden. "I just wanted a nice lunch with my family."

Azure frowned. She could understand that. It had been a relief to sit with Rus and let the chaotic energy of her and the girls settle Azure's frazzled nerves. Which was almost funny, considering once upon a time she might have thought this kind of thing would make her more anxious. It didn't, though. Rus and the girls' chatter, the way they moved around her, left space for her, made Azure feel like she fit in a way she hadn't thought she would a year ago when Rus first returned to Moondale.

"Was she scary?" Aihuan's tone was cautious, unsure, and Azure looked over at the little girl whose eyes were wide and a little afraid. Fuck. She'd forgotten they had a bit of an audience here.

"No, little monster, she wasn't scary." Rus smiled softly, shaking her head. "She just wanted to give me a warning," Rus said meaningfully, her silver gaze meeting Azure's. "To let me know that maybe we should look after your Aunt Vi a bit better."

Azure's skin prickled, gooseflesh rising with every hair on her body. Vi. Her sister. She'd been foolish to think the soul jumper would be done with her once they chased it from town. To think that maybe the reason Violet had been chosen for Taryn's wife wasn't because of the soul jumper. What did that mean? Did it care for Violet? Or was there something else? Something worse going on?

"Aunt Vi?" Meiling blinked at them, a plate in her hand.

"Az's sister, Violet," Rus explained, and Azure almost winced at the fact that she had to. "She's your doctor remember?"

The girls had met her a handful of times over the last year, but Violet hadn't been as present in their lives as the others in her family. They didn't know Violet the way they knew Indigo, Sunila, and her aunts. And most of that was because she and Violet had fought when Azure decided to leave the Circle of Jade Waters, and they hadn't properly made up. She would have to rectify that.

"Oh." Meiling set her plate down and sat beside her sister, but she still looked unsettled by this information. "Is she okay?"

"I'm sure she'll be fine, A'Ling." Rus's tone was gentle and warm. "We're going to stop by her place after we're done the celebration today. Do you two want to come with?"

The girls shifted, unsure. Which was perfectly reasonable.

Azure wondered if Violet realized what she was missing out on by being so closed minded and keeping herself separated from them. It was a pity.

"If you don't want to go, you don't have to," Azure assured. "There will be plenty of chances to visit with her some other time." When the tension between Violet and the woman Meiling and Aihuan considered to be their mother was less prevalent. It wouldn't be fair to ask them to sit through that.

"We'll go home with Uncle Nando," Meiling said after glancing at Aihuan. "If that's all right?"

"It is." Azure nodded.

"We'll have to meet with Aunt Phyre after, too, so I need you both to not give Nando any trouble, am I clear?" Although Rus didn't sound like she actually thought they would. They were good kids. "You have to stick to your school-day bedtime."

"But Auntie Rus, it's Friday!" Aihuan groaned, throwing her head back with a flair for the dramatic that she had clearly learned from Rus.

"Nope. None of that. We have to be up early again tomorrow to man the table. You know that. And I can't have you both in bad moods. I need bright, happy children to convince people to join our coven," Rus teased. She stood to lean over the table and push the corners of Aihuan's mouth up into a smile. "There we go, that's better."

Aihuan grumbled and swatted Rus's hands away, but Meiling was doing her best to cover her laughter.

"You too, Meiling. No grumpy teenagers."

"Fine." Meiling rolled her eyes.

"Good. Now finish your lunch. We've got to get back to the table before Ava glares away all our potential coven members."

"Don't you mean *scares* away?" Meiling snorted.

"I said what I said."

Chapter 12

Azure's hands would probably smell like crab for the rest of the day, in spite of the fact that she'd washed them at least five times and used lemon on them. But that was the least of her worries after leaving behind her little family at their table outside Necromancer's.

The hiccups of the morning seemed to have been ironed out through sheer force of will. It wasn't perfect, not by a long shot, but Azure supposed some things were bound to go wrong. That was the nature of events on this scale.

Still, the appearance of Mazarin Elwood felt like a harbinger of something much worse, and her warning echoed through Azure's mind as she wove between the stalls, checking in with the vendors. It took about an hour and a half for her to make her rounds completely and wind up back where she'd left Rus and the girls.

Rus's stall was packed now. A cluster of eager faces crowded all the way around the tables as people made their purchases and chatted with the members of the Coven of the Forgotten. While Hunter and Ava were there helping, it was Rus who stole the show. Her hands flapped about as she spoke, her eyes shining.

Azure wasn't close enough to hear what she was saying, but she didn't need to be to imagine Rus's voice in the back of her head as she explained something to the three young folk in front of her. Two witches and a fae, Azure guessed based on their auras. College age. Maybe they were some of Rus's students?

All she could hope was that they didn't already belong to one of Moondale's clans or covens. If they did, then Rus would refuse to add them to the Forgotten. Which was foolishness, in Azure's opinion, but things like recruitment weren't up to her, and Rus had drawn a hard line on this discussion in particular. They would not take from any of the existing families. They would not make an enemy of those that surrounded them. Azure could see the wisdom in it, but that didn't make it any less annoying. Especially when she was very much aware that one day there would be no choice but to do that.

Still, she supposed it was nice how small and intimate their coven was at the moment.

"Az!" Rus called, waving her hand to draw Azure forward, like reeling in a fish. And the same as a fish, Azure was helpless but to go. "There you are." Rus beamed at her like she'd missed Azure unbearably, even if they'd only been apart for less than a couple of hours at this point.

Not that Azure didn't feel the same, because she did. She knew it was silly, and absurdly co-dependent, but it was like making up for lost time. They'd spent eleven years apart, and Azure didn't want to waste another moment if she could help it. She couldn't help it, a fact made abundantly clear by all the shit that had gone wrong so far that day.

"I was just showing these three my phone case," Rus babbled as Azure got closer, but not close enough to get between the pack of twenty-somethings and Rus. They were all looking at her like she was some kind of techno-magic goddess. Which she was, in Azure's unbiased opinion. "I still need to make one for you."

Azure hummed with a nod. "When we have more time."

Although when that would be, she had no idea. After they dealt with the soul jumper, at the bare minimum, but Azure couldn't help but think that even then there might not be time. It was as if the universe at large had seen fit to test them at every turn. She would worry that Moondale didn't approve of her and Rus's relationship—as she tended to make her displeasure known when she thought two people weren't meant to be together, Azure's sister and Taryn being a prime example—but the town herself had done nothing but try to sink her teeth into them more and more each day. Maybe there was something else at work? Not that it mattered. Azure wouldn't let go of Rus, and Rus seemed to feel the same.

Rus had fixed her with a soft smile, then she shook herself to return her attention to the little crowd she'd gathered. "As I was saying, phone cases are the easiest way to protect your devices from magical attacks like scraping for hexes and spying spells."

She popped her phone out of the case to show the group the intricate web of sigils and characters in a variety of different languages from all over the world. Each had their purpose. One braided over the other to form something damn near impenetrable by any folk trying to use Rus's device against her.

"Makes the phone weigh more than a brick, but it's definitely saved my bacon more than once." Rus handed the case over to one of the witches, and the twenty-something's hand dropped under the weight of it.

"Holy shit, you weren't kidding." They laughed and passed it to another of the group.

"Is that the magic doing that?" one of them asked, their

head tilted in interest. "A consequence of the spellwork, a bug, so to speak? Or is it intentional?"

"Excellent question!" Rus crowed with all the excitement of a professor in front of a lecture hall of young minds who were seriously engaged with the material. This was why Azure had talked her into being a guest lecturer at Moondale University all those weeks ago. Not just because Rus had knowledge that should be shared, but also because she genuinely enjoyed sharing it. She liked passing along something she'd learned to others, no matter what age they were. Rus coveted knowledge, but she wasn't miserly about it.

Rus took the phone back and tilted it to the light so she could point at two characters scrawled into the corner. "You see these?"

The group nodded collectively.

"These are a weight charm. They add heaviness without adding mass." Rus's grin had spread so wide, it made her eyes squint. Azure was arrested by the happiness that shimmered from every pore of Rus, her heart lodged somewhere in her sternum as she watched. "Any guess why?"

The group all shifted around, looking at each other, then the tallest of them, the fae, raised their hand. When Rus nodded their way, they said, "Because if someone goes to pick up your phone when you aren't paying attention, they're going to react oddly to the weight and draw your notice?"

"Exactly!" Rus laughed. "It's nothing more than that. Some magical precautions are a little less magical, and a little more practical, and that's okay. Not everything has to be shrouded in mysticism. Sometimes the easiest safety measure is the most effective."

A murmur went through the group, and Azure stepped closer to mumble gently to Rus, "Tell them about your courses at Moondale U."

"Right!" Rus grinned broadly at her. She looked as if she wanted to reach out and kiss Azure for her reminder, but Azure refused to get any closer. She'd already interfered enough. "Thank you, Az."

Azure nodded and turned to slip back into the crowd as Rus moved on to tell the twenty-somethings about the course she would be teaching at Moondale University come next semester. Her gray eyes sparked with enthusiasm. Azure hoped they would show up, at least some of them. She hadn't recognized them, so odds were that they weren't from Moondale. Maybe Ironport or even Eventide. That made them fair game, as far as finding a coven was concerned. And clearly, they were eager...

Azure stumbled forward as someone bumped into her back and kept going without a single apology. She spun, trying to see who it had been, but the crowd was too densely packed now to know. A good sign for Moondale's ley lines, but an annoyance for her. She was just about to head back the way she'd come, make another round of the vendors, and check in over at the fairgrounds when her eyes caught on the table outside Elwood & Co.

Sunila had set up a sidewalk sale in front of the big bay window, leftover stock from the last couple of years littering it with red sale tags fluttering in the breeze. And there, one hand stuffed into his back pocket, the other holding out a to-go cup, shoulders hunched forward, was Fernando. His body curled toward Sunila but also shied away from her. At odds, it seemed.

Azure knew she shouldn't. Being nosey was a terrible habit, and if her aunt Carmine caught her eavesdropping growing up, there was always hell to pay, but the punishments had never broken Azure of it. Besides, it wasn't like Fernando and Sunila were trying to hide the way they felt about each other from anyone. It was just that neither seemed to know how to act on it.

"For you," Fernando said, thrusting the to-go cup closer. "I know our chocolate chai is your favorite, and it's supposed to get chilly later. It has a warming charm on it, so it should last." Even as he spoke, he didn't meet Sunila's gaze, his head ducked.

Sunila, for her part, seemed unaccountably charmed by Fernando's kindness and his shyness. It was a wonder they hadn't made it further along yet, with how forward Sunila could be, but perhaps she was afraid of scaring him off. A valid concern, although from what Azure had seen of Fernando, he wasn't exactly flighty.

Timid, yes. But also steady.

Azure wondered sometimes if he had learned that from Rus or vice versa. They were so different in every other way, but in their steady there-ness, they were the same. It was a relief and a comfort now that Azure was living with them full-time.

"You're so sweet," Sunila murmured, heat coloring her cheeks. "You know, Fernando." She said the name gently, like one might call a scared animal, and Azure got the distinct impression that she was seeing something private, something maybe she should look away from. But she was much too nosey to do so, and even if she weren't, Rus would probably scream at her if she did. They'd both been rooting for Fernando for months by that point. "Would you maybe like to do dinner sometime? After the centennial is over, of course. And things have settled down. I know you're very busy with coven business, and I—"

"I'd like that," Fernando said, cutting Sunila off mid-ramble. "I'd like that very much."

Sunila's face darkened further, her eyes went wide, and Azure had the pleasure of watching her always flirty, always ridiculous cousin stumble over her words. "Friday!" Sunila squeaked. "I mean— What I mean to say is— You don't have—"

"Next Friday works perfect." Fernando unfurled, his voice leveling out into something Azure would almost call smooth. This, she recognized, he had learned from Rus. Even the casual slouch was something Rus had employed many times when she flirted. "Eight?"

"Eight is good." Sunila nodded a little too quickly and knocked into the table, sending several things tumbling to the ground. "Shit."

Fernando laughed warmly and bent to scoop the items up, putting them back carefully exactly the way they'd been. Conscientous and kind. "I was thinking maybe..." He twitched a little, and although Azure couldn't see his face from this angle, she could imagine him chewing on the inside of his cheek as he tried to draw on the slowly growing confidence he'd acquired since coming to Moondale. "Maybe I could come to your place and cook for you?"

"That sounds great. If you wouldn't mind?" Sunila tilted her head, her artfully tousled hair falling across her eyes as she got back into the swing of things.

Azure pulled away. She had seen enough. They were on the right track now. All that was left was to leave them to it. Whatever was meant to happen now, would.

Chapter 13

Blue rumbled around them, the music from her speakers cut low, not by Rus's hand, but by the car herself. She seemed to sense that Rus and Az needed to talk, and she wasn't willing to give Rus the distraction she wanted to avoid it. Which was just fucking peachy. Not that Rus wasn't fully aware that it was a bad idea to cop out of this conversation. It was just that she didn't like the idea of having to tell Az about her sister.

Still. She did.

When Rus was done telling Az everything Mazarin said, they sat in silence for a while, the car idling at a stop sign as a large group of tourists crossed the road. Moondale had never been so busy before in Rus's life. Sure, they had festivals, and markets, smaller events. Enough to bring visitors to the town and keep the economy going. But never anything on this scale. They were always smaller, more niche, drew less people. Nothing like this. She supposed a once-in-a-hundred-years celebration was enough of a draw.

"Hey, Az," Rus said just as she was pulling away from the crosswalk. The silence had stretched on for too long, and while she knew they both needed to seriously think about what they were going to say to Vi to convince her to let them help her, she didn't want Az to get too caught up in her head. That way led disaster for them both, as Rus was deeply familiar with the way Az could take the blame for things that weren't her fault.

Az hummed in question, turning her attention from where she'd been staring into the middle distance to look at Rus.

"Do you think we were together in our past lives?"

It was a ridiculous question. Silly and frivolous. New souls were born all the time. Not every folk family knew or cared to perform the rituals necessary for reincarnation. The Huntsmen, for example—the progenitors of the vampire hunting Venator—had never bothered when it came to their Venator children. They were treated as expendable things—weapons, exterminators—instead of the folk they were. That might have been why Rus had been so willing to help Eric and his boyfriends. Because she knew, in her bones, they wouldn't get another chance at it. That also might have been why it was so hard to bring Eric back— he'd assumed there was no returning once he died.

That was neither here nor there. The point was, there was no reason to believe that she and Az had been together in their previous lives, if they'd even *had* previous lives. But Rus couldn't help but wonder...

"I have little doubt," Az said, her voice firm and sweet. Full of the kind of conviction Az had developed while Rus was gone. It was good to see her so sure, so certain, comfortable in her own skin. Rus didn't think she'd ever loved Az half as much as she did now.

"Yeah." Rus's laugh was breathless, her ears hot. "Me either."

Az reached across the center console and pulled Rus's hand from the wheel, threading their fingers together in a hold that sent a zing of sensation skittering along Rus's nerves. Goddess, if they weren't on their way to Vi's to warn her about a revenge plot by the soul jumper in habiting her estranged wife's body, Rus would pull over the car this instant.

Instead, Rus lifted Az's hand to her lips and pressed a kiss to the back of it. A reminder that she was there, whatever came next, and Az returned her attention to the house down the street where her sister had once lived with her wife.

What the soul jumper had done to the place left its mark. The spirits that once crowded the front yard were gone, but the grass where they'd stood was devoid of any color or life. The whole place, it seemed, had been sapped of it. Like someone used a desaturation filter, but in real life. It made Rus uneasy, and that was saying something, considering how frequently she interacted with the dead.

But this place wasn't just dead, it was... it was a *void*.

"Why does she stay here?" Rus couldn't help asking, even if she already knew the answer. Vi had loved the soul jumper. Loved her so much that even after she'd learned of her betrayal, Vi still couldn't let go. Couldn't move on. Not that Rus could blame her, really, she'd be the same way.

"I think she believes she is serving penance," Az said, looking at the little house through the windshield. Her face was pressed into careful impassivity, but she couldn't fool Rus. This bothered her. Knowing that her sister was aching and not allowing anyone to help, not allowing herself to move on. It was slowly eating away at Az.

Well. Enough was enough.

"We should have brought Brenton with us." Rus should have given this some more thought before they came out here. Brought back up. Especially when Vi's heart was still painfully bruised from losing her wife. But there hadn't been time to give the situation the due consideration it clearly needed.

"To what end?"

"Don't be purposefully obtuse, Az, it doesn't suit you." Rus scoffed a laugh, giving Az's hand a tight squeeze to assure her that she was only kidding, before dropping it to parallel park by the curb outside Vi's house. "You know he's been in love with your sister since he was, like, five."

That might have been an exaggeration. But it didn't feel like one. After all, she'd spent so much of her childhood with the Elwood sisters that it was kind of hard to miss the gruff, serious, severe little boy whose eyes followed Violet Elwood like a flower seeking the sun.

"We are here to warn my sister and offer whatever protection we can. Not matchmake." But there was a playful chiding in Az's voice, like maybe she found the whole thing amusing. She probably did. She could be mischievous when she wanted to be. A trait Rus liked to think Az had learned from her.

"I can do both. It's called multitasking."

"Of course." Az climbed from the car and waited on the sidewalk for Rus to join her before they made their way up the path to Vi's house, their footsteps seeming to echo in the silence. There was hesitation in her movements as Az lifted her hand to ring the bell, and Rus settled her palm onto Az's lower back, a comforting weight. She was here, she would stay here. She would not let any family complications chase her away.

It took a while for Vi to answer the door, and when she finally did, she had a robe wrapped tightly around her as if to ward off a chill despite the weather not yet changing to fall. Her long, dark hair was woven into a messy braid with several strands pulled loose, and there was an indent on her face, as if she'd been asleep. Guilt churned in Rus's stomach. They should have checked in earlier. Vi was clearly going through it, and it was wrong of them to keep their distance just because she was being prickly.

"I wish you'd called," Vi said with a sigh, but she turned and headed for the kitchen, leaving the door open for them to enter.

"It's a bit of an emergency, I'm afraid." Az followed behind her, with Rus at her heels.

"It always is with you two," Vi muttered so quietly, Rus couldn't tell if she was petulant, annoyed, or just tired. Maybe a combination of all three. "Tea?"

"Yes, thank you," Rus said, because Vi was already filling a kettle with water, and she didn't want to be rude. It was bad enough they were about to upend Vi's entire world a second time in as many months.

"You'll have to excuse the mess." Vi gestured to the sink full of dishes, the stack of mail sprawled across one of the counters as if it'd been stacked there and fallen over, the dust bunnies in the corners, the little table with empty wine bottles and takeout containers, but she didn't offer an excuse or an explanation. Not that she needed to. Rus knew very well what heartbreak could do to someone.

Rus opened her mouth to offer assistance, to try to be the good sister-in-law she knew she ought to be, but Az reached for her, giving her wrist a warning squeeze. They couldn't overstep, not in this. And they didn't want to make Vi feel looked down on.

"It's all right," Az said instead.

Vi hummed noncommittally and pulled down three non-matching teacups, something Rus had never seen her do before. She was an Elwood. She was upright. Prim. Proper. Always. Rus ached for her. There was no love lost between them—Vi had never approved of Rus and Az's relationship—but that didn't mean she deserved *this*. No one did.

"What is it this time?" Vi asked, and now Rus was sure of it: She was exhausted. Maybe there was something to the idea that they should set her up with Brenton, after all. Just as friends, at least for now. He'd always been good for Vi when they were kids. Rus wondered what happened there, but she had her suspicions.

"Mazarin appeared to Rus again." Az stayed at Rus's side as they both moved to stand against one of the counters, Rus leaning against it in a slump that she hoped looked relaxed when she was anything but. They needed to put Vi at ease. Needed her to listen to them instead of going on the defensive. And that would never happen if they came at this the wrong way.

Vi went entirely still. Her shoulders tightened and the line of her back straightened. Rus didn't have to see her face to know what played across it. Upset. Shock. Fear. What she didn't expect was the rage that came from Vi when she next spoke. "What did *she* want?"

Az glanced at Rus, clearly discomfited by Violet's reaction, but Rus couldn't blame her, honestly. Vi had been happy. She'd thought her wife loved her. She didn't know the soul jumper was even *there*. And Mazarin's—the soul jumper's ex-wife's—reappearance had likely been what pushed the soul jumper to act as she did. Forced her hand. It had burst Vi's pretty little bubble.

Biting down on the inside of her cheek, Rus raised her brows at Az in question. It was sort of taboo to tell someone about their former life. One could speculate. One could daydream. But to know for certain? It wasn't exactly forbidden, but it wasn't the done thing. Still, when was the last time Rus bothered with such conventions? It was those unsaid rules that had gotten them all into this mess.

"Mazarin worries the soul jumper targeted you specifically." Rus kept her tone gentle, quiet, but still she could see how the words struck Vi. A subtle jerk that Rus might have missed had she not been looking for it, like someone had slapped her.

"*Why?*" Violet choked out through a throat that sounded like it was thick with tears, but she didn't turn around. She didn't look at them. Which might be for the better.

Az shook her head subtly, but Rus forged on anyway. She'd deal with Az's chiding later. "You're the reincarnation of Mazarin Elwood's eldest sister, Hyacinth Elwood. The eldest sister that led the charge to punish Mazarin and the soul jumper after Mazarin brought her back from the dead. Mazarin feels this was a vendetta. Revenge."

"For something I don't even remember doing." Defeated, sad, heartbroken. If this were anyone else, anyone who Rus was actually close to, she might have reached for Vi and pulled her into a hug. Assured her that she wasn't alone in this.

"It would seem so." Az lifted her chin. She looked a little annoyed by Rus's lack of tact, but she probably wouldn't give Rus too much shit about it. She trusted Rus's judgment.

Rus nodded to her, then in the direction of Vi. A subtle gesture meant to encourage Az to go to her sister. But Az hesitated. She took a step forward, her hand lifted, but she couldn't breach the divide between them. Not yet. Maybe Violet wouldn't have accepted comfort from her sister. They were both still healing. Rus wouldn't push them. Not if they weren't ready.

"What am I going to do?" Vi whispered to herself.

"I'll be setting up a sentinel before we leave," Rus said, even if she knew that Violet hadn't been talking to them. "I have a couple of ghosts not patrolling who can stay here with you and make sure nothing comes for you. They won't be inside, of course, but they'll be perfectly happy to hang around your yard and keep an eye on things. They'll let me know if anything comes up." Rus shrugged, unbothered.

"And I will put some extra warding on your house," Az volunteered.

Vi stilled and turned to look at Rus and Az over her shoulder, dark eyes wide, brows drawn up, surprised. Flabbergasted, really. Which was fair. After the way Vi treated them both when they'd first gotten back together, it would be within their rights to ignore her and any danger she was in. But they wouldn't. "You don't—you don't have to do that."

"It is not a hardship," Az said at the same time Rus shrugged and said, "You're family."

Violet's jaw fell open in an expression Rus had never seen on her before.

"Right then." Rus rubbed at the back of her neck awkwardly. She wasn't used to people looking at her with that kind of gratitude, especially those who didn't like her. "We should get to work, aye, Az?"

"Yes." Az nodded, fixing Rus with a tiny smile. Barely noticeable. But it was there. A *thank you* shining in her eyes that was entirely unnecessary, because as Rus said, Vi was family.

"I'll finish getting your tea ready. Can I—" Violet's eyes flicked between them, unsure. "Can I get you anything else?"

"Dinner would be swell. Pizza, maybe?" Rus grinned,

ignoring the flat look Az gave her. "Haven't eaten since lunch, and after this we've got a meeting with Phyre."

Violet blinked for a moment, as if confused by Rus. She probably was. Rus never did act the way people thought she should. It's what gave her an edge, she thought. "I think I can manage that."

"Super!" Rus gave her a thumbs-up, then trudged out into the yard to get started.

Chapter 14

The air outside had shifted, grown colder, in the twenty or so minutes Rus and Az were inside, speaking to Vi. Not entirely unheard of for this time of year —just on the cusp of fall—but still strange. Rubbing her arms, Rus walked to the short white picket fence that lined the front of the yard, separating it from the sidewalk. She didn't think Vi wanted ghosts on her property again, which was completely valid. but Rus could get her spies close enough to sense if something was off.

There was a gurgle from the trees lining the sidewalk, and Rus looked up just in time to see Darcy swoop down to land on her shoulder in silent admonishment, his talons digging into her skin beneath the thin long-sleeved shirt she wore.

"Maybe she will, maybe she won't." Rus shrugged, jostling him. Although he was probably right. Violet likely wouldn't thank her for what she was about to do. She likely wouldn't even think twice about the energy Rus had to expend to bring souls forward and convince them to remain stationary in a place like this, on land that Rus could feel like a splinter under her skin. The soul jumper had left a curse, a blight, on this place that would take years, perhaps decades to root out. It might almost be better if Vi just left it behind. But "It's the right thing to do."

Darcy clicked his beak, nipping at her ear.

He was right about that too. She'd get no recognition for this from the Board of Magic, or from the clans and covens as a whole. The Elwoods would care, Jade Waters might feel indebted to her for looking after one of theirs, and Az was already grateful—that had been clear in the way she squeezed Rus's hand before she left the porch. But Rus never did anything for recognition. It wasn't her way.

Still, she couldn't hold his pettiness against him—crows were well-known to hold grudges for upward of a decade, it was in his very nature—even if she was always the type to forgive too easily. And there was a certain level of loyalty in it she was grateful for. Darcy acted like an unaffected asshole most of the time, but he cared for Rus and her little family. He'd give his life for them if he had to. And Rus appreciated that more than she'd ever be able to put into words.

Good thing she didn't have to.

The connection between a familiar and their witch was a unique thing. They were able to communicate, to share magic, to be one in a way no other living creatures could. So when Rus raised her hand to stroke through Darcy's feathers, she knew he understood what she was trying to say to him.

Unfortunately, he was also more emotionally constipated than any other creature Rus had the displeasure of knowing. So instead of leaning into the gentle affection from his witch, he bit her fingers, his sharp beak slicing through the tips, just before he flew back to the tree to watch her with irritation.

"That fucking hurt, you little bitch," Rus hissed at him, cradling her bleeding hand close to her chest.

Darcy chortled from where he settled quite happily on a branch, his eyes gleaming. Fucking bastard.

"Cutting my arm with an athame to get the blood I need would have hurt less, and you know that damn well." She grumbled, rolling out her shoulders, before she squeezed her fingers so the blood welled closer to the tips, forming droplets. They hit the sidewalk on the other side of the fence with a hiss that echoed through the sucking silence of her magic forming. It would anchor her spy here, giving them the magic they needed not to drift like tumbleweeds on the breeze. Then there were the whispers, rising with the green magic that floated around her like toxic fumes.

"I need someone to watch this place," she told the spirits. "Someone who can hide themselves from not just the living but also the dead. Someone unafraid to face off against a soul jumper, should things come to that."

Rus could force one of them to do it. Drag them from their rest and make them stand guard outside of Violet's door if she wanted to. She knew how. And honestly, it wouldn't be the first time she had. But she'd learned a long time ago that it was better to ask for what she wanted. To get volunteers. To build a reputation among the dead as someone willing to help them, to work *with* them. Then they were less likely to turn their rage on her when something went wrong. She had enough scars on her body from pissed-off spirits who hadn't come willingly to know better.

The whispers hit a fever pitch. Growing in power. Talking over each other.

Then the spirit of a younger person stepped forward. Holly. Rus recognized them immediately from the apartment building in Ironport all those months ago, even as they looked different now. The After had been kind to them, allowed them to rest, to take shape. Their eyes were no longer empty pits. Their mouth a firm, set line, instead of the yawning dark.

"You don't have to do this," Rus pressed gently. "If you want to remain at rest, that is understandable." It hadn't been long since Holly moved on to the After. Not even a full year. Rus never meant to call one so recently gone. It wasn't fair. Especially one like Holly, who had languished so long among the living before finding a way to move on.

"I want to help you," Holly said, lifting their chin. They were still childlike in appearance, too young to have died, but there was a knowing to their eyes now. Like they hadn't gone to the After and rested, like they had gone and learned. Watched Rus and what she was doing. "You gave me a gift. I want to return the favor."

"You don't have to," Rus repeated. "My helping you was never conditional."

"I know that." Holly nodded, their long hair brushing across their face in an unfelt breeze. "I'm here anyway."

Rus sucked in a breath, hoping it didn't shake on the exhale. Holly shouldn't feel the need to do this. They'd been through enough. They couldn't be much older than Meiling—eighteen, early twenties at best. They had died *so* young. She couldn't ask this of them.

"You're not asking," Holly said, seeming to read what was going through Rus's mind. "I'm volunteering." They stepped forward, their body phasing through the fence until they stood before Rus, and their hand settled over top of Rus's in a cold touch that held no solidity, like touching Jell-O. "You helped me. I want to help you."

Rus's next inhale *did* shake, her eyes burning with an emotion that was better swallowed. "All right." She scrubbed her nose, hoping it would hide the way she was on the verge of tears, and sniffed. "But the moment you see it, you come to me. Don't try to fight it. Don't stand against it. Report to me."

Holly cocked their head, still birdlike in their movements even months later, like they'd forgotten how to be human in the years since they'd died. "But you said—"

"And now I'm saying *this*. You come to me. Understood?"

Holly smiled, soft and knowing. "Understood."

"Good." Rus flapped her hand through the air to dissipate the remaining whispers.

"I will also help," Cecil said, stepping through what remained of the green magic before it could float away.

"You've just *gotten* there!" Rus choked. Her eyes popped wide at the boy she and Meiling helped cross into the After not but a few days prior. He looked better rested now, more put together. But that didn't change the fact that he should be at peace. They both should be.

Cecil shrugged, clearly unbothered.

Rus blew out a breath, her hair puffing away from her face with it. "Fine. But you heard what I told Holly. Don't take any risks."

"Of course," Cecil and Holly said as one, both dipping their heads, and all Rus could do after was huff and turn on her heel to head back to the house where Az was waiting for her, her cheeks hot.

Really. Where did these children get off treating her with so much *respect*?

VIOLET ALREADY HAD some wards in place, because she wasn't an idiot. But they weren't nearly enough, in Azure's opinion. And as she sat on the porch swing, her senses reaching out to test their strength, she realized they hadn't been updated since before Taryn was found to be the soul jumper. It was almost like Violet wanted the soul jumper to return to finish what it'd started.

Azure shook that thought aside. She understood Violet's heartbreak. The depression she was feeling was entirely reasonable in the wake of finding out that her wife wasn't her wife, but some evil creature intent on taking over their town. Violet's reaction was warranted. Azure couldn't fault her for it. After all, she'd lost the woman she loved once, too, but at least Rus hadn't turned out to be a monster. So there was that.

Still, Azure released a tired sigh, and her fingers tightened around her knees as she began to hum gently. Magic rose from her, soft and cooling, to brush against her skin. Calming. She closed her eyes to focus, to feel the world around her, the way it shifted.

There was something wrong with this parcel of land. Something hungry and dark had been there, and it left behind a mark. She could feel it. Raw and gaping. All she could hope was that whatever magic she pumped into Violet's wards wouldn't get eaten up by it.

Maybe Rus was right. Maybe they should convince Brenton to check in with Violet. His magic had more brute strength than either of theirs did. Different enough that it might make more headway in protecting Violet. Maybe they should also talk Greer into coming over to check the wards too. That was his specialty, after all.

Azure nodded to herself, decided, and let her magic flow from her into the wards, shoring them up. It took no time at all, but once she was done, Rus was on her way back up the walk.

"Some talismans wouldn't go amiss." Rus smiled conspiratorially and sat down next to Azure, their shoulders brushing, a comforting weight at Azure's side. Right where she belonged.

"No, I suppose they wouldn't."

"Every little bit helps."

Azure nodded, pulling her purse up onto her lap to dig out a pad and a pen.

"The one you used at 157 will have to be modified," Rus advised, her head on Azure's shoulder as she worked. "Since Violet's house isn't sentient the way our home is."

Our home. It still cut through Azure like a knife some-times—hot and aching—the realization that she finally had everything she'd ever wanted. A home. A family. Rus. The Goddess had smiled upon her, and she wasn't going to squander her blessing. With a small smile ticking up the corners of her lips, she rested the pad on her knee and pulled the box from her pocket. "Will you marry me?"

Rus squeaked, looking down at the ring, then let out a soft, happy laugh. "Az, we still haven't talked about all the things you missed while I was gone. There is—" She paused, taking a breath. "There's a lot."

"You said you'd tell me in your own time." Azure shrugged, unbothered.

A long, slow breath left Rus, and she reached down to snap the box closed. "Tonight. I'll tell you some of it tonight. We'll talk about Sage."

"Okay." Azure pressed a kiss to her forehead in reward, tucked the ring back into her bag, then returned to her talisman work, taking Rus's suggestion in mind.

"The symbol for a home needs to change based on square footage," Rus continued.

"Single occupancy is also important."

"Right. Where will you put them?"

"Someplace she won't notice, and neither will anyone else." Azure twisted around to look at the pot next to the door. The plant inside of it was dead, another victim of the soul jumper's hunger, but it would do.

"Good idea." Rus nodded her approval.

"I would also like for Evander to come out here and check the Crimson Tide–provided wards. I think they've been damaged."

"Ugh, you want me to talk to *Greer*?" Rus groaned, flopping back further onto the swing in a heap.

"I thought you two had made up." Azure bit back a laugh at Rus's dramatics, shaking her head. She wasn't fooled. They were well on their way to being friends again, and she wasn't about to give Rus an out.

"We did. That doesn't mean I like him." Rus's eyes narrowed on her, as if she knew exactly what Azure was doing. "You're scheming."

"I am doing no such thing." Azure returned to the talisman, her pen marks careful and precise. "Brenton ought to come by, too, to set his own wards."

"You said we couldn't matchmake. I remember very clearly you saying I needed to keep my busybody nose out of it not but an hour ago."

"Those weren't the words I used." Azure finished up the talisman and ripped it from the pad, letting her magic flow into the paper so it would better stand up to the elements before she stuck it to the back of the flowerpot, where no one would notice it. "Come. We've still got to meet with Phyre, and the pizza will be here soon."

"Fine." Rus grumbled, but she let Azure pull her to her feet and lead her back inside for what would no doubt be a very awkward supper. But at least she and Violet were talking, for the first time in weeks. Azure would not look this gift in the mouth, especially not with Rus at her side, leaning subtly against her like a particularly persistent cat.

So inside they went.

Chapter 15

The quiet that settled between Azure and Violet was nothing like the companionable stretches of silence she'd known growing up. There was a sadness, a heaviness to this one. Made only more awkward by the way Rus shifted around in her chair, the legs creaking beneath her. Rus had never been particularly adept at staying quiet, but she seemed determined to let Azure and Violet work this shit out themselves. Which Azure found particularly annoying.

So it was no real surprise that the first full breath she managed to take was when they were standing on Violet's front porch, saying goodbye. Rus's hand was warm and firm on the small of her back, the pressure an easy weight that had Azure's spine relaxing.

"We'd like it if you came by to see our girls soon," Rus said without any prompting from Azure.

Our girls. It made Azure's body hum with a contentment she didn't know how to put into words. A warmth that spread through her veins like syrup. Aihuan and Meiling were her daughters as much as they were Rus's now. Wasn't that just... *wonderful?*

When Azure looked at Rus out of the corner of her eyes, she saw Rus looking back, a soft smile on her face like she could see right through Azure's carefully neutral expression. Like she'd felt the shift in Azure, had said it that way deliberately to have that effect. Like she knew what she was doing.

Violet, too, seemed to know what was happening when her sister's heart clenched in her chest before beating so quickly she could feel it pounding in her temples. Because she tilted her head, a light of amusement dancing in her eyes that hadn't been there during their entire visit. "Yes," Violet agreed. "I think I'd like that."

"Great!" Rus chirped, her smile spreading further.

Yes. Rus knew *exactly* what she was doing.

"We have a meeting," Azure reminded, hoping to curtail any further teasing from her sister and girlfriend.

A soft laugh burbled up Violet's throat that seemed to surprise all of them, Violet included, who blinked wide eyed for a moment after it had finished. She cleared her throat. "Well, I'll see you all soon."

"Will you be coming to the centennial celebration? We've got a table set up outside of Necromancer's." Rus planted her feet subtly, obviously unwilling to move until she decided it was time for her to go. Azure wasn't sure what Rus was looking for or trying to achieve. But sometimes it was better to let Rus do what she felt she had to. "The girls are helping sell these cute little crocheted ghosts."

Violet's eyes grew wider. "I—" She paused, her gaze flicking from Rus to Azure, as if seeking Azure's help to head off whatever Rus was doing. She had to know that was impossible. Icarus Ashthorne was a force of nature. A menace. A typhoon. She would do as she pleased, and none could stop her. Not that Azure had ever wanted to. There was something kind of beautiful about watching Rus lay waste to people's plans and perceptions by simply being who she was. "Yes," Violet said finally, when no help was offered. "I think I will. Maybe tomorrow around lunch?"

"Perfect! We'll see you then." Rus's grin grew into a bright, shining thing that was honestly hard to look at. Then she spun on her heel and hauled Azure behind her toward where Blue was parked on the curb.

"What was that about?" Azure asked once they were inside the car and Rus was pulling onto the road to head toward Phyre's.

"She needs to get out of that fucking house," Rus said simply. "You saw what it was like. She's surrounded by Taryn. Photos. Clothes. Shared dishes. She can't stay there, and I didn't think I could convince her to go stay with your aunts. Not yet, anyway. But maybe some time with the girls will help. And we can always shove Brenton at her once we get her out and about too."

The warmth that tingled through Azure's veins turned into a fever pitch, molten and hot, at the realization that despite what Violet had done, Rus was willing to forgive. More than that, she was willing to help Violet dig herself out of the hole of depression she'd buried herself in.

"Pull over."

"Why? What's wrong?" Rus glanced at her with a frown.

"I need to kiss you. Right now."

Rus laughed, her turn signal already on to pull off the road even as she said, "Az, we're gonna be late."

"It won't take long."

"I think we both know that's a lie." But the car was in park a second later, and Rus didn't do anything to dissuade Azure as she climbed across the center console into her lap.

Rus let out a startled laugh that rumbled against Azure's chest where they were pressed together but cut off the moment Azure hooked her fingers under Rus's jaw and drew her lips up to meet her own. It was a slow, heady kiss. The kind they wouldn't have had time for when they were younger. Unhurried, but thorough. Maybe the setting of the car was eerily similar to when they'd made out a few times in her vehicle, hoping for a little bit of privacy from her siblings, her aunts, and the house packed with roommates where Rus lived. But the act itself was different.

Azure was breathless when she finally pulled away, her body singing at the contact. "Marry me?"

Rus frowned, leaning forward to bite at her lower lip in admonishment. There was some fear in her voice when she said, "The last person I brought back from the dead—before Eric, that is—was four years ago. They were a part of one of the Mafia families in Eventide, and we had to take another life for it to work." Rus wouldn't meet her eyes as she said it, her shoulders drooped forward.

"The life you took," Azure spoke carefully, "were they also from one of the families?"

"Yes." Rus closed her eyes as if she were afraid of watching Azure when she told her this. Maybe she thought that Azure would judge her for it. "The person I brought back was looking to get out of that life. The one helping them wanted an out too. The life we took wasn't a good person. They were a murderer in their own right, a dealer, a —but that doesn't excuse—"

"Did you take their life, or was it the one helping?"

"I—" Rus opened her eyes, frowning. "What?"

"Were you holding the blade?" Azure clarified, because clarity was important.

"No. But I definitely told Corey we had to—"

"Then you didn't kill that person," Azure said simply. "Those you were working with made their own decisions.

They would have done so had you not been there. You were complicit, yes. But I can see your reasoning."

It was murky at best, but Azure was finding it harder and harder to judge Rus for the things she'd done in the past. For the morally gray way she lived her life. She was slowly coming to understand that if she were to be with Rus, she was going to have to accept all of her. The blood on her hands included.

"Why did you help them? Apart from the fact that they wanted to escape that life?" Which was reason enough, in Azure's mind. Anyone who wanted to change should be allowed to. Rus had just been a vehicle for that.

"Sage had this kid…" Rus frowned, her brow creasing in confusion. "They didn't take her with them, but they kept up with them, protected them, even from afar. I just couldn't imagine not being there for my moonkids like that, even if this was before they lost their parents. And Corey had younger sisters, too, who were in danger."

Azure nodded. She thought she was beginning to understand Rus a bit better. To see the gray area she lived in. It had never been Azure's desire to live in such a way. For most of her life, she'd seen things as black and white. To the point that when Rus brought Darcy back, they'd had a fight about it. Azure still remembered how she called the act evil. How she condemned Rus for saving Darcy at the cost of another life. She cringed at those memories now, felt shame at how she reacted. How she shut Rus out and refused to listen.

She would not make the same mistake again.

The longer she'd lived without Rus, the more she'd begun to see that people and their actions increasingly fell into a spectrum of gray. Necromancy was considered evil magic, but the way Rus used it was usually to help, not to hurt. Taking another life was wrong, but Azure could see Rus's reasoning, could understand it. And above all else, she trusted Rus to do the right thing, even when the right thing looked like the wrong thing.

"Okay," Rus said on a long breath. "Okay."

Azure perked up. Did that mean—

"I'm not saying yes. Not yet. There's still more. But... thank you for listening? For understanding?" It was said as a question, like Rus wasn't sure how Azure had taken that so well. To be fair, Azure wasn't sure either. It was a lot to learn that the woman she loved had been complicit in what added up to a murder. If the Board of Magic ever found out, Rus would be run from the town. But Azure couldn't find it in herself to see the problem, not when she knew that Rus only ever did what she thought was right, however twisted her logic.

"Of course." Azure leaned forward to press a kiss to the tip of Rus's nose. "Thank you for being honest with me, even though it's scary."

"You're really cool with the fact that I essentially killed someone?" Rus raised a skeptical brow.

"You didn't kill them. Whoever you were working for did. And even then, it sounds like they had a good reason and picked someone who the world was better off without. I'm not going to judge their decisions. I don't know their lives. I don't live in Eventide." Thank the Goddess for that, for as much as Azure was beginning to come to terms with the moral ambiguity of being folk, she didn't think she could handle the bloody streets of that city on the misty island off Moondale's shores. She pressed her forehead against Rus's and inhaled deeply, closing her eyes. "Nothing you can say will scare me off."

"Don't be so sure."

"Fight me." Azure pressed hard against her lips, luring Rus into another deep kiss, her tongue forcing its way past Rus's lips until the other woman melted back into her seat, a groan vibrating her throat. Goddess, Azure loved her.

"YOU'RE LATE," Greer grunted when he opened the door to Phyre's little rambler near the center of town. The front yard was littered with children's toys, and Azure could hear someone squealing further in the house.

"We got held up," Azure offered, daring Greer to challenge her. "We stepped in to see my sister and had dinner with her."

Greer scoffed. His eyes raked over them, no doubt noticing the way Azure's neatly pressed shirt was now a wrinkled mess, and Rus's hair looked distinctly rumpled. Not that Azure gave a single fuck what Greer thought of her and Rus. She'd made that quite clear to him.

"Violet? You went to see Violet?" Brenton asked, bodily pushing Greer out of the way so his wide shoulders and considerable height could fill the doorway almost completely. "How is she?"

Words escaped Azure. She didn't want to give out too much of Violet's private information, especially when she was in such a fragile state. But she didn't want to lie either. Lying wouldn't be conducive to getting Brenton to reach out to Violet and possibly rekindle what they'd had before Taryn.

"Better than expected," Rus supplied, leaning her shoulder against Azure's in a way that let her know she'd noticed Azure's confliction and was taking it upon herself to deal with the situation. Because they were a team. "But still not great. We think maybe you and Greer should go by and check her wards."

"*Me?*" Greer asked from where he'd been shoved aside to stand next to the door. "Why me?"

"Is Crimson Tide not in charge of the wards on Moondale properties?" Azure's voice was calm, cool. Greer could get pissy all he liked, but he knew he'd never win against her. Mainly because she refused to rise to his ire. "My mistake. Perhaps we'll just—"

"Fine." Greer grunted, then stomped off to return to the others.

Brenton glanced over his shoulder and shook his head before turning his attention to Rus and Azure. He took a step back to allow them space to enter the house, but Azure could tell he wasn't done asking them about Violet, so she took her time removing her shoes to place on the rack.

"Do you think she'll even talk to me?" He sounded uncertain, something Azure would never have thought he could do. The Brenton Ironwood she knew had a loud, booming voice. He had serious opinions on things, and he didn't back down from a fight, never had, even when they were children. It was what she admired about him, what she thought her sister loved about him.

"No reason not to try." Rus shrugged, kicking her own shoes off more quickly so she could turn to face Brenton, her arms crossed over her chest. "Unless you want someone else to—"

"No, no. I'll do it." Brenton ran a hand over his long, dark hair. It was pulled into a tight bun at the back of his head. "Someone needs to look after her."

"Perhaps you could come by our table in front of Necromancer's tomorrow," Azure supplied. "Violet will be stopping by around lunch. Then it wouldn't look like it was staged."

"Plus, I kind of need to borrow a nail gun," Rus added.

Brenton huffed a laugh. "Now you sound like Nesta."

"Don't drag me into this!" Nesta called from where they had rounded the corner, likely to see what was taking them all so long in getting inside. "I'm not even *in* the match-making business anymore, remember?"

"Right." Brenton snorted. His eyes flicked to Rus and Azure like he knew something they didn't. Or maybe he thought they did know, and he expected them to be in on the joke. Azure couldn't tell. Nor was she sure what he might be alluding to with the glance.

"But if you want to buy a house," Nesta said. "I've got you covered."

Another shake of his head, and Brenton turned on his heel to head down the narrow entryway hall and turn left, expecting them to follow.

"He's in a mood, isn't he?" Rus stepped forward to throw her arm over her friend's shoulder, leaving Azure to bring up the rear.

"When *isn't* he?" Nesta fired back.

"Fair."

Chapter 16

Rus knew they were looking down the wand of an uphill battle. What they were proposing had never been done before, at least not as far as Rus knew. People came into power as elders of their clan or coven, chosen by the previous elder, and did not leave until they decided it was what they wanted. There had never been a time where the other elders stepped in and removed someone. Never been any recourse for an elder acting badly or being corrupt.

The system was inherently broken, and it was amazing no one had taken advantage of it to this point. Or, at least, not as overtly as Brant clearly was. How it had taken this long for that to happen, Rus wasn't sure. But now that it had, they needed to make it clear that it was unacceptable, and that those in Moondale wouldn't bow down to someone who clearly didn't have their best interests at heart.

"How do you know he's working with the soul jumper? He could just be an asshole?" Cagney raised one red eyebrow, her expression as unskeptical as they come. She knew what Rus was saying was correct, and she agreed, but Cagney had always been the type to play devil's advocate. And really, they needed that right now. They needed someone to poke holes in their plans so they could fill those holes and make this airtight.

"Why not both?" Greer muttered. "Both is good."

Rus choked on a laugh and cleared her throat.

"We have no direct proof," Az acknowledged, though it was said through clenched teeth. Which was fair. It annoyed Rus that they had no hard proof too. They had no paper trail, no way to concretely show the board what Brant was up to. But that didn't mean it wasn't happening.

"So then how are we supposed to turn the rest of the elders against him?" Brenton frowned. So far, he hadn't argued that they shouldn't do this, just that he didn't understand how they would, which Rus respected but hadn't expected.

Her little family unit, the people closest to her... She knew why they were on board. They had seen the way Brant did everything he could to push her out, had encouraged Az to be set up with someone else, and put her and her children in danger. Even if he wasn't working with the soul jumper, that would have been all the proof they needed that he didn't deserve the position he'd been gifted. Brenton, on the other hand, wasn't close to Rus like that. They'd been acquaintances at best and had only really known each other through Az's sister once upon a time.

She understood why Phyre was including him—he was her brother and also under Brant's thumb—but that didn't mean she understood why he was so willing to hear them out. So willing to side with them.

"I don't think it's the elders whose minds we need to change." Phyre's voice was always soft, gentle, kind, but it carried in a way few others could. She had a quiet command of any room she walked into when they were children. It's why Rus gravitated toward her. Well. That and the fact that when the other kids in their group home were bullying her for seeing ghosts, Phyre stood up for her.

Putting herself in between Rus and anyone who dared attack her.

Rus made a sound of interest, her eyes flicking to Phyre's face in question.

Phyre tilted her chin back a little, her dark hair falling off her shoulders. She was a lovely woman, always had been. With skin like burnished copper and eyes so dark they looked almost black but were still somehow not cold. The warmth and kindness she held within her radiated outward, all encompassing. And she'd been the best big-sister figure Rus could have asked for.

Once she was sure she had everyone's attention, Phyre's face split into a slow, easy smile. "We need to convince the other members of the Silver Flame that he is no longer fit to lead us."

"And how are we supposed to do that?" Brenton asked, his tone gruff, but even the faux annoyance couldn't hide how intrigued he was by this idea.

"We're going to provide them with an alternative." Phyre's gaze fixed on Brenton, her smile growing slowly, eyes taking on a level of mischief Rus hadn't seen since they were children and Phyre agreed to help her prank the rest of the kids in their group home. But only if Rus let her take the blame when they were inevitably discovered. It was enough to keep Rus from spilling the itching powder into everyone's pajamas, because she didn't want Phyre getting into trouble. And maybe that should have been the moment she realized that for as quiet, and kind, and gentle, and unassuming as Phyre could be, she was also a mastermind.

"An alternative?" Brenton cocked his head, his brows drawn up. All the eyes in the room had drifted to him. And Rus could see the slowly crawling grin on Nesta's face where they sat next to him. Like they were very much on board with this idea. "Like who?"

There was a beat, a long one. Where everyone just looked at him, and his dark gaze flicked between them, as if he'd find someone else in their little group who could take on this role. Logically, it could have been Phyre, but she wasn't blood born Ironwood. She was adopted into the family. That would make her standing more precarious. Not to mention the fact that so many thought she was a weak witch, hardly enough magic to power her own wards. It wasn't true, of course, Rus knew that from experience. But Phyre seemed to appreciate being underestimated. It meant people left her the fuck alone to raise her kids, and work at the forge, and live the life she wanted. It also meant people weren't knocking on her door, trying to marry her when she was so clearly uninterested.

Brenton finally seemed to catch on. "No. Uh-uh. Nope. Not happening. I'm not doing that. I can't go against Uncle Brant. I don't even—"

"Are you scared of him?" Greer asked with enough disdain in his voice to show that he thought it was patently ridiculous.

"Of course I'm not scared of him! I just—"

"Is it because you actually *respect* him?" Cagney scoffed her own displeasure.

"No! He's definitely not worthy of—"

"Then what *is* it?" Nesta tilted their head, their brows raised high in question, as if genuinely curious, but their eyes were keen and assessing.

Brenton shifted, uncomfortable with being put on the spot.

Rus leaned back in her chair and turned to smile at Az

beside her, unable to hide how interesting she found the dynamic between Cagney, Nesta, and Greer now that they were bullying someone else. She had to admit, for as much as she didn't understand them, and actively disliked Greer on principle, she could see how this might work. They were so similar, but also so different at the same time. All of them stubborn and unwilling to bend to the ways of the world around them—even Greer, though she hated to admit it. They were good for each other.

"I don't—" Brenton swallowed sharply, the sound loud in the ensuing silence as they all waited for him to spit out whatever foolish objection he seemed to have so they could counteract it and get on with the planning phase. "I don't know if I'd be a good elder."

Everyone blinked at him for a long moment, the silence drawing into something distinctly uncomfortable before Phyre choked on a snort and wound up coughing so hard, her eyes shimmered with tears.

"Don't make fun, Phyre!" Brenton grumbled, his arms crossed over his chest. "You know I don't like being in charge!"

Rus coughed, trying to hide her own laugh, but there was nothing for it. The sight of a man like Brenton, who had always seemed large and in charge to her, sinking down in his chair under the scrutiny of his adopted sister, who just kept laughing at him, was too much. And honestly, it was sweet to know that for all his bluster, he'd never once wanted power. It would make him an even better candidate for leadership than Rus first thought.

"Good thing you've got me, then. Right, big brother?" Phyre asked, her head tilted to the side, eyes crinkling with her joy.

Brenton scoffed, looking away from all of them, but he didn't deny it.

"Now that that is settled," Azure said after a moment, "we must think of what tactics we'll use to convince the rest of the coven you should replace Brant."

"Can't we just send out a bulk mailer like he tried to do with Rus?" Cagney's disgruntled tone was obvious, and Rus flushed a little under the knowledge that her friend was still pissed someone had tried to ruin her chances at a new coven a while back. With bulk mail, no less. It was strange sometimes to see how the people she'd left behind all those years ago remained loyal to her.

"No." Phyre shook her head.

"And why not? He was more than happy to use dirty tactics to push Rus out of town. I don't see why we can't—"

"Because we want to prove we're better than him," Phyre said simply. "We can't do that if we're mudslinging."

"Then what are we going to do?" Rus leaned forward, her eyes alight. She would much rather have dragged Brant's name through the mud, but there was a viciousness in Phyre's gaze that told her whatever Phyre had in mind might be more fun.

"We're going to tell the truth." Phyre shrugged easily. "It's always more effective." Phyre looked over at Nesta, a knowing smile passing between them. "Right, Nesta?"

Nesta hummed, picking at their brightly colored nails. "Yes. I think the truth will do quite nicely."

Silence settled between them again, only broken after a moment when Greer asked, "Okay, but what does *that* mean?"

"Don't you worry your pretty little head about it, darling." Nesta cooed, patting his cheek placatingly.

He grumbled in return, his cheeks turning red at the contact, but didn't bite back.

"Riiiiight," Rus said, her eyes darting between all of them, trying to avoid the casual intimacy as if she were seeing something private. But also, she wanted to know too. What did Phyre and Nesta know that they were planning to use against Brant? And would it come back to bite them all in the ass?

"I think we can trust them with this." Az reached over to take Rus's hand and give it a firm squeeze. "We have other things we need to focus on, after all."

She was right, of course she was right, but Rus didn't like the idea of leaving something so important in the hands of others. Even others who she trusted implicitly.

"She's right, Rus." Phyre reached to take her other hand, pulling it toward her so she could pat it gently. "You've got enough to worry about with the soul jumper getting ready to make its move. Focus on that. Let the rest of us deal with the political hellscape."

Rus groaned, leaning her head back. "Fine. Fine." Then she turned to look at Az from where she was still craning her neck up to the ceiling. "We should go home?"

"We should go home," Az agreed readily, already on her feet and pulling Rus from her chair.

"Bye, everybody!" Rus waved. "Don't forget to bring your nail gun by the booth tomorrow, Brenton!"

Brenton grunted his agreement.

"And Phyre, I need some warding nails. I'll send you pictures," she called over her shoulder as Az tugged her toward the door at a steady pace, hardly looking back, and if Rus didn't know any better, she'd think Az had been waiting the entire hour and some minutes they'd been talking to pick back up where they left off in the car. "Az, slow down!"

Az turned to fix her with a heated expression and handed her her shoes. "No."

Okay. So maybe that was *exactly* what was going on.

Chapter 17

"Marry me?" Az pressed the question into Rus's throat, the words sending a buzz of sensation along her nerves. Goddess, if Rus didn't already know that she was going to say yes eventually... Az sure knew how to wear a woman down.

"There's more still," Rus argued, her head thunking back against the door that Az had pushed her up against the moment they made it to their bedroom. The whole house was asleep again, Nando taking care to make sure the girls adhered to their bedtime even when Rus and Az were out trying to save their little town. It felt almost normal, how much of a routine that had become over the last year. Rus wondered if they'd ever know peace.

"Marry me, anyway," Az insisted. Her fingers dug into the skin above Rus's jeans, where she'd rucked up her shirt to reveal her soft stomach. This skin, like everywhere else on Rus's torso, was littered in scars from where she'd been attacked by the demon fox all those years ago. Az's thumb brushed over a faded silver line near her hip with a reverence that made Rus's knees give out under her.

"You should marry someone more acceptable. Someone who doesn't play with the dead for a living." But even as she said it, Rus's arguments were drying up on her tongue. There was still one more big secret she needed to tell Az. One more thing that might drive her away. But Rus had already spilled enough of the big things for one night. She was wrung out and running on empty. That didn't mean she was going to agree before Az knew all of it.

"No." The word was soft, but firm. A quiet command

Fuck, she was so hot. For some reason Rus had thought Az would stay the same while she was gone. It was one of the things she'd loved most about Az back in the day. She was steady, never changing, where Rus seemed to shift with every passing day. It had calmed her then. But eleven—almost twelve at this point—years spanned between the woman Az had been and the woman she was now, and Az had changed. For the better. She was still steady, unwavering, but she had grown into herself.

"Az, come on." Rus laughed as a shiver raced down her spine from the spot where Az was worrying the skin beneath her ear. A soft pinch of teeth and brush of lips. She'd leave behind a mark that hopefully Rus's hair would cover tomorrow. Not that it mattered. "Don't you want a nice little witch who isn't likely to bring a ghost home for dinner?"

"I do not," Az insisted, her grip turning bruising as she pulled Rus's hips into her own for a slow grind that lit every nerve in Rus's body on fire.

"Not even a little bit?" Rus teased. At this point she was almost wondering if the babbling was just pillow talk. They both knew they weren't getting anywhere in this argument tonight. But it was fun to rile Az up a bit. To feel the way her body wound tighter and tighter against Rus's own. "Someone sweet. Someone who isn't cursed."

Az stopped abruptly and pulled back to glare at Rus. Her pupils were blown so large they had almost entirely eaten up her irises. A thin sliver of warm brown only just visible. Color rose high on her cheeks, painting the brown skin a warmer shade. Rus loved her so much it made her teeth ache.

"Cursed?" The word was careful, almost like Az was afraid to ask, and Rus felt herself already caving. How couldn't she? She was always going to tell Az. Always going to lay herself bare at her feet. This might have been the wrong time, but they were here now. A crossroads. Where Rus could either bury her secrets and hope they didn't come back to haunt her, or make a deal with the beautiful witch standing in front of her.

Fuck it. There was never any choice, was there?

"Not exactly. Just—" Rus's next swallow was dry, her tongue sticking to the roof of her mouth. "We should sit down for this."

Az frowned but took Rus's hands, gently, so fucking *gently*, and guided her to their bed. They sat, side by side, their hips pressing together, warm and cozy. Rus didn't look at Az. She couldn't. She stared out the window at the darkened graveyard behind their house. This could be it. Az could leave her because of this. What would she do then? Would this all be over? Would she—would she lose the coven as well? What would be left of her without Az and her strength? Would she crumble?

She sucked in a breath. No. No, she wouldn't. She'd been through worse. She'd survived *worse*. And she had her girls. Her friends. If Az decided this wasn't for her anymore because of what Rus was about to say, then Az didn't deserve her. Simple as that.

But for all that Rus could tell that to herself, her gut still twisted.

"I will not judge," Az murmured gently, her hands still holding Rus's in a firm grip, giving them a squeeze.

"You say that now." Rus laughed, high and nervous. She

wanted to duck her head into Az's neck and never come out again. To hide there until the world stopped trying to pull her apart at the seams. She couldn't.

"I will always say that." There was a surety to Az's words. A firmness. Like she'd thought about this a lot over the last decade or so and had come to the conclusion that to love Rus was to love all of her. Scars included.

Tears pricked the backs of Rus's eyes. She'd just have to come out and say it. "When I brought Aihuan back—" She nearly choked on that sentence. Because although she'd referenced it before, although it wasn't exactly new information for Az, it still felt heavy to say the words out loud. To tell someone that her little girl died, and Rus sacrificed so much to bring her back. "When I brought Huaner back," she continued, "I didn't have someone there to sacrifice. The witch hunters who took her had already moved on, left her behind. And there were no animals anywhere near there. Not that they would have been enough when it came to the balance of things. I did what I had to."

"And what did you have to?"

This was it. This was the part where Rus's world fell apart. She couldn't explain why she thought this was worse than her involvement with a murder. It just was. Maybe because the blood on her hands from bringing Sage back didn't change her down to her marrow, and this did. She didn't want to examine it too deeply.

Rus sucked in a breath and tore herself open. "She needed chances, a lot of them. More than even my own life could give. More than any adult life could give. There was no other way to balance it out, no other way to keep the scales from tipping. I gave up my ability to have children. All those chances, all that possibility, I gave to Aihuan."

It still hurt to think about. And the magic she'd had to

use to do it, to pull Aihuan back, had left its mark on her in more ways than one. Still ached down to the bone.

"So if you were hoping we could have little witchlings all our own... we *can't.*" Which honestly, hadn't been something Rus had known she might have wanted until after the opportunity was gone. She sucked in a shaking breath, squeezing her eyes shut.

"But we do have little witchlings all our own," Az said, her words quiet but certain. "We have Aihuan, and we have Meiling."

"I know that. But it's different. It's not—"

"It's not different." Az's tone grew firmer. "It's the same. You're their mother. You gave Huaner life. It's the same. And if we wanted more... If we wanted babies, there are always orphan witches in need of family." Az's words grew more and more sure as she spoke. She leaned closer to Rus, pulling her in again, her arms tight around her. "And if we wanted to try to get pregnant, there are methods. You may not be able to carry children, but I could. This doesn't stop us. It just makes things different."

"Yeah, but Az—"

"No. This changes nothing." There was a fierceness to the way Az was talking now that drew Rus's eyes open. She jerked her head to look at Az and found her staring back, unflinching. "This. Changes. Nothing."

Oh.

Rus hadn't known she needed to hear that. Hadn't realized the way fear had spread through her veins until it was gone. Like a breath of fresh air after being sick, her chest expanded fully for the first time in what felt like ages.

"Nothing?" She couldn't help but to ask. That didn't sound right. It had to make Az feel differently about her.

"Nothing," Az confirmed, then she pulled Rus in close,

her arms engulfing her in a safe warmth, and Rus leaned more against her, resting her head on Az's shoulder, burying her face in her neck. She smelled like their laundry detergent. Like her sandalwood shampoo. Like skin and sweat and Az. She smelled like *home*.

"I love you," Rus said, as easy as breathing.

"I love you too." Az's arms tightened around Rus, pressing her in closer, like she never wanted to let her go.

They stayed like that for a while, sitting on the edge of their bed, 157 Mourning Moore creaking and groaning around them in the slowly rising wind outside. Comforting. And soft. Rus breathed in deeply, let herself settle into this new world where Az knew the secret that scared her the most and accepted her still. Or maybe not *still*. Maybe it wasn't *in spite of*. Maybe it wasn't anything like that. Maybe it was just that Az loved Rus, and this was a part of Rus, a part of who she was. She was the kind of person who would give any hope she had of having her own children up for a child who was already living. One who she already loved so deeply. Maybe that was just it. Maybe this was just who Rus was, and Az understood that, maybe she always had.

Fuck. It felt good.

It wasn't even a relief. It just felt *good*.

Rus let out a choked-off sob, burying herself further in Az's long, plum-colored hair, breathing her in, taking her time to come back to herself. And when she had, she pulled away from Az and gave her a shaky smile.

"We should get some rest." And not just because Rus was wrung out, stretched thin. But also because tomorrow was another full day of centennial celebrations, and the day when the soul jumper would likely show itself.

"Marry me?" Az asked again, her lips ticking up at the corners in a sly smile.

Rus groaned, throwing herself back against the mattress. "Really, Az? Now? We don't have time for this! We've got the soul jumper to deal with. And I still haven't figured out how in the name of fuck I'm going to combat it."

"You'll think of something." The bed shifted as Az rose from where she'd been sitting to head toward their wardrobe. "You always do."

"Yeah. I do." She didn't have any other option. Either she thought of a way to protect herself, her family, her coven, her town. Or she lost them all. And losing them just wasn't an option she was willing to consider.

"But first, you'll need some rest. We've had a late couple of nights," Az reiterated. Rus's pajamas landed on her chest in a soft *thwump*. "Get dressed for bed."

"So bossy." A snort left Rus as she sat up and started to struggle out of her clothes. Az was right, of course. She needed her rest. She wouldn't be any good to anyone if she ran herself completely ragged. Better to sleep now, so in the morning she could think.

"You like it."

"And what if I do?"

Az shook her head, her slippers scuffing on the dark wood floorboards to come and stand between Rus's spread legs, where she could bend down and kiss her lips gently. No heat. Just warmth. "That's what I said. Now do as you're told."

"Yes, ma'am," Rus muttered, dazed.

Rus jerked awake, suddenly on high alert.

She was in her room.

The space was warm and cozy.

Az was pressed against her back, her arm draped over Rus's middle as her breath tickled the back of Rus's neck.

She was safe. She was home. And there wasn't a whisper of a spirit in any of the corners that surrounded her. Then what had ripped her from her sleep?

Another gust of wind howled through the trees outside, rattling the glass of 157 Mourning Moore's windows. That must have been it. She was so used to that sound preceding some kind of attack, her body had responded on instinct. The way it would if she were still out in the world, not protected by the wards of Moondale.

There was nothing keeping her from snuggling back into Az's warmth and ignoring the storm until morning. She could deal with what it meant that there was wind but no rain when the sun came up. She could—

Her eyes fell on the velvet ring box Az must have sat on her nightstand after they changed into their pajamas. It was dark in their room, but still that item carried a significant weight, drew her attention. She hadn't said yes. Yet. But Rus knew beyond a shadow of a doubt after their conversation before bed that they'd be married before the new year.

Not if the soul jumper destroyed everything they loved.

"Damn it," Rus hissed to herself. She didn't have time to lie in bed and enjoy the heaviness of Az's sleep-warmed body behind her. Not when the Heart of Moondale said they had two days, and one was already gone. They needed a plan. A way to pull the soul jumper out of Taryn and send it to the After before it could do anymore damage to Moondale. Hopefully before the actual hour of the centennial rolled around. But that probably wasn't possible. Still. She had to try.

Squeezing her eyes shut for a moment, Rus tried to memorize the feeling of Az curled around her. It was a nice feeling. One that would bolster her through the next however many hours she'd lose sleep. Then she took a deep breath and slowly began to extricate herself from Az's hold. Harder than one might think, considering Az had more arm strength than she looked like she should, and an unwillingness to let Rus go even in sleep.

Rus's heart clenched with that knowledge, but she continued to wriggle out of bed. Once freed, she turned to brush a few strands of Az's hair from her face and press a kiss to her forehead.

Az mumbled something unintelligible.

"It's all right, Magpie, go back to sleep."

Another sound of irritation, but the crease in Az's brow smoothed, and she settled back into a deeper sleep.

That done, Rus moved to the desk set into one of the small gables of their room. It wasn't the best option. It would be far better to head down to her office to think about this. Then the light wouldn't wake Az. But she couldn't pull herself away from the sleeping form of her soon-to-be wife, not when there was so much at stake.

She settled into the chair, twisting one way, then the

other to stretch out her back, and turned her mind to the problem of the soul jumper.

The fact that Taryn made a deal with it was going to be a big problem. It meant that she'd invited it in, that she'd allowed it to possess her willingly. That made the hold it had over Taryn's body much stronger. Couple that with the fact that it had control for at least a decade or more, and Rus wasn't sure if Taryn was even still in there.

There had been a moment when they'd last faced off against it that it seemed like Taryn surfaced. That she'd begged for help Rus wasn't able to give her at that point. But Rus couldn't be sure that wasn't a trick.

Still, Mazarin had given her an idea of what to do about it.

Names. Names and history.

She might not be able to get her hands on the soul jumper's name, as the creature had hexed it.

But any being that was that long-lived would leave behind a trail of blood, of death, of unfairness and unkindness. There would be other spirits who wanted vengeance against it. Others who could help her. She just needed to find them.

A quick glance at her phone told her it was nearly three in the morning. Too late for some. Too early for others. She could go down to the rounded room where she kept Xueming and Eamon's tablets, and see if she could summon them. Maybe they would have some more insight into the spirits in this area. But with how long they'd been dead, how settled they were in the After, she had no idea what kind of door that might open with the magic running as dangerously low as it was in Moondale. Better not to chance it.

That left one option. Research.

And there was no one she knew who was better at research than Hunter Delacroix. Would he be awake? If he wasn't, would he be pissed that she'd called?

He did owe her a favor. A *big* one. But that didn't really excuse waking someone up at three in the morning, not to her mind.

"Fuck it." He could be pissed at her if he wanted. They didn't have time for this. She pulled up his contact, then dialed his number.

Hunter picked up on the fifth ring. "What happened? Is everyone okay?"

"Nothing yet." Rus leaned back in her chair, tilting her head to stare into the shadows of the high-vaulted ceiling. "But I've got a job for you."

"All right." His voice was a little rough, groggy almost, but he sounded alert enough to at least take instruction. "Just let me—"

There was shuffling on the other end of the line, a murmured "I'll be right back" to someone in the room, followed by the distinct sound of a door shutting. Rus could imagine him climbing out of bed much as she had, leaving behind the people he loved, just as she had, so they could both turn their minds to this thing together. Because they were coven. And coven meant family.

"All right, what do you need me to find?" Hunter asked after a few minutes. Maybe he'd gone down to the basement to his lab. Maybe he'd just headed into a different room. But wherever he was, he was giving her his full attention, and Rus was impossibly grateful.

"I need a list of names." Rus rubbed at her face, brushing away the crust still lingering in the corners of her eyes. "Of the dead."

"What sort of names? I'm going to need more to go off than just the dead thing. Do you have a radius? Do you have some kind of search parameters? Car accidents? Suicides? What?"

She hadn't really gotten that far, she just knew she needed names. Damn it. "The soul jumper has been around for five hundred years," she said instead of providing those things outright. "I imagine in those five hundred years, they hurt plenty of people. It's kind of part and parcel of what they are. They're malevolent, malicious. Suicides might be a good start. But I don't want to rule out deaths that look like an accident but might have been curse magic."

"That's not going to be easy to narrow down." But she could hear a keyboard clacking in the background like he was already working on it.

"No. It won't. But I feel like someone with your background in vampire research might know what to look for when it comes to deaths that don't really fit the mold, right?"

Was she above a little flattery? No. No, she was not. And she knew Hunter was the proud sort, just like she was, the kind of witch who held his work in high regard. Plus, she had no illusions that Hunter and Ava hadn't figured out her background before they'd come to her, asking for help with tracking vampires all those months ago. They were too comfortable with the whispered voices of the dead not to know most of what she'd gotten up to over the years.

"Well obviously." Hunter huffed. "Out of curiosity, what is this for?"

"I need vengeful spirits to help me deal with the soul jumper. I couldn't get rid of it myself a few weeks ago, and I doubt I would be able to now with how low the magic in

Moondale is running. I'm going to need a hand." She didn't like the idea of putting spirits in the path of that creature, but at least with those that held a grudge against it, they would be getting what they wanted in the end. They would be seeing their vengeance come to fruition.

"You need their names for that?" The clacking stilled, like Hunter had paused in whatever search he was putting in to listen to her. "I thought you could just send out a call in the After and ask those spirits who'd suffered to come forward?"

"I can." And she would. She was also going to need a place to hold them while they waited for the soul jumper to appear. That was a problem for after her call with Hunter. "But to send them along after the fact, I need a name. I can't call that many spirits up from their resting place, or even drag them away from where they are haunting, and put them all in one place if I don't have a method to free them afterward."

"Why not?" It wasn't asked the way Aihuan sometimes did when she was asking just to see how far she could push boundaries. It was asked out of academic curiosity.

"It's dangerous." And oh boy, was it ever.

Hunter made an interested sound, like a question, or an invitation for her to expand, and Rus sighed, rubbing the back of her neck.

"That many unsettled spirits in a small vicinity, all turned to a singular task, can coalesce and morph into something *else*. Something maybe worse than the soul jumper. I've only ever actually seen it happen once, and thankfully I was quick enough to realize something was wrong before it fully amped itself up, but there have been stories." So many stories. Too many. And Rus knew most of them, because it was her job to know. "About these like..." She paused, trying to think of an accurate term. There wasn't one in lore that she'd found, because it was a phenomenon that hardly ever happened naturally, and when it did there weren't many, if any, left to tell the tale. "Cyclones of malevolent spirits. They whip themselves up into a torrent and feed off each other."

Rus shivered at the memory. The only one she'd ever come face-to-face with hadn't even been that far along yet, but the way the spirits' faces vanished, the way they lost definition and twisted into something *else*, still made her a little sick.

"What do you do with something like that?" They had gotten off topic, but the earnest curiosity in Hunter's voice was heady. Rus loved teaching other people, and it was rare someone found medium work and necromancy so interesting. Most people were skeeved out by it.

She blinked up at the ceiling, trying to get her bearings again. Drag herself out of the memory. Her next words left her from a throat that felt distinctly raw with grief. "You have to destroy them."

Hunter was silent on the other side of the phone, but she heard the slight intake of breath when he realized what that meant.

"They don't go to the After. They don't enter the reincarnation cycle, no matter what their burial was like. They just... they just stop existing." It was perhaps the worst thing she'd ever done in her entire life. And that included giving Corey the name of the fae they killed to bring Sage back. It was a fate worse than anything else. And the universe agreed, based on the havoc it had wreaked on her body to do it.

"I'm sorry you had to do that." There was a kindness to the words that caught Rus off guard. People didn't— They didn't usually do that. They didn't look at what she had to do and see what it cost her. At least, people who didn't know her well enough to see what kind of person she was. And Hunter certainly didn't know her well enough.

Sucking in a strangled breath, Rus forced herself to sit up. "Right, so I need names. To keep that from happening. Do you think you can manage that?"

"Sure." Hunter's fingers were clacking against his keyboard again. "How do you want them?"

"Notes doc, and a spoken clip so I can make sure I get pronunciations right." Hopefully Hunter would manage to get most, if not all, the spirits that would come forward. "Veer on the side of too broad if you have to. I'd rather have a name that's not there than miss one."

"Got it. I'll get that to you before this evening?"

"The sooner the better."

"Got it," Hunter said again. "I'll give you a buzz when I've got something for you. Mind if I pull Ava in on this?"

"By all means. Vanessa, too, if you think she'll help. I'd do it myself, but I don't have time for it. I need to figure out how the fuck I'm going to draw so many spirits to one place and hold them there."

"They're not all going to come from the After?"

"No. Probably not. Most unsettled spirits never make it there. The ones likely to hold a grudge against the soul jumper will be on this plane somewhere, or in limbo. But I also need to think of a way to keep them up near the Heart of Moondale, so they're waiting for me when I face off against the soul jumper." Goddess, she was fucking tired already. She just wanted to crawl back into bed with Az and pass the fuck out. There was no way she could, not if she wanted to keep all she'd gained in the last year.

"All right. I'll let you get to that then. Later."

"Bye."

The line went silent, and Rus dropped her phone onto the desk beside her before leaning in to flick on the lamp and grab some paper from the drawer. An array might work. She'd just have to build in some magic to keep the spirits inert in the interim.

Chapter 19

When Azure blinked awake, it was because she reached out for Rus and found a cold bed instead of the warm body she'd fallen asleep against. A wrinkle creased her brow as she rolled over to search the room for her wayward fiancée. With a grumble, her gaze landed on Rus bent over her little desk in the corner, head resting on her arms as if she'd put it down for a moment to rest and promptly fallen asleep. The watery, dreary light from outside made her look impossibly softer than even just sleep should achieve, and Azure's heart clenched.

Sighing, Azure stood, pulled the crocheted blanket—a gift from her younger brother, Indigo—from the end of their bed, and made her way across the room, banking on 157 Mourning Moore to hide her approach so as not to wake Rus. She clearly needed the rest, and if Azure had to leave her at her desk to ensure she got it, so be it. Rus would complain about being sore all day, but she knew that if she woke her now to send her back to bed, she'd be up. So there was little point in trying.

She draped the blanket across Rus's shoulders carefully, and nodded a silent thank you to 157 Mourning Moore that it was keeping the howling wind from entering through the window in front of the desk. Rus didn't need the cold on top of the way she'd curled herself over her paperwork to leave her sore. Frowning, Azure leaned in a little closer to try to make sense of what Rus had been so desperate to get done that she'd left their bed in the middle of the night and not returned.

It was hard to parse.

Rus's handwriting was a messy scrawl at the best of times, but when she really got into the zone—and was tired—even Azure had trouble translating the words on the page. It seemed to be some kind of containment circle or array. Although Azure couldn't make out what for exactly. There was symbology for luring, and some markers in the language of the dead that, even if Rus hadn't been half-asleep writing them, Azure would never have been able to understand.

Shaking her head fondly, Azure turned to head downstairs. She needed to get the girls up and started for the day. Not that they would be any more trouble than Rus. In fact, the girls seemed to be morning people, as opposed to their mother, who was most decidedly not. But it would be easier to drag Rus away from her work if everyone else was already up and ready to go. Or at least convince her to pack it up and take it with her.

Azure stopped at Meiling's door, knocking lightly before she pushed it open.

"What's up?" Meiling called from where she was rummaging around in her drawers, pulling out clothes.

"I just wanted to make sure you were awake." Azure stayed at the door, unwilling to encroach upon the teen's personal space without an invitation. "Rus was up late last night working on something, so I assume she'll be having breakfast on the go today."

Meiling snorted. "Doesn't she always?"

She wasn't wrong. Rus tended to sleep in until the last possible moment when she could. Especially on weekends. She was better on school days because she knew the girls had to be up and out the door, and even if Fernando and Azure were both there, they also had their own things going on. But like some weird kind of magic, her body seemed to sense when it was the weekend and decide breakfast wasn't a priority.

"Are Nando and Huaner up?" Azure queried instead of engaging with Meiling's slight attitude. It was better not to participate in it when it happened, Azure had found. Acknowledging that Meiling was being a bit of a shit seemed to make it worse, and that held even more true in the mornings. Azure wondered if Meiling's sleep patterns would change once she was well and fully a teen. She had just recently turned fourteen. Would she take on Rus's infamously bad habits? Azure hoped not. One of Rus was enough for her.

"I think they're already downstairs, making breakfast. Uncle Nando said he was going to make pancakes." Meiling kept digging through her drawers, likely looking for that one specific shirt that she'd been wearing for the last couple of weeks.

"Check the hamper."

"You mean it's *dirty*?" Meiling threw herself back on her bed dramatically.

"I'm afraid so." There had been little time to deal with laundry over the last couple of days with everything else going on. "You'll have just have to wear something else."

Meiling's eyes shifted to the hamper, her lips pursing, considering, and Azure knew exactly what she was thinking without the words ever having left her mouth.

"You can't wear it anyway. It's a wrinkled mess and has been in there with your clothes from gym class." Azure let her words dip into something sterner, parental. The idea of being a parent to the girls was still new to her, but she found it came rather easily when Meiling acted so much like a teenage Rus.

"But Auntie Az," Meiling groaned, and Azure's chest seized.

It didn't matter how many times the girls called her that, how natural it sounded, she would never get enough of it. Never get over the feeling of being a part of this little family. With pancakes in the morning, and laughter before bed, and movie nights on the weekends. Rus had built a home that was warm and safe for her girls with the help of Fernando, and Azure was just lucky to be there.

"That's my comfort shirt," Meiling added a moment later in a voice so small it pulled Azure up short.

Why would Meiling need her comfort— "You've heard about the soul jumper?"

"They're not calling it that, exactly." Meiling picked at a loose thread on her comforter, not looking at Azure. "But there's rumors going around."

Azure nodded, guilt settling into her belly. They should have talked to the girls about this earlier, when they knew it was coming. Should have prepared them for the possibility of something that had almost taken both Rus and Azure from them not too long ago. But time was so short. They'd only had their fears confirmed by the Heart the night before last. And since then, all manner of problems had arisen at the centennial celebrations that both she and Rus had to turn their minds to.

With a deep inhale, Azure picked her way across Meiling's messy bedroom. They would have to have a talk with her about cleaning up her clothes and school materials another day. Today Azure needed to put her at ease. She had never had a child of her own, but she'd helped raise

Indigo enough to almost feel natural sitting on the bed beside Meiling, their shoulders brushing.

"You know you're protected, right? You have so many strong, powerful folk standing between you and this threat, you likely won't even know it came and went." Or, at least, Azure could hope so. She would prefer their children think of Moondale as the safe place it was meant to be, even for all the hardship they'd known since coming there. She'd prefer they look at that hardship and realize that although bad things had come for them, they had been protected by the town they lived in. The land of Moondale had offered her power to their family and made it easier to protect them. But she knew they couldn't hide from Meiling all the bad things that happened around her.

"I'm protected, but what about Aunt Rus?" Meiling asked in a voice so quiet, Azure wouldn't have heard it if the house weren't silent around them.

"Your Aunt Rus has me, and her coven, and her friends. She's protected too." Even if she liked to act like she wasn't sometimes. Even if she liked to go rogue every once in a while and try to take shit on by herself. She was never alone. Not anymore.

"Does she know that?"

"I'll make sure to remind her whenever she forgets." Azure patted Meiling's shoulder lightly.

The girl threw herself at Azure, her arms wrapping tight around her waist as she buried her face in Azure's shoulder. "We can't lose her too. Don't let Huaner lose her mom."

Azure blinked for a moment, her heart lodged in her throat. Then she wrapped her arms tightly around Meiling, pressing her face into the girl's hair as she curled herself protectively around Meiling like she could keep the world from touching her.

Aihuan might not remember their parents, she might only know Rus, but Meiling remembered. She remembered all of it. It was like the difference between Violet and Azure, only Violet had decided that instead of letting herself see their aunts as their mothers, she would just see them as aunts. She would marry and move out as soon as she could. She would stand on her own after they lost their parents. While Meiling was open and willing to let Rus in, to let her be her parent.

"I won't let that happen," Azure promised. She wasn't sure how she'd keep that promise, but she would. Because she had to. "I'll make sure she has someone with her when things get dark. I'll make sure she's not alone against this thing."

Meiling sniffed, clearly trying to disguise her tears as she kept herself hidden in Azure's shoulder. But that was all right. If Meiling needed a place to hide, Azure was willing to be that for her. They sat like that for a long moment, the sounds of Aihuan and Fernando down in the kitchen eventually filtering up the steps to invade the quiet bubble that 157 Mourning Moore had formed around them.

"Okay." Meiling sucked in an unsteady breath, but when she pulled herself back, the only sign of her crying was her red and puffy eyes.

"Okay." Azure let her go, although she didn't want to. She wanted to keep herself as the barrier Meiling and Aihuan needed against the world around them. She thought she'd never understood her Aunt Carmine so much in her life. "You should finish getting ready, or Huaner will have eaten all the pancakes by the time you make it down."

"Probably." A laugh burbled up Meiling's throat that

sounded far more like herself than anything she'd said so far. It was a relief.

BREAKFAST in 157 Mourning Moore was always chaotic. With five people living under one roof, there was really no way it couldn't be. Even if three of them were adults, that didn't account for the teenager and the steadily growing toddler who were both agents of mischief so lively, Azure knew she'd never be bored again.

But even for all the noise and the bumping up against each other in the kitchen, Azure found she loved it. She loved the way she and Fernando had learned to dance around each other while he filled a plate with a steadily growing stack of pancakes, and she made coffee for Rus. They had turned into a kind of team. Two people working as a unit to get Rus and the girls ready for the day. It was nice.

The stairs creaked, and Rus came into view, the blanket still wrapped around her shoulders. "Time's it?"

"Still early yet," Azure said, moving to hold out a mug for her. "You've got a little bit. Why don't you tell me what you were working on last night?"

Rus huffed, dropping into one of the chairs at the black kitchen table. She chuckled as Aihuan pushed a plate of half-finished pancakes toward her. "Thanks, Huaner, but you should finish those. Uncle Nando made them for you. They've even got chocolate chips in them."

"Are you sure?" Aihuan asked, her head tilted to one side.

"Positive. Now be a good girl and eat your breakfast."

Rus slid the plate back to her and sipped from her cup of coffee with a soft hum before turning back to Azure. "I was trying to combine a summoning array with a containment circle with little success."

Azure turned to lift a brow in question and found Rus scrubbing her nose thoughtfully. "What for?"

Gray eyes cut to where Meiling and Aihuan were sitting at the table as if unsure how much of this they should hear, but after a moment she sighed. "I'd like to use some vengeful spirits to help me deal with the soul jumper. Preferably those who have some grudge against it."

Why would she want to do that? That sounded *dangerous*.

Fernando set some pancakes in front of Meiling, nodding. "That makes sense. Then you'd absolve their grudge while also dealing with the soul jumper. If you timed it just right, they might take the soul jumper to the After for you."

"Exactly!" Rus crowed, pointing at her friend, a proud light in her eyes.

"But how would you summon them without a séance?" Meiling stilled where she'd been cutting into her pancakes to frown at Rus. "I thought that was the only way to contact the After."

"It is. But the spirits who are holding a grudge against the soul jumper aren't likely to be in the After. They're either on our plane, or in limbo. That makes them much easier to draw out." Rus took a deep drag from her coffee, looking suddenly energized despite the dark circles around her eyes.

"Isn't putting that many spirits in one place... dangerous?" Fernando was frowning now, too, his eyes flicking around Rus's face as if searching for something.

"Oh, it is." Rus's flippant tone made Azure's hackles rise. "But that's where Az comes in."

"Where I come in, how?" Azure was pretty sure she didn't like the sound of this plan, but as they were tight on time, it wasn't like they were going to get the chance to think up something better.

"I need something to sedate the spirits. To keep them from forming a single consciousness. I thought, maybe, given how amazing you are with talismans, you could figure that out. I mean... talismans and arrays work on the same basic principles."

Azure's cheeks heated. "I'm adequate at talisman work."

"Don't lie, Az!" Rus smiled broadly up at her, pride shining in her eyes.

Azure exhaled, her cheeks puffing out as if that would hide the flush. It didn't, and the delighted laugh Rus let out told her as much.

"So," Rus said, leaning forward, her gaze dancing, "can you do it?" But she asked it in such a way as if to say *I know you can.*

"I'll need to get to work right away." Azure glanced out the window and frowned. It still looked like it was early, but she knew better. Why was the day turning out so dreary? That had not been in the forecast. "I'll have to call someone to have them cover for me with the celebration committee."

"Nesta would be good for that," Fernando volunteered.

Azure nodded her agreement. "Where do you want this array set up?"

"As close to the Heart of Moondale as we can get it." Rus's eyes flickered with something worried.

"Okay." Because Azure was always going to agree, but that expression on Rus's face made it impossible to argue.

"If you can get me the language you need for the dead, I'll have Evander take me up there."

"*Greer?*" Rus grumbled, flopping forward over the table and nearly knocking her mug over in the process. "C'mon, Az, what do we need him for?"

Azure ignored her dramatics and pulled her phone from her pocket to text the sheriff.

"Fine," Rus grumbled when it was clear she wasn't going to get her way on the Evander front. "I'll go with you. Hunter and Ava will be by shortly. They're going to man the table for us while we work. We don't have much time."

Azure's stomach dropped. Hours. They had mere *hours* to set this up before the soul jumper struck. No room for error. No time to experiment. Goddess willing, Moondale would do the heavy lifting and ensure it didn't blow up in their faces.

Chapter 20

"Why did *he* have to come?" Rus cut Greer a hard look. Her annoyance was running particularly high today. Irritability was not a new thing for her. Being tired always made things worse, then there was the cold that seeped into her joints to make them ache. When this was all done, she was going to sleep for a week and not move from their bed, apart from the need to go to the bathroom. Az and Nando would just have to handle the rest.

"Because," Greer said like it was the answer. Like he didn't have to explain his presence to her. Sure, maybe they weren't enemies anymore. Maybe Rus didn't feel like cursing him every other day for the way he'd almost taken Az from her. But that didn't mean they *liked* each other. Gross.

Az sighed, stepping carefully over a fallen log. "Greer knows the woods of Moondale better than anyone, and we're less likely to get in trouble for going near the Heart without board permission when we have the sheriff with us."

"Okay, yeah, but he's just going to get in the way," Rus pressed. She knew talking about Greer like he wasn't there was just going to piss him off more, but honestly? Good. He wasn't coven. He had no business being a part of this. Even if he was Nesta and Cagney's boyfriend.

"Get in the way *how*? I'm not even doing anything!"

Rus was too fucking tired for this. She was too fucking tired for a lot of things right now. Her entire body felt like one big bruise. The only small mercy being that Az had bullied her into wearing her knee brace and bringing along her cane. She hated to admit it, but the cold wind whipping through the trees around her was chilling her to the bone even through the thick sweater Az had wrangled her into. Making every joint in her body want to lock up like a fucking corpse.

The way Az looked over at her said that even if Rus hadn't said so out loud, she knew. And she was feeling smug about it. She could be such a petty bitch sometimes. Rus loved her so much.

"Ugh," Greer groaned, clearly catching the shared look between them. "You two are so gross with each other. Honestly, the amount of longing on your faces, you'd think you—"

"Shut up." Rus cut him off. Her body had gone rigid without her say so, and it took her a moment to realize why.

Greer's mouth clacked shut. He didn't make another sound.

They were approaching the clearing that held the Heart of Moondale. The large ore deposit that fueled the entire town had been discovered hundreds of years ago; it's why the folk who chose Moondale as their home had settled there. Why the town was so easy to hide and protect. An ore deposit of that magnitude, connected directly to the ley lines, made all the difference. That's why Rus brought her little family here to hide a year ago. Because she knew the power of the ground beneath her.

But what pulled her up short, made her feet feel like

they were glued to the earth, were the shades lingering in the wood around the Heart. They weren't doing anything, just standing there. Just like the ones from Taryn and Violet's house had been all those weeks ago. They were staring straight toward the Heart, their shapes flickering in and out. The difference between those spirits and these were that these were clearly not from the After. They hadn't been ripped from their final rest. They had come from limbo, or from the town, their edges ragged with age, their lines indistinct from years of slowly forgetting who and what they'd once been.

"Fuck," Rus rasped. She hadn't even realized there *were* so many disquieted dead in Moondale. Where had they all come from? How hadn't she noticed them before now? She'd clearly been sticking too close to home over the last year if there were this many spirits lingering in the town without her notice. She'd have to make sure to rectify that if they made it out of this thing in one piece.

"What is it?" Az stepped closer, her presence a comforting weight at Rus's side. Maybe she felt it, the chill in the air that hadn't been there a few minutes ago, even though she couldn't see the spirits the way Rus could. Not if she wasn't focusing. Not if they didn't want to be seen. Sometimes being a medium really fucking sucked.

Something moved out of the corner of Rus's eyes, and she whipped around to glare at the spirit trying to wrap their arms around Az. Likely looking to leech off her body heat, and her life, to fuel itself. Az shivered at the touch, clearly feeling it even if she didn't know what it meant.

"You knock that shit off." Rus growled, and her magic rose from her skin like mist from the ground, except it was green and deadly.

The spirit stilled, turning their head slowly to look at Rus with a blur for a face. Just a wash of gray skin. It'd be terrifying in its own right if Rus wasn't so used to seeing things like this.

"You heard me," she hissed warningly. "These two are not here to act as kindling. They're with *me*."

The spirit let go of Az, backing away from her with their hands raised in surrender.

"And that goes for the rest of you too!" Rus whipped her head around to stare at the mass of spirits dotting the woods like saplings, her gray eyes glowing with an eerie green light. "No one touches them, or I'll give you a one-way ticket to the void of nothingness that awaits spirits who don't make it to the After."

The other spirits in the wood turned slowly to look at her as a single unit, their attention drawn to her power and her words. Their heads all tilted to the side at the exact same time, the exact same angle, as if curious at this intrusion into their space.

"Okay. That's not good."

"What is it?" Az asked, but she hadn't moved from where she was watching Rus. Her eyes were wide and worried, even if there was an underlying heat at the display of Rus's power.

"You remember that discussion we had about spirits coalescing and forming a single consciousness?" Rus wanted to step away from this situation. To turn her back on it. Pack up her car and run. This wasn't her and her girls' problem. They weren't the ones who had very clearly been leaving the spirits of Moondale to rot. This was someone else's fault. But she'd built a home for herself here, a place where the girls felt safe, where she had people who knew her, where she had a routine, a soon-to-be wife, and a family. She was loath to give that up now after so many years of longing for it. Not without a fight.

"Yes."

"Well, I don't," Greer said, but much of the brashness had left his tone. He was scared, and with good reason. He couldn't see the spirits either, but he had to know what Rus's sudden carefulness meant. Maybe he even retained some of that old instinct to trust Rus that they'd had when they were children. Before whatever ember of friendship they'd been building was snuffed out by the Crimson Tide elders.

Rus ignored him. It would take too long to explain. "This place is cluttered with restless dead." She let her magic flow out around them, creating a barrier between them and the spirits who were now looking at her with such intensity that she knew they didn't have long to wait before they came for her. "Not pulled from the After. Why didn't anyone tell me Mooncale had such a big shade problem?"

"No one knew." But Az's words sounded more like *no one cared*. Which was probably closer to the truth. "How many?"

"A *lot* a lot." Rus's skin was starting to tingle with the rising tension. With the way the spirits were slowly coming to understand what her power might mean for them. They needed to stop her before she stopped them. "And they're all kind of... moving the same."

Kind of was putting it lightly. They hadn't merged yet, but it was clear they had all come to the wood with the same purpose, drawn by the same thing. From there, it would be easy for them to form a single consciousness and become a much bigger problem. Especially since it didn't appear that they were being drained the way those in front of Violet's house had been.

"But they haven't started to merge together?"

"No. Not yet. But it's a matter of time. You don't happen to have extra stunner talismans that I could use to gather some of them up and send them into the After before this thing gets out of hand, do you?" It was a gamble. Literally *anything* Rus did at this point was. There was one of her, and from what she could see, there were over twenty spirits. And that was just on this side of the Heart.

"I do." Az slowly moved her purse to her stomach and began digging around in it.

"What's the plan here?" Greer had gotten closer to her, so she could pull the circle of her magic in tighter. She was grateful for that. She knew she couldn't keep the spirits at bay long, and the wider the circle, the more power she was using. She'd need blood eventually, too, probably. Good thing she'd brought her athame just in case.

"We're going to stun as many of them as we can, and I'm going to try to send some of them over to the After. If some of them are vengeful and have a grudge against the soul jumper, then we can put them in the containment array with the ones we'll be calling forward. But I'll have to be quick, and so will you. Do you know a good warding circle that can keep the dead out?"

None of this was ideal. If Rus were alone, she would be less worried about this. It wouldn't be easy, and she'd likely wind up having to bleed—a *lot*—for it, but it would be better than the spirits having living people to feed off. Rus was half dead. They knew they could pull her under easily, but she wouldn't supply much energy. Greer and Az, on the other hand, would fuel them further. Make them angry, and more powerful.

"Yeah. I'll get it started." Greer didn't wait for further

instructions. He pulled out his athame and started carving symbols into the ground beneath them.

"Az?"

"Rus." Just her name. Only her name. But it was enough to let Rus know that Az was there with her, that she wasn't going to leave her to face this alone. It was a comfort and a terror all at once.

"I need you to stay in the circle with Greer." She took the talismans from Az's steady hands, her own trembling with fear.

"You'll need help laying the talismans." Az lifted her chin, unyielding. "It will be quicker with two."

"Az." Rus groaned, leaning forward so she could bump her head against Az's. "Just trust me on this, it'll be safer for all of us if the two of you stay in the circle."

Az scoffed but nodded. "If things become more dangerous, I'm following after you."

Rus stepped from the circle Greer had just finished building. She felt the ripple of his magic slide over her as she exited his protection. Tilting her head to the side, she let her movements stay careful and unhurried. All she could hope was that there weren't spirits all the way around the Heart, but she knew that was probably wishful thinking.

"I need your names," Rus called to the first small group of spirits, hoping they wouldn't immediately attack her. Their stances weren't combative, but that didn't mean anything for the dead whose emotions could shift on a dime. She had to seem as nonthreatening as possible.

Why. Why. Why.

The whispers drilled into her head in a way no spirit had in over a year. She'd come to Moondale, and she'd gotten used to the calm, mostly sad shades of this town. To the old graveyard behind her home. To the ones who weren't looking to take a bite out of something living. But these spirits, for all they might be of Moondale, were also distinctly different. More powerful. Likely because of the way they were slowly growing into something dangerous.

"To set you free from this."

We are *free.*

"Ah. Fuck."

Chapter 21

*T*hink Icarus. *Think. Think. Think.*

But fear and doubt had crawled in at the edges, making it hard to hear anything in her head past the pounding of her heart in her ears.

This was bad.

This was *so* fucking bad. How had someone allowed this to happen? How had someone not done something about the spirits wasting away around town? She knew the answer, of course, it was the same reason the board fought so hard against letting her stay, against letting her form her own coven. They didn't want to think about the dead. Because mortals, no matter how long-lived they might be, were all instinctively afraid of death and what lay ahead of them. Even those who were likely to be reincarnated. They clung to their current flesh like leeches, hoping to suck every ounce of life from it before they had nothing left.

She'd have to do something about that in the future. But right now, she needed to deal with the spirits that were slowly inching closer and closer together without lifting their feet. Sliding across the ground like they were on wheels. She had to put a stop to this before they merged and became an even larger problem. But *how?* If they didn't want to move on, the only other options were to contain them in a ghost box or obliterate them. Neither of which were good options.

A twig snapped behind her, and she looked back to see Greer and Az creeping through the woods, applying talismans to the trees as they went. Going against her orders, because they were foolish and brave.

There was a whoosh of air, and Rus turned back just in time to realize that she wasn't the only one who noticed the movement. The shades had all begun to move at top speed toward the two living witches trying their best to keep their distance while also working to contain them.

"Ah. *Fuck*," Rus said for perhaps the third time and dropped to the ground just as one of the shades lunged for her head. She had just enough time to reach up with one of the talisman papers and stun them before the next came their way, more than happy to go through Rus to get to the witches behind her.

Clenching her teeth, Rus grabbed her athame from where it was tucked into her boot and sliced open her hand without a thought. It hurt like a bitch, and normally she wouldn't do it this way, but there wasn't a whole lot of time. She needed blood, and she needed it on her hands. With a hissed breath she clapped her palms together hard enough to sting. Green magic built from where the blood was on her skin. Expanding. Swirling. Into a ball that grew as she pulled her hands apart.

First the size of a softball. Then a globe. Then bigger than a Hula-Hoop.

Blood trickled from her palm in a steady flow, drawn out by the magic she was expending. Rus breathed through the lightheadedness of it, allowing the ache in her bones to sharpen her focus.

When the ball of magic was taller than she was, she held it up high, flinging it into the air, where it continued to grow.

Sweat trickled down her back.

There was a wetness under her nose.

Goddess, it had been so long since she'd done something like this. Probably more than five years. And the last time she had, there were other witches to draw from. And she hadn't been weak from giving up so much of herself to save a child. It didn't matter. Either she stopped these spirits, or they tore Az and Greer apart. There was no other option.

She swayed on her feet. Her ears rang.

Almost there. So close.

There was metal on her tongue. Bile crawling up her throat.

Just a little more.

There!

Rus stumbled to her knees, slamming her aching palms into the ground. The ring of magic above her head followed. It hit the ground with a *bang* louder than a bomb, making the earth beneath her jolt.

The spirits froze where they were, watching the barrier of green mist go up like a wall. Their eyes were wide and hungry. They were contained and stunned. For the moment.

But she wasn't done. She wouldn't be done. Not until Greer and Az finished setting up the talismans.

Her energy flagged, and she was losing grip on her control. The circle of green magic flickered like a candle in the wind. One wrong move, and this would all be over.

Her phone started buzzing in her pocket. "You've got to be fucking *kidding* me."

She could ignore it. She probably should. But there was always the chance that it was one of the girls, and she wasn't willing to risk that. Balancing her weight on the hand still bleeding into the ground, collecting dirt and detritus from the forest floor, Rus reached into her pocket to check the caller ID.

Hunter Delacroix.

She hit speaker and dropped the phone to the dirt, returning her other hand to pumping magic into the ring of power keeping the spirits at bay. "This isn't really the best time, Delacroix."

"Sorry." But he didn't sound apologetic. "I tried to call Azure first but couldn't get through."

Rus exhaled sharply. Her hair flopped out of her face before settling back to stick to her sweating temples again. The inability to call Az was probably because of the latent negativity in the area. It had likely drained her phone battery. Rus would have to sit down and work on building her a phone case like hers so that didn't happen again, and soon.

"What did you need?" she asked through gritted teeth as she struggled to keep her breathing even. Goddess, she was going to pass out. If Az and Greer didn't hurry the fuck up, they were all going to die in these fucking woods.

"I couldn't get you a list of the dead like you asked. And before you yell at me—" he said, cutting her off as she opened her mouth to do just that, because that wasn't so important that he couldn't have waited until she was down the fucking mountain! "The search criteria was too broad, and there was no way to tell which deaths were caused by the soul jumper and which weren't. For all we know, some of them could have been other folk fucking around. You know how petty they can get. Someone doesn't hold a door once and—"

"Delacroix! The point!"

"Right. I couldn't get you the victims, but I do think I

found the hosts. All I needed to do was look for witches who died of old age."

"That's not unusual." In Moondale, most witches died of old age. It wasn't like there were witch hunts anymore, and the community was relatively peaceful, so there weren't hexes or curses flying around on a whim.

"They were all less than a hundred years old."

Rus's eyes widened, her shoulders tightening. Witches lived a long time. Even the ones who didn't take care of themselves well could live for a couple of centuries or more before they succumbed to age-related complications. They aged slower. Lived longer. It was unheard of for any witch to die from old age before a hundred.

"Say their names," Rus ordered, her gaze fixed on the shuddering shades in front of her. They were moving, like a flip book, a little at a time, her brain filling in the space they covered. "Loud."

Hunter, to his credit, didn't ask why. "Aster Donovan. Eden Elias. Carson Forrest. And Julian Bennet."

The spirits stopped, their heads tilted in interest.

"These are the names of the ones the spirit jumper used to torment you," Rus called out, forcing her voice to remain steady even as her body began to tremble from the force of her magic. "I don't know its name, but I know these names, and I'll use them to pick it apart. To remove its strength until all that's left is that first witch. If you want vengeance on it for yourselves, for the people you loved, and for these witches who may or may not have given themselves to it willingly, you need to stop."

Vengeance?

"Yes." Goddess, her knees were on fire, her arms shaking. But Az and Greer were almost finished their work. The magic buzzed through the ground, reinforcing the seal she'd made to hold the spirits at bay. "It will come for me and mine. It will be here in a few hours. Whatever called you here, it can't give you what I can. It can't send the soul jumper to the After."

We should believe you?

Fair question. Rus was just some rogue necromancer they'd never had contact with before. They didn't know what she was about or how she'd helped so many. She had to think quick. She had to give them some guarantee. Something they could use to hold her accountable.

"I'll allow two spirits to possess me until this is done."

"Icarus!" The outraged shout from Az wasn't enough to stop Rus from doing what she planned. Because there was no other way, not as far as Rus could see.

"The others will have to wait here. My companions have created a holding array that will allow you to rest while you wait. It won't dispel you, nor will you be trapped forever. Just a few hours until I can figure out a way to get the soul jumper up the mountain." She was talking so fast she was almost breathless with it, fighting dizziness and exhaustion. Just a few more hours. Then the soul jumper would come, and this would all be over one way or the other.

You would allow us to possess you?

"Yes," Rus breathed at the same time Az shouted, "No!"

But it was too late, the deal was struck. Rus felt it the moment the promise locked into place. A witch's word was her bond, and Rus had made a deal with something that was no longer living, something she couldn't lie to, even if she wanted. She sucked in a shallow breath and lifted her bloody hand from the ground.

"Only two," she reminded sharply. "Any more than

that, and I will dispel all spirits that attach themselves to me. Am I clear?"

Only two.

The agreement rang true. A promise sealed in blood. Rus let out a long, shaky breath, and the barrier she'd constructed dropped just as the one Greer and Az made snapped into place. Rus slumped forward, her arms barely holding her anymore, but her exhaustion wouldn't stop the spirits. She'd made a deal with them.

She felt more than saw the two shades move forward and slip beneath her lowered chest to tuck themselves between her ribs. A chill raced down her spine as they settled in, but they were surprisingly quiet, polite ghosts. At least, for the time being. All she could hope was they stayed that way.

"What the fuck did you *do*?" Az asked from where she'd dropped to her knees beside Rus in the dirt, her hands gentle but trembling as they lifted Rus to lean heavily against her.

"Don't worry about it. I can handle a couple hitchhikers for a few hours. It wouldn't be the first time." Rus shrugged but let herself curl closer to Az's warmth.

"When this is over, we're going to have a very serious conversation about your reckless need to use your body as a ghost box," Az hissed. She brooked no argument as she scooped Rus up by the underarms and helped her limp back to where she'd dropped her cane in the rush, where Greer was waiting.

"Later. Later." Rus patted Az's hand placatingly, her body lolling heavily against Az. Az was stomping along beside her, clearly pissed by what Rus had done. But there was nothing for it now. It had been the best of a lot of truly fucked-up options, and Rus didn't have time to regret it. "In the meantime, we need to call Nixie Vernan."

"Why?" Greer moved up to her other side, not touching her, but it was nice to know that he was there in case she stumbled. Even if he was arguably an asshole who may very well let her fall on the ground.

"Because I need to have a talk with the board about their lack of tending to the spirits of Moondale." Anger lit her on fire at the mere thought, chasing away the chill. How long had this been going on? Had no one noticed? Or had no one cared? Maybe they just didn't think it was a big deal because human shades were unlikely to cause problems, being as they were less powerful. Which was true, to an extent. But stopped being true when a community left them to pile up for five hundred fucking years. "This is unaccep—"

An alarm rang through the silence that had gathered around Rus's fury, and Greer muttered a quiet, "Fuck me, what now?" as Az pulled Rus's phone from her bag.

"The Ghost Tracer." Az handed the phone to Rus for her to unlock and pull up the app.

With the radar in front of her nose, Rus could see the scatter of little dots cluttering the screen on the outskirts of town. Popping up one right after another as the app fully loaded. It wasn't a lot, not yet, but it was more than the norm. She sucked in a breath and sped up her pace as they hobbled back toward the car. "We have to get down the mountain. ASAP."

"I'll meet you there." Greer nodded.

"No." Rus shook her head, her mind already working a mile a minute. "Head to Violet's place, check on her wards again. Make sure she's all right. Let us handle the rest, at least for now." Then she turned her attention to Az, who was watching her through narrowed brown eyes. "We need to get to the car."

"We need to get your hand cleaned up first." Az looped Rus's arm over her shoulder and started dragging her back the way they'd come, clearly still pissed about what Rus had just done.

Chapter 22

"I'm fine, Az. I'm fine." Rus chuckled, trying to pull her hand away from Azure. Her skin was clammy beneath Azure's fingers. Her muscles twitching and jumping with either pain or exhaustion from the magic she'd just performed.

The magic that had been—very fucking sexy, seriously, what the fuck—a risk. A *huge* risk. And then she'd had the sheer *audacity* to invite spirits to possess her! Azure knew Rus was strong and capable. She knew Rus had years of experience dealing with the dead and doing things exactly like this. But if Rus said she was fine one more fucking time, Azure was going to grab her by the shoulders and shake her until her teeth rattled.

"Az, I'm fi—"

"Do *not* say you're fine," Azure growled through clenched teeth and held her hand out for the water bottle Greer had dug out of the back of his car. "That was both reckless and stupid."

Rus hissed as the water washed over her skin, clearing away some of the debris that had stuck to the now-congealing blood. It wasn't enough. They needed to clean it with something a bit more disinfecting. But she didn't have all the proper equipment on her, so this would have to do for the moment. Next time—hopefully there wouldn't be a next time—she'd have to make sure they had a proper first aid kit in Blue.

"I can't believe you would just invite that kind of trouble into—"

"Az," Rus murmured gently, her uninjured hand moving to grasp the one holding the water bottle that Azure hadn't realized was trembling. The water sloshed around inside its container. "I'm okay."

"That doesn't change how utterly moronic that was."

"No. It doesn't," Rus agreed readily. With a firm squeeze on Azure's still-shaking hand, Rus dropped the grip to take hold of her chin and force Azure to look away from the cut, meeting her eyes. "Trust me?"

Azure exhaled deeply, the air from her lungs rustling their hair as she leaned forward to press her forehead to Rus's. "I'm going to be so pissed if this goes wrong."

"I know." Rus's smile crinkled her eyes near shut, which just wasn't fair. She shouldn't look *happy* after what just happened. "But even if something does go wrong, we'll be okay. We'll figure this out together, right? Like you said, we're all a team now."

Azure wasn't sure she had said that, not in so many words, but it was true. Neither of them were alone in this. They had each other. They had their friends. They had their coven. "Hold still and let me finish cleaning this up."

Rus let out a long, beleaguered sigh, but she held her hand steady as Azure went back to trying to clean out the wound, hissing only occasionally when Azure had to pick pieces of leaf or bark from it. Greer left them to it, in spite of the fact that he was normally the first one to complain about any obvious tenderness, and Azure quickly lost herself to the task. Someone needed to take care of Rus. To make sure her wounds were cleaned and bandaged, to make sure she went to sleep at a reasonable time. It would just have to be Azure.

"Here," Greer grunted, holding out a roll of bandages.

"Thank you." It still wasn't as clean as Azure would like, but it would have to do. They'd already wasted enough time in the woods. "We can have Ava and Phyre look at it once we're back in town. Between the two of them, I'm sure they can at least keep you from getting an infection."

"Solid plan." Rus pulled her hand away, her ears heating a little. "Az, I—"

A loud, sharp ring broke the quiet of the clearing, making Azure's heart kick up in her chest. She'd almost forgotten for a moment that there was a world outside of this. That they were still running on a timetable so crunched, she didn't know how they'd ever get everything done before disaster struck.

They had solved one problem, but it was one in a long list of them. Chaos and discord were sown through every second of the centennial, and it made the world around them hum with unrest. Moondale was not happy about this turn of events. And the question that was rapidly coming to the forefront of Azure's mind was *What if all the things that have gone wrong ruined the charging of the ley lines?*

Rus pulled her hand away quickly and fished out her phone from Azure's bag before answering it and putting it on speaker phone. "What's up, A'Ling?"

"There are..." Meiling let out a shaky breath on the other side of the line. "There are ghosts down here."

"How many?" Rus met Azure's gaze, and they both nodded, moving as one to the blue sedan parked near the edge of the woods.

"I'm headed to Violet's." Greer's footsteps were loud in the silence as he climbed into his truck. It was interesting how quickly he had melded into their little group, become one of them. He'd probably hate it if he realized, but Azure was intolerably grateful for his presence. It made things easier.

Their doors closed behind them, and Rus repeated her question. "How many, Meiling?"

"A *lot*." Meiling's voice shook with the words, her fear so evident Azure wanted to reach through the phone and pull her into her arms. Her muscles ached with it.

"Okay." Rus's tone was calm, controlled, but Azure could see the way her hands shook around the key in the ignition as she got the car started.

Blue didn't even sputter. She roared to life around them, already ready to go.

"You and Huaner are okay," Rus soothed gently, backing out of the parking space. Maybe Azure should have offered to drive, but it was a little late now. "You're both wearing the pendants Az made you. The ghosts can't touch you so long as you're wearing those. Remember?"

"Right." Relief colored Meiling's next breath. "Right."

"Make sure neither you nor Huaner take them off," Azure added. She didn't feel as calm as Rus sounded, but she tried just the same, understanding that Meiling needed them to be steady right now. They were her guardians. She needed to know that someone would take care of this, and that she'd be safe. She wasn't even fourteen, for fuck's sake.

"I'll remind her."

"Good." Azure's approval warmed her words, and she nodded when Rus shot her a grateful smile.

"What are they doing?" Rus continued, turning onto the narrow two-lane road that would take them away from the Heart, back toward town. It wasn't a short drive, but

Azure could already tell that between Blue and Rus's anxiety, they'd make it in record time.

"They're just... they're just *standing* there," Meiling said with what sounded like a frown. "It's like they don't even notice anything around them. They're just staring straight ahead."

"Weird." Rus scrubbed at her nose thoughtfully.

"Do you know where they came from?" Azure pressed. They needed as much information as they could get on these spirits before they touched down in town. Maybe then they'd be able to formulate a plan.

"They just appeared. Out of nowhere. Like..." Meiling huffed, annoyed. "Shut up, Huaner, I'm trying to think."

"Be nice to your sister," Rus chided at the same time Azure said, "We don't say *shut up* to our family."

"Fine, *moms*," Meiling drawled sarcastically, but it lit a fire in Azure's belly. Her nerves buzzed with the word. *Moms*.

She shook herself. Now wasn't the time. She could deal with whatever existential crisis that single word caused later. After they dealt with the spirits in town. After the soul jumper was gone for good. Then there would be time to dig deep and figure out how she felt about being a mother to Meiling and Aihuan when all she'd been to this point was an aunt, and even that was relatively new.

Rus's own breath seemed a little shallow, and her swallow was loud in the silence of the car around them before she moved on to her next question. "So they popped up out of the ground like daisies?"

"No. They just appeared. Flickered into being like when you turn on a TV. It was super weird."

"All at once?" Rus pushed the car faster, over the speed limit, a little too close to what could be considered dangerous on a narrow, winding road through the mountains, but Azure wasn't going to chide her for it. Not when they were both clearly afraid of not being near the girls during what was happening.

"Not sure. All the ones near us appeared close to the same time, but maybe it hit in waves?" Meiling was frowning again, although now it sounded less like she was unsettled and more like she was thinking through what happened. Turning it over in her head the way Rus did.

"Has anyone noticed them, apart from you and Huan-er?" Azure wasn't sure which answer she was hoping for. On the one hand, if the humans noticed, it would clear them out of town and probably get them to safety before whatever was brewing finally struck. But on the other, that would be pandemonium. Chaos. Someone would get hurt.

"No. Not even the other folk can see them. I was able to touch Hunter, Ava, and Uncle Nando, and let them borrow some of my ability so they could see what's going on, but as far as I can tell, everyone else is walking around like it's just another day at the celebration."

The uncertainty in Meiling's voice had Azure grinding her teeth. She shouldn't have to deal with this. Moondale was supposed to be a safe place for her and her sister. That's why Rus brought them here. And yet, since they'd come, they'd dealt with witch hunters, abusive exes possessing their guardian, a soul jumper, and now this. It made Azure angry—and not unreasonably so—to know the girls had yet to find peace. How was that at all fair?

"People are just... walking through them," Meiling whispered, unsettled.

"They don't notice the chill?" Rus's own frown deepened further, her brows wrinkling.

"They might if the ambient temperature hadn't already dropped so much."

"How much?" Azure didn't think she wanted to know. It had been chilly up on the mountain, surrounded by the spirits drawn to the Heart of Moondale, but before they left town, it hadn't been that cold yet. Even for October, even with the wind.

"Ten degrees? Maybe fifteen? I could check a weather app and do a comparison?" Meiling sounded less afraid now. Like being given questions and a problem to turn her mind to distracted her from the fact that she was surrounded by spirits.

"Do that," Rus ordered. "Text Az any data you've got. And have Hunter send along anything the Ghost Tracer is kicking out on the back end. We're on our way down the mountain. We'll be there in twenty, maybe fifteen, if Blue cooperates."

Blue beeped the horn. Whether in affront, protest, or agreement, Azure didn't know. She hadn't spent enough time with the car.

Meiling inhaled deeply, the breath seeming to calm her down entirely. "All right."

"That's my girl."

"I'll see you soon," Meiling said, and Azure could tell that Rus's approval had eased whatever was left of her fear.

"You will." Rus waited until Meiling hung up before she dropped her phone into her lap and let out a long, shaking breath. "Fuck me. That's not good."

"The girls will be all right with Fernando and the others," Azure offered, trying to soothe some of Rus's concern, but she knew it wouldn't do much. Especially with the fact that they were still so far away. Too far.

Rus nodded, but the crease between her brows didn't

ease. Azure wanted to reach for her. To pull her into her lap and curl around her. To hide her from the world and the things that were coming for them. But there wasn't time. "A'Ling will feel better with a puzzle to solve."

"She will." Azure let herself breathe for a moment, focusing on Rus instead of the road speeding by them. It was the eye of the storm. The beginning of something much worse, much more dangerous. But she had no doubt that they would make it through this. "Do you think the spirits in town are the same as those that were drawn to the Heart? Were they also drawn from the unsettled dead of Moondale?"

"I won't know till I get down the mountain and see them for myself. But the prophecy did say the dead would walk among us."

"We thought it could be a metaphor."

"I wish it had been."

Chapter 23

"No," Rus gasped the moment the town came into view through the trees, her hands so tight around the steering wheel, Azure could hear the faux leather creak. "No. No. No. No!"

"What? What is it?" Azure squinted through the front windshield to try to see what Rus was seeing. But it was just a dreary, overcast sky, and a town packed full of tourists from all over enjoying the fall chill, watching the leaves, and letting their energy infuse the land with power.

Rus made a soft sound of upset unlike anything Azure had ever heard before, and a chill raced down Azure's spine. Was that actual fear in her fiancée's trembling breaths? She'd seen Rus unsettled plenty since she'd returned to Moondale, but she didn't think she'd ever seen her *afraid*. Not in the face of the things that went bump in the night, at least.

"Give me your hand." Rus pulled one of her own from the steering wheel and held it out to Azure, who wasted no time in threading their fingers together, squeezing tightly.

"What are—" The words cut off in a sharp intake of breath as Azure felt the slow crawl of cold magic travel up her arm. It wasn't cold like the winter wind that could cut through to the bone when it kicked up. Instead, it was like the cool side of the pillow on a warm summer night. The first popsicle under the midday sun in June. It was nice.

Refreshing. But it still raised every hair on her arm in its wake as it traveled along her shoulder to her face. She shivered, squeezing her eyes shut, just before it settled across her brows.

"Open your eyes, and tell me what you see," Rus ordered softly, as if she already knew what Azure would find when she finally allowed herself to look. Which wasn't making the fear that settled into Azure's stomach any less pronounced, but there wasn't much she could do about that.

Azure peeled her eyes open forcefully, and her breath lodged in her chest. Instead of just the overcast sky of a chilled fall day, there was a dark, dense cloud hanging over Moondale. It might have been a snow cloud but for the way it twisted and writhed. The shape morphed and changed constantly, and Azure thought maybe she saw faces in it, but they were too far away for her to know for sure.

There were shapes along the side of the road, too, as they approached the edge of town that abutted the woods. Standing unmoving and near translucent. It took Azure a moment to process the fact that they were ghosts, for her brain to catch up with what her eyes were seeing. And when it did, she held tighter to Rus.

"Are these spirits like those in the woods?" Even if they weren't malicious, even if they weren't moving, the sheer enormity of their numbers was enough to make terror grip Azure's chest in a vice. There was no way Rus could send this many over to the After. Not in the mere hours they had before the soul jumper returned to Moondale.

"I don't know. The ones in the woods have very clearly been left by the board to languish, and gathered up by someone or something." Rus sounded angry, and Azure didn't think she could blame her. Even if the Board of Magic couldn't see the spirits of Moondale that had been left to rot, they should have been able to feel them, and they should have done something about them. It was irresponsible not to. Just like it had been irresponsible to drive the only medium out of town.

"I don't think Moondale has this many unquiet dead." At least Azure hoped not. If they did, then there was a bigger problem in their town than just the soul jumper.

"Five hundred years is a long time for the Board of Magic to avoid thinking about caring for the spirits of the humans and folk outside their purview. These things tend to add up." There was a cold calmness to Rus's voice now that Azure didn't think she liked. A decision made.

"You can't send them all to the After alone." Even if she was capable, powerful—and she *was*—this was too many for Rus to handle. "Even with the help of Meiling."

"Meiling can't help. She hasn't done it before." Rus shook her head, letting out a long, slow breath, but she didn't release Azure's hand, didn't pull her magic away. And as much as Azure wanted to stop seeing what was right in front of her, she knew she couldn't. She needed to look. She needed to understand the depth to which they were all royally fucked. "And even if she had, she's going through puberty. That will make her connection unstable. It's too big a risk to let her handle it without my supervision."

"Then what should we do? No one else can—" Azure stopped, her grip tightening around Rus's to the point that she was sure it was near painful. Mediums were witches who could see spirits. They were rare. Rare enough that they should have been held in high regard. The Board of Magic made an error when it treated Rus with anything but.

"No one else can what?" Rus pressed.

"No one else can see them." Which was the crux of why

so few folk dealt with the dead. Or perhaps not the crux of it, not really, because there was also the matter of their unfounded fear of death itself. Which was silly when one thought about how many folk traditions there were to ensure reincarnation. Death was never the end. Rus taught Azure that.

Rus turned her head to blink at her, and Azure stared steadily back, giving Rus a moment of quiet to let her mind work. "Even if a witch could see them, it won't mean the witch has a direct link to the After to send them there."

"No," Azure agreed readily. "Are there not other methods of convincing a spirit to cross over?"

"It depends on the spirit." Rus sighed softly, her hand twitching where Azure held it as if she wished to run it through her hair nervously, or scrub at the tip of her nose, but she also didn't seem to want to let go. "Sometimes you can get them to go over by themselves, if you give them what they want. Or if you remind them that they don't belong here. But having a direct connection to the After makes the process quicker and easier for them. They don't have to try to open a connection themselves."

"Would there be a way to set up some kind of..." Azure pursed her lips in thought, her mind working over the problem. It wasn't exactly something she'd turned her thoughts to. Rus was always good enough at what she did that they wouldn't need extra help to free the spirits of Moondale— or, at least, that's what she'd thought. "Some kind of portal, or touchstone, or something that they could utilize once they were convinced to cross."

"Maybe. But that hinges on the folk being able to see them, like you said."

Azure hummed, her brow creasing at the reminder. Of course there were times when every folk could see and talk to spirits. But they were few and far between. It wasn't like with Rus and her girls, where all they had to do was look around and find them. Rus's thumb brushed across the skin of her knuckles, and an idea struck Azure. "We were able to create a tattoo that tied Hunter and Ava to the land, making it so they could access the magic of Moondale without having to live here."

Rus made a sound of interest in the back of her throat as she drove carefully through the neighborhoods of Moondale.

The tattoo was a talisman Azure designed. One that would be used specifically for their coven. One that every member would have. It would tie them together as much as it would tie them to Moondale. Make their shared power greater by extension. But what if they could— "If we change some of the characters, we might be able to make it so that instead of tying them to the land, they were tied to you."

She didn't know what effect that would have on Rus. She was powerful, sure, but if they drew on her magic, how far would her power stretch? Azure didn't think she wanted to find out.

"I couldn't charge up that many witches." Rus sounded annoyed at that admittance of weakness, even if it wasn't really weakness, per se. Most folk didn't have that kind of magic at their beck and call. It would go against the natural order of things. Not that Rus went *with* the natural order of things even on a good day.

"No. But could we use it to...mirror your power in a way? Take the magic already in their bodies and twist it into something that functioned like yours?"

Rus was quiet for a long moment, her brain working through the problem, turning it over and over again in her mind, the way she did when presented with something interesting. It sent a little thrill through Azure's body to be working with her like this, their minds playing off each other as they fired ideas and pitfalls back and forth. She didn't think she'd ever get tired of this. She'd spend the rest of her days with Rus like this, letting her mind be sharpened by Rus's, and it would be wonderful.

"It wouldn't be permanent," Rus said as she pulled into a parking spot just off Main Street.

Azure's eyes flicked to the spirits again. Meiling had been right. They were everywhere. Standing there, unmoving, staring straight ahead. Letting the humans and folk who couldn't see them walk through them with not much more than a shudder. It was eerie. She could see why it made Meiling so afraid. Especially as she was only just now beginning to get a handle on her abilities as a medium.

"Eventually," Rus continued, "their innate magic would discard the mirroring. Like working through an infection."

"We wouldn't want it to be permanent. Folk are very protective of their magic." Which meant there may not be any willing to alter their abilities, even for a short while, to deal with this problem. Their coven, of course, would take no issue with it. But they would need more than just them.

"Yeah. They are." Rus blew out a long, slow breath. "All right, I think I have an idea. Do you have a pen?"

Azure, still refusing to release Rus's right hand, dug through her bag until she produced a pen and held it out to her. Rus frowned down at their connection and slowly released it, one finger at a time.

"Using ink will make it less permanent, less powerful," Azure warned.

"Yes. But I think there might be a way to create a tattoo that's half finished, then the folk could add the final stokes later, if they're willing. But we need to try it first. And this is..." Rus frowned, shaking her head. "This is a *real* rough draft. It's not going to be great, and it might even feel... uncomfortable. It also might not work."

"That is all right." Azure turned her arm over to bear the underside to Rus. It was the only part of her skin free from tattoos that might otherwise interfere with the talisman. "We'll have time to perfect it later."

"This also doesn't deal with the whole touchstone thing. We'll have to think of a way to open a line to the After so you can send them over. But at least this way you'll be able to see and hear them."

Azure nodded firmly and gritted her teeth when the cool press of ink on skin turned jagged and hot as her magic fought against the idea of looking like someone else's. A cold burn rushed her veins, lighting her up from the inside. Every nerve ending in her body screamed so loudly, she wasn't sure she hadn't joined them. She was panting by the time Rus was done, her eyes squeezed shut.

"We will definitely have to think of a way to make it less invasive," she huffed around her ragged breaths.

"Yeah. Sorry about that," Rus mumbled, then leaned forward to press her lips to the talisman.

Azure flinched.

"Sorry. Sorry. I had to brute force it a little bit. With more time, I can finesse it. But first... Did it work?"

With a deep inhale, Azure opened her eyes. Her vision wavered for a moment, almost as if she were seeing double, then it settled, and she was seeing the world perhaps as Rus always saw it: full of spirits. "I can see them."

"Okay. That's a start. We'll have to ponder on the second half. But first, let's go get the girls. Meiling was freaked out enough. We need to get them back to the house, out of harm's way." Rus was already climbing out of the car even as she spoke, and Azure followed on much less steady legs.

"I should check on my sister, be sure that she hasn't been targeted." But even as she said it, she hoped that Brenton Ironwood had done as he'd agreed to and taken care of Violet. There was so much else she needed to worry about; having Violet's safety off her list would be a big help. "Our girls first, though."

Rus nodded and led the way down the street.

Chapter 24

The words *our girls first* settled into Rus's veins like something warm and solid. Hot cocoa on a cold afternoon. Warm showers in the morning. Their bed nice and toasty while the wind howled around them. It was everything that Rus had ever wanted, and everything she never thought she'd be able to have. And it was perfect.

"Yes," Rus agreed. "Our girls first."

The trail through the spirits that had appeared was a winding, twisting one. Rus knew she could walk through any and all of them, but she didn't want to take any chances on what that would do to her or the spirits themselves. Especially when there were two already in her head, whispering low and dark. They were a quiet hum in the back of her mind. She could ignore them, but she was constantly aware of them. A ringing of her ears she couldn't make stop. So far, they weren't causing any trouble. That might not hold true if she cut through one of the spirits standing around Moondale.

As she passed by them, she tried to catalog how old they were. Where they might have come from. They weren't ragged around the edges, lacking definition and humanity the way those who had been left to ferment were. But they also didn't seem as if they had been freshly ripped from the After. They were clean, and bright eyed.

It was... it was strange.

And for perhaps the first time since she was a teenager, Rus felt real fear curl its fingers around her insides and close its fist. Something wasn't right about these spirits, and it wasn't just that they'd appeared from nowhere.

It was...

It was like they'd been kept somewhere. Like when someone stored their things in a storage facility that was temperature and weather controlled to protect them. These spirits had been preserved. But not by the After. There would be no degradation at all if they had been in the After. And while it was minimal, Rus could see signs of years passed. A subtle softening around the edges.

The question was, *who* had been storing them? And *why*?

She was reasonably sure she didn't want the answer to that question. She was also reasonably sure that she was going to get it whether she liked it or not.

"Auntie Rus!" Aihuan's tiny voice called Rus back to the present, and she pasted on what she hoped was a convincing smile for her youngest.

"I'm here, little monster. Auntie Az and I are both here." Rus bent to scoop her up when she ran the rest of the distance from their booth to her. Aihuan buried her face in Rus's shoulder, her little body trembling slightly. She'd never been afraid of the spirits before, but this was different.

Meiling followed a second later. Not quite running but definitely speed walking until she could wrap her arms tight enough around Rus that Rus could hardly breathe through the hold. It didn't matter. Her girls were safe. That's all that mattered.

"I'm here," Rus repeated, wrapping her free arm around the teenager, who was shaking just as badly as her sister. It was good to have them both close, to know they were safe.

But it couldn't last, and she knew that. Because the soul jumper would be there in a matter of hours, and before then they had a whole list of things that needed to be handled to ensure the town didn't fall to it.

Rus gave her girls another reassuring squeeze before she patted Meiling lightly on the shoulder and turned her attention to the other adults. She hadn't noticed before how they were kind of drawing a crowd. Hunter, Ava, and Nando were all behind the tables of their booth, watching with pleased smiles. But they weren't the only ones paying attention. Not that it mattered. Rus had no shame in how she loved her girls. They were the world to her.

"What did you find?" Rus asked gently, tapping Meiling again on the shoulder. If she could keep her mind on the problem in front of her, maybe Meiling wouldn't notice the things Rus had about the spirits. She was a clever one, though, so there was no guarantee that she hadn't already put those pieces together the way Rus had.

"Hunter scrolled back on the radar," Meiling said, straightening up and surreptitiously rubbing her eyes. "They all appeared at the exact same time."

"Not in a wave," Az concluded, her brow creasing with the information. It wasn't good news. Although nothing about this would be. "The prophecy did say the dead would walk among us."

"Yes, but we have no way of knowing if this is happening because of the centennial or if it's happening because of something else." Ava shook her head, her nose wrinkled.

"Ava's right. We don't know if they were pulled from their resting place by the celebration, and this is all part of the process of Moondale recharging herself previously unrecorded because Moondale didn't have a resident medium, or if this is the soul jumper gearing up for something worse." Hunter didn't sound any happier about the prospect of them not knowing than Rus felt.

"Nando, I need you to take the girls home," Rus said without waiting another moment. What she had to say next she couldn't say in front of them. It would only scare them further. "Take Blue, take them home. You'll all be safe behind the wards of 157. I'll send Greer and Cagney by to reinforce them once I find them."

"I'm not leaving you." Meiling's fists tightened in Rus's sweater, where they hadn't yet let go of her. Poor kid.

"Me either!" Aihuan's fingers twisted painfully in Rus's hair, but she didn't bother to try to pull her away. She just lifted her head to look at Az helplessly before returning her attention to her girls.

"You have to," Rus hushed them softly. "I can't deal with all of this and protect you two at the same time. And you're both the most important thing to me and Auntie Az, right, Az?"

Az stepped closer, letting Rus pull her in to smash Meiling between them in a family hug. "You don't need to worry about your Auntie Rus," she murmured gently. "I'm going to be with her the whole time."

"And besides." Rus puffed up her chest, going for bravado she didn't really feel. "Who do you think you're talking to, huh? I am Icarus Ashthorne." She tickled Aihuan, who giggled while Meiling rolled her eyes in fond exasperation. "Famous necromancer. World-renowned medium. The most talented crow witch to—"

"Infamous, more like," Cagney's voice cut through her little speech, dry and bland. "Are you done?"

"Not really."

"Too bad." Cagney shook her head at the entire scene.

"Nesta and Phyre want to meet with Az before the Board of Magic meets tonight for the elder ceremony. They found some... stuff."

"Stuff?" Az asked, pulling away from their huddle but not going far.

Cagney nodded. "Stuff."

"Okaaaay," Rus said slowly, sounding the word out. She didn't know what Phyre and Nesta had been up to, but maybe it was for the better. If it was someone outside of her coven digging up dirt on Brant, it would be more believable. Hopefully.

"Have Brenton and Evander been by to check on my sister?" Worry etched itself across Az's brow. Rus wanted nothing more than to reach up and smooth it away, but there wasn't time for that kind of tenderness. Not right now.

"They're on their way. You can meet them there." Cagney sounded like a general ready to go to war. Rus wondered if she knew about the unsettled dead that lingered around them, staring unseeing into the middle distance.

The air shifted. The hair on the back of Rus's neck rose. Something was coming. Something—

A scream went up from somewhere in the crowd. Rus struggled to tell if it was a person or one of the spirits. Something moved out of the corner of her eye, and when she looked for the movement, she saw the spirit to her right whip its head in her direction. Its neck twisted in an unnatural way.

Then it screamed. The rattling wail of something dead and forgotten.

Right into her fucking ear. Rus jolted at the noise.

Meiling and Aihuan jerked their hands up to cover their

ears, not that it would do any good—the sound wasn't coming from outside of their heads.

"Enough," Rus whispered, her magic flaring out around her and silencing the spirit, putting it back into the holding pattern it had been in, if just for a moment. Just long enough for her to get the girls out. Hopefully none of the others would start screaming. But just as she thought that, she heard another from farther away.

"The humans still can't see them," Hunter said in a whisper.

"See what?" Cagney asked.

"We'll explain later." Rus motioned for Nando to come closer and handed Aihuan to him. "Get the girls home."

The crowd of people around them had begun to stir, disquieted. They might not be able to see the spirits, but they knew something wasn't right. Their instincts told them that maybe it was time to start heading home. Even without the wind, the temperature dropped another couple of degrees.

"What's going on?" Sunila asked as she pushed through the people still milling about Main Street to get to their booth in front of Necromancer's. "The door to Elwood & Co. just locked itself, and I can't get in."

That wasn't good.

"Was there anyone inside?" Az frowned.

"No." But there was fear in Sunila's eyes, and Rus was reminded all over again how vulnerable the folk around her were. They couldn't see the spirits. They didn't know the rising threat. But they were still in danger from it. What they couldn't see *could* hurt them.

There was another scream.

"Go home," Rus insisted. "Get behind the wards. Call Indigo and Maureen to stay with you." There wasn't time to wait. If the spirits were starting to get physical, it was just a matter of time before the crowd around them panicked and became a weapon all its own. They would have to deal with what the negativity of this did to the Heart of Moondale later. For now they needed to get to a place where they wouldn't be crushed by a stampede of scared humans.

"Where are you going?" Nando took the keys for Blue but didn't move right away. The same dawning of dread filled his expression that Rus could see reflected on the faces of the rest of her coven. Rus wished she could take it all back and tell them all it was a terrible prank. But she couldn't.

Another scream. Rus winced and rubbed her ear against her shoulder.

"I'm taking Hunter and Ava to create a touchstone, someplace to herd the spirits and send them to the After. Az, I need paper."

Az dug around in her purse again and quickly produced the pen and pad.

"Draw this onto your arm." Rus's handwriting wasn't the best, but Nando had learned to decipher it a long time ago. She had no doubt he'd figure it out. "Then let Meiling channel a small bit of her magic into you. Not a lot. But a little. It'll give the talisman something to mirror. It's going to hurt like hell, if how Az looked says anything, but it'll let you see the spirits and talk to them if need be." She was speaking so quickly she was hardly breathing between sentences, needing to get Nando and Sunila on their way before shit really hit the fan. "Don't," she said, meeting Meiling's eyes seriously, "try to send any of them to the After. Just ask them to leave if they get inside the wards."

"What if they don't want to leave?" Meiling's voice was small, afraid.

"Then Maureen should have methods to make them. But I don't think they'll be able to get beyond the protections I have in place at home."

Or, at least, they shouldn't. She'd spent the last year funneling magic into the land there so that it would recognize her, would protect her and hers. Add to that the way Cagney had spoken to the plants in the area, and the wards already in place by Greer's family, and 157 Mourning Moore should be the safest place in all of Moondale. It was a gamble, sending the girls off without her. But she'd stacked the odds in her favor. And they wouldn't be alone. They would have three fully grown witches already connected to the land, and two nearly adult witches to protect them.

Not to mention the fact that Moondale ought to know better than to let anything happen to her girls. She wanted Rus here. All but dragged her home, kicking and screaming. If Moondale wanted to keep Rus and her fledgling coven, then she'd have to work for it.

"Be good for Uncle Nando." Rus pressed a kiss to Aihuan's temple, then hugged Meiling in spite of her complaints recently that she was getting too old for Rus to baby her. "Now go. We need to pack up here and get to work."

More screams. They grated at Rus's ears.

Nando didn't waste time arguing. He nodded and wove through the crowd, Aihuan in his arms, Meiling with her hand fisted in his jacket as Sunila brought up the rear. Rus waited until they were out of her sight before she turned her attention back to the others.

"All right." She clapped once, wincing when it burned the wound still on her palm. "Az, you're going to check on Violet. It might be better if she went to 157 and stayed there with the rest of them until we deal with everything else. I'll meet you at the board meeting later."

Az nodded, leaning in to brush a kiss to Rus's lips before stepping back. "Be careful."

"Aren't I always?" Rus scoffed.

Az fixed her with a bland look, then turned on her heel and disappeared into the crowd as well, likely already making a plan on the quickest route to Violet's. Once there, Rus had no doubt that she'd have enough good sense to take Violet's car over to 157 versus walking.

"What do we do about the humans?" Cagney tugged Rus with her into the quiet of Necromancer's, where Ava and Hunter shut and locked the door behind them. There were enough wards on this place that the spirits hadn't invaded it yet, a relief, but Rus didn't know how long that would last. Warding a business wasn't the same as warding a home, especially not one that was as new as Necromancer's. Elwood's would probably be safer, but Rus wasn't willing to fight with a distressed spirit to get in there right now.

Rus peeked out the front window to look at the humans in question. For all there was a nervousness to their movements, they were still going about their business as if nothing at all had changed.

Another scream rent the air, and she hissed. They were getting louder. More unsettled. Each unhappy wail drilling into her skull.

"Call Greer. We need him and his people to start going through the festival table by table and talking to the folk. We need the tables to pack up early. It'll get people to start clearing out." Greer wasn't going to like following orders sent out by Rus, but there wasn't a lot of time to argue. She trusted he'd understand that and make himself less of a pain in her ass.

Cagney nodded, already pulling out her phone.

"What about the humans staying overnight in Moondale?" Ava frowned, her eyes fixed on the people outside.

"Greer will have to handle that too. He'll have to go to the others in Crimson Tide, and they'll need to reinforce any wards on rentals, inns, and so on. It would help if they could see the spirits." Rus frowned, rubbing her temples. She didn't know that they had time for her to put the talisman on that many people.

"We could set up a talisman station at the coven house," Hunter offered.

"We could, but there needs to be a medium to power them. And I need to be with you to set up the touchstone. You can't open a portal to the After without me. I'm not putting Meiling in charge of powering the talismans. It's not her responsibility to make sure the adults around her know what they're up against. She's just a kid. And I can't be in two places at once."

"Let me see the talisman," Hunter ordered, then held out his hand and waited impatiently for Rus to sketch it for him so he could examine it.

"It's rough," Rus warned. "I didn't have a lot of time to think about it in the car. Az needed to see what we were up against."

Hunter hummed thoughtfully, bending over the notebook with Ava while Cagney issued orders to Greer rapid fire. There was a lull, however brief, before Hunter asked, "What if we connected them all together?"

"What?" Rus scooted closer to look at her work again.

"This character," Hunter said, pointing, "means

connection. Means a binding. It's similar to the one we used to tie Ava and me to the land."

"But a little different," Ava agreed.

"Right." Rus was starting to see where he was going with this. "But if we change it closer to something like the binding to the land, and instead make it a flesh binding…"

"It'll burn a fuckload more." Ava shook her head.

"It will. But it'll allow us to pump magic into only one person. The rest will be taken care of via domino effect." Rus chewed on the inside of her cheek thoughtfully. "It won't last as long that way. The magic will be spread thin."

"But if you keep the original person everyone is tied to with you…" Hunter murmured thoughtfully.

"Or if I tie them to myself." It would suck. It would *royally* suck. It would hurt. And it would be draining. And it would no doubt leave her open to the influence of any spirit the others came across.

"I don't like it," Cagney said when she rejoined them.

"It doesn't matter. We're out of options." Rus shook her head. "Ava, make a copy of it that's easier to read. Then I want Cagney to send a picture of this thing to Greer and get his people to put it on their forearms." Already she was sketching out an updated talisman for Ava to rewrite, the cap of the pen between her teeth.

"You should wait to power it on," Ava offered, her hands working quickly. "To reduce panic and strain."

"Right. Until we've gotten the streets clear, at least." Cagney nodded.

"Fine. But in the meantime, we need to find a place for the touchstone." Rus didn't exactly love that Ava and Hunter already seemed to know her well enough to realize how reckless she could be.

"I think I've got an idea for that," Cagney volunteered. "But the Board of Magic isn't going to like it."

"Yeah. Well. We wouldn't be in this mess if they took care of their shit. So. Fuck 'em." Rus sneered.

Chapter 25

"What do you mean I'm not safe in my own home?" Violet's voice had gone up several octaves, her panic and upset clear. A fact that Azure found rather disconcerting as she'd always thought of her sister as having better control over her emotions than that. But even if she did, the last few months had been a *lot* for Violet, Azure supposed.

"Brenton can't stay with you during the Board of Magic meeting. We need him there." Even though he obviously wanted to be with Violet. When Azure showed up, he wasn't holding Violet like maybe he had once upon a time, but he seemed to curl around her like something large and protective, an animal shielding its mate. More proof that the more things changed, the more they stayed the same.

"I don't need Brenton's protection." Violet scoffed, indignant, crossing her arms over her chest. It was the most like herself she'd been in weeks now. Who knew all it would take to draw that out was for her younger sister to tell her what to do.

"I didn't use the word *protection*."

Brenton snorted from where he stood, leaning against the counter in Violet's kitchen, his eyes following Violet's every move as she washed the dishes that were piled high in the sink last Azure was there. She could only hope that was an indication that maybe Violet was starting to feel better, starting to drag herself out of the pit that was her despair. Now all they had to do was keep this business with the soul jumper from putting her right back where they'd found her.

To be clear, Azure was still angry with her sister for what she'd said when Azure decided to leave the Circle of Jade Waters to start a coven with Rus. She would not forget being called *selfish*. But that didn't mean she wanted her sister to suffer. That didn't mean she felt Violet deserved the pain of finding out that the woman she'd loved was possessed by a centuries-old witch who was more poltergeist than folk these days and was only with her to get back at their family. No one deserved that.

"You didn't have to," Violet said, her tone shifting to annoyed.

Which wasn't fair, really. Azure was trying to keep the soul jumper from taking a bite out of Violet like it'd tried to do with their aunt. She glanced back to the window over the sink. There were spirits lined up outside the fence of Violet's house. They couldn't get any closer, thankfully, because of the heavy warding she, Brenton, and Greer had put into place, and the two spirits Rus had set up to monitor the property. But Azure wasn't sure how long that would hold.

Moondale's magic flexed and stretched around her, a rubber band pushed beyond its breaking point. If it snapped, any wards not actively maintained by the person who set them, or some other means, would disappear in an instant. Then the dead would invade the homes of the living.

A scream rent the air, sending a shiver down Azure's spine. They'd been doing that on and off since they started while she was on Main Street with Rus and the others. She didn't even want to know what it meant.

"Why are you so worried, anyway?" Violet asked, not bothering to turn to look at her sister.

Her hands were elbow deep in sudsy water, pink rubber gloves pulled up over her arms to keep them dry. All she needed was an apron, and she'd be the picture of the woman Azure remembered from all the times she'd visited her sister before. The doting housewife. Azure's stomach churned at the image. How much of that had been what Violet wanted? And how much of it was her trying to squeeze herself into a box the soul jumper placed her in? To keep her weak and subservient. To chain her to this place so the soul jumper could use her when the time came. Fuck. Azure was going to be sick.

She looked at Brenton, her eyes wide and pleading. He had to do something. He had to talk some sense into her sister, because she clearly couldn't. And they were running out of time!

Brenton sighed, his shoulders slumping as he moved closer to Violet and bumped her hip with his own. "Maybe we should listen to your sister."

"I just don't understand why? What's the danger?" Violet tilted her head back to look up at him, a soft look on her face that left Azure feeling like she was watching something private. Goddess, had she and Rus been this stupid when Rus first came home?

Azure could tell her about the ghosts. About the way they had appeared all at once all over town. She was sure Violet felt Moondale's magic stretching thin too. Any folk who was paying attention would. But they likely brushed that off as being just hours away from the end of the centennial, when all the energy from the celebration would complete its cycle and head back to the Heart of Moondale to be dispersed through the clans and covens. It was a reasonable explanation, but Azure didn't think that was the case.

Biting the inside of her cheek, Azure debated what to tell her sister. She didn't want to make her panic, not with how on an athame's edge she'd been of late. It might tip her the wrong way. Send her spiraling. But she needed to stress the importance of this. Maybe if she—

"Don't you want to spend time with your nieces?" *Dirty pool, Azure.* But Rus would likely approve of this tactic. It wasn't exactly fair, and she knew that. But none of this situation was fair. If it were, none of this would be happening.

"My nieces?" Violet turned slowly from the sink to look at Azure with wide eyes. Brenton, too, stared at her, his jaw hanging slack.

Oh. Had she not told anyone that she'd proposed to Rus yet? Well, outside of Phyre, who helped with the ring. Oops. It was too late now. She was in it already.

"I have proposed to Rus." The language was stilted, and Azure stood up a little taller under her sister's scrutiny. She knew Violet didn't approve; she'd made that abundantly clear. But there was no way that distaste for Rus would carry over to Meiling and Aihuan. They were adorable. "Which means that soon Aihuan and Meiling will be my daughters as well. Making them your nieces."

"She said yes?" Brenton asked, his tone half incredulous. Goddess, she forgot what a fucking asshole he could be sometimes. It wasn't on purpose, she knew that. He was just a cynical fucker. Which was probably partly Violet's fault, because he'd been head over heels in love with her for most of his life, and she'd not even fought the Board of Magic when they'd paired her up with Taryn. Her sister was a fool.

"She hasn't said no." Which was as good as a yes in

Azure's book. Besides, she knew Rus wanted to say yes. She knew that once they got past all of Rus's insecurities, once the soul jumper was in their rearview, Rus would agree to marry her. It was just a matter of time.

"She hasn't said yes either." Violet narrowed her eyes, and Azure resisted the urge to snarl at her sister or curl up under the assessing way she was being watched.

"Rus has some insecurities about it. We're working through them. I told her if she really didn't want it, she just had to say no, and I would stop asking."

Brenton barked a laugh. "How many times have you asked?"

"I don't think that's anyone's business outside of Rus and I." Azure straightened her spine and lifted her chin.

"Oh, it's been a lot, hasn't it?" Brenton chuckled with dark delight.

"The girls would like to get to know their aunt a bit more, and I think it would be good for you to be around them. They would—" She paused, thinking over her next words carefully. Saying that they would cheer Violet up would be acknowledging that she was currently anything but happy, which was likely to set her off again. That would be counterproductive. "Everyone would benefit from the family being a bit closer."

"You said Maureen, Indigo, and Sunila are also there?" Brenton raised an eyebrow, and Azure could see his mind working. He'd moved past the teasing into something she could work with.

"Yes. Having another witch there to keep the wards up would be good as well." Azure nodded, hoping this was the track he'd been on. "To protect the girls and the witches not pledged to a coven."

Violet's head jerked as she looked between them, but

even as she watched, Azure could sense the defeat. Violet knew she'd lost. She sighed, her shoulders slumping. "I'll get my things."

She slapped the gloves next to the sink, clearly annoyed, and left to gather everything she'd need for an overnight stay at 157 Mourning Moore, leaving Brenton and Azure to their own devices. Brenton didn't wait before grabbing the gloves and settling in to finish up the dishes.

"I wish you'd told me sooner to come over here," he said after a few minutes of quiet only broken up by the splash of water.

"I wish I had too." Especially seeing how his presence settled something within Violet, allowing her to start moving forward. It wasn't much, but it was something. "I'm hoping she won't have to face the soul jumper again. It'll only set her back."

Brenton glanced at her over his shoulder, a conspiratorial light in his eyes. "The kids will just have to keep her busy."

"I'm sure that can be arranged." She pulled her phone from her bag and sent a quick text to Meiling to make sure she understood the assignment before returning her attention to waiting for her sister. "You'll take her to the house."

"Right. I'll meet you at the board meeting."

Relief flooded Azure at the words. She might really be able to do this. Unseat Brant. Stop the soul jumper. Save Moondale. Get married to Rus. All of it.

Brenton seemed to notice, and he lifted his chin in acknowledgment. "Go check in with your necromancer. I've got things taken care of here."

"Thank you."

"Of course."

"HOW OLD DID you say this tree was?" Rus asked. Her feet crunched in the slowly browning grass as she made her way around the thick trunk.

"No way to know for sure." Cagney's arms were crossed, her eyes following Rus's movement from where she stood off to the side with Hunter and Ava. "Trees don't understand years the way we do. Even with the cycle of the seasons."

"But it's at least a century or two?" Two hundred years was a long time by human standards but not really by folk standards. It would make a decent anchor to the After. Not the strongest touchstone, but they were running out of time.

"The roots run deep" was Cagney's answer. "And they spread for a ways."

"Which is why the board would be super pissed if I used it." Rus nodded in understanding.

"I'm sorry, why's that?" Ava asked. "You're just doing what you have to to protect the people of—"

"They'll spout some bullshit about my contaminating the land of Moondale, disturbing the natural ecosystem." Which was just fucking stupid, because the natural ecosystem of a place was one of life and death. It was a circle, a cycle. That was something the board never seemed to fully understand—that they wouldn't have one without the other. They couldn't have life without death. It was foolish. She tilted her head toward Cagney. "Are you sure about this? Herne could have you pruned from the grove for this."

"Herne could try." Cagney scoffed. "Brant Ironwood

isn't the only one too stuck in their ways to be on the Board of Magic these days."

"What do we need to do to create a touchstone?" Hunter asked, pulling them back to the problem staring them in the face. They could deal with the issue that was the Board of Magic being full of folk who didn't like change later. Probably that very evening. But Rus couldn't focus on that. Not right now. One problem at a time.

"Well first, we'll need to set up an array to make sure the door is one way." Rus paced thoughtfully in front of the tree. She'd never done this before, not on this scale, and not when she was planning to leave the opening to the After unattended. It was a risk. A big one. "We'll also need wards to keep anyone who shouldn't be here away. Especially humans."

Goddess, she wished Az were there. She would be able to look at this problem and figure out a talisman that would work for it. Know exactly the right way to balance the symbology and how to force the negative space to do double time. Rus's ink witch was so clever. But she wasn't here. It was just Rus.

"Could we reuse some of the ones we've set up on the coven house?" Ava frowned, her eyes dancing from the tree to the spirits that littered the small park where Cagney had brought them. The sky was slowly turning darker, even though the sun had yet to set.

"Yes. We can." Rus nodded. "They'll make for a good jumping-off point, but I think even with that we might need someone here to reinforce them, should things go wonky."

"Like how?" Hunter tilted his head, his brow creased.

He probably couldn't feel it—he wasn't as closely tied to the land as Rus was—but it had started up almost as soon as they got to the base of the mountain: this thing inside of her stretching and getting thinner and thinner by the second. It had taken her far too long to realize it was Moondale herself, letting her folk know that she was doing her best, that she would protect them as much as she could. But that time was running out.

Rus shook her head and didn't answer his question. "Cagney, could you do like you did at 157? Ask the land and the plants to help protect this place?"

Cagney rolled her eyes. "Why the fuck do you think I brought you here? Great Elm, I swear sometimes you don't even fucking think, do you?"

With a shrug, Rus pressed on. "If you can get me any more information on the tree in the meantime, that'd be great. An age would help, then at least I know what I'm working with. Hunter, Ava, let's get the wards set up. Then we can focus on connecting the touchstone."

"Should we let Azure know where we are?" Hunter already had his phone out, typing up a message.

"Yeah, but tell her not to rush. I don't want her cutting her time with Vi short if she doesn't need to." Hopefully they'd be able to handle this themselves without Az's impressive ink witch knowledge, and without the rest of their coven. Rus sent up a silent prayer to the Goddess and settled on the ground with her pad and paper to get to work.

Chapter 26

"It really wasn't necessary for you to come," Rus mumbled, fondness lining her tone. She couldn't help it. She would never *not* be happy to see Az. Even when the world was falling down around their ears, she would be happy to see Az. More proof that she should just give in and agree to marry her already, probably. "You should look after you sister."

"Violet is fine." Az moved in close, wrapping an arm around Rus's hips as she pressed a kiss to her temple. Soft and companionable. A *hello*, like they hadn't just parted ways only a little more than an hour ago. Was this what Rus's life would look like when she married Az? She could get used to it. "Brenton is taking her to our home. She will be safe there."

Our home.

The words swooped into Rus's chest like a hook sinking between her ribs to tug her forward, the line pulled tight between her and Az. Connecting them in a way that had likely always been there, but she'd never noticed before. Maybe it was this that pulled her back to Moondale. The fishing line of her heart tied to Az's. Strange. But comforting.

"Are you sure?" Rus didn't like the idea of Az not doing something she felt she should just because Rus needed her.

"I can handle things here. If you need to be with your fam—"

"You're my family." Az's fingers pressed into her hip, a warning and a promise all in one. "My coven."

"Well, that's settled then," Cagney said, cutting into their happy bubble with no remorse. Her green eyes were sharp when they met Rus's.

Rus wanted to fucking kick her, but she recognized that there wasn't a whole lot of time for her to settle into the feeling of warmth that Az coming for her provided. Hopefully after this was all over, she'd have a moment to really let herself feel it. The knowledge that Az had come for her, would always come for her, was something she could hold on to for the rest of her life, however long that turned out to be.

"Now that you're here." Hunter stepped away from where he and Ava had been working on setting up the perimeter that would keep the touchstone safe once Rus created it. "You can help me and Ava set up the array. We need something to keep people from wandering over on accident."

Az pressed another kiss to Rus's temple, then pulled back. "Let me see what you have so far."

Rus watched Az for a long moment. Watched the way she squatted beside Ava and Hunter as they showed her the symbols they'd been working with. Her skirt pooled on the ground. She was beautiful. She was *always* beautiful. But never so much as when she was in her element like this. Never so much as when she turned her mind to her craft. Rus wondered when Az would officially take the title of ink witch. Maybe they should throw a party when she did.

Cagney cleared her throat, drawing Rus back to the matter at hand.

Rus said, "We should check in with Greer. See how everything is going with closing down the celebration." She didn't envy him that task. No one liked to leave a party early.

"I already did that. While you were mooning over your girlfriend swooping in to rescue you like some damsel." Cagney rolled her eyes and let out an amused huff.

"Not a damsel." Rus scoffed. "It wasn't like I was fainting or anything."

Cagney didn't dignify that with a response, which was probably for the better. "Some of the folk weren't keen on packing up early."

"Yeah, I thought that might be the case." Rus ran a hand through her hair, hissing when her fingers snagged on knotted strands. "I don't know what ending it early will do to the recharging of the ley lines."

"No one does. But we don't have a lot of choice. We can't let the humans stick around and potentially get attacked by shades. That would be a fucking disaster."

"Right." Rus rubbed her sweating palms on her jeans and turned back to the tree before calling over her shoulder, "How's the warding looking? I need to get started on the touchstone if we're going to get it done before the board meets."

"Five more minutes," Az reported. "You should be able to get started now. The basic wards they've set up will be enough to hold people out, at least during the initial process."

Rus nodded. "And the trees aren't going to give me any trouble?"

"You might get a little pushback." Cagney shrugged. "But I've done my best to communicate to the plants here what you're doing, so it shouldn't be too bad."

"Right," Rus said again, nerves settling low in her belly. She didn't want to do this. It was asking for trouble, and she knew that. And it was going to fuck with her own system more than she'd like.

Fuck it. They didn't have a choice.

"If it fights back, I'll be here." Cagney reached for her hand and gave it a squeeze, the gesture so familiar it tore at something inside of Rus. How long had it been since Rus had been this close with her friends from Moondale? This close to the family she'd built here before she'd left. Even in the year since returning, they had danced around getting back to where they were before. Only now was it finally starting to feel normal. Was it finally starting to sink in that she was staying. Possibly forever.

"Okay." Rus returned the squeeze, then tugged until she and Cagney were both sitting on the cold, hard ground in front of the thick trunk. It took them a moment to get settled into a lotus pose, their knees knocking together. Rus let her eyes drift to Az and their small coven as they worked for another moment. Let the sight of them center her, remind her why she was doing this, then she pulled her athame from her back pocket and yanked up the sleeve of her henley.

The metal bit into her arm, blood pulling to the surface before it dripped onto the ground. Magic hissed from the wound, resistant to being summoned so close to the last time she'd done something big with it. She probably should have eaten something before trying this. Or at least pumped herself full of caffeine. But it was too late now.

Rus swayed with the feeling, swallowing around bile that burned her throat on its way up. She hadn't pushed herself this hard in such a long time. Hadn't needed to. Even when she'd been up against a soul jumper, a possession, and a crew of witch hunters, she hadn't needed to expend this much power. To get this close to the bounds of her abilities.

But that was all right, because the only way to expand her capabilities was to get close to the edge, to push past it. To force herself to grow stronger.

Sucking in a breath, Rus forced her magic into submission and channeled it into the ground beneath her. It didn't go willingly. Not that she'd thought for one moment it would. The ground wasn't dead enough yet for it to not fight back against the rotten feel of her magic.

Cagney grunted at her side, and the scent of decomposing leaves filled Rus's nose. A reminder from Cagney that this was the cycle. That the earth, like those who inhabited it, was not exempt from the pull of death. That death was natural. Good.

The ground stopped fighting, the plants and the dirt accepting Rus's magic finally as it settled like mist into the earth, as if it would dampen it, cause mud and dew. Only it wouldn't, because water brought life, and all Rus's magic did was handle the dead.

There was a whisper of something there, when she finally connected to it. The spirits of foliage and saplings that hadn't survived the summer's heat and lack of rain. Small things. Not negative in nature. Things that would likely have dissipated on their own come winter, along with their kin. But they couldn't take that chance, not with so many unsettled shades popping up all over Moondale.

"Let me send you over," Rus whispered, lifting a hand from her leg to brush her fingers through the grass. "Let me set you free."

The spirits of nature didn't respond in words the way those of people would, because they didn't understand language. But they also didn't cling to life the way that others might, given the chance to leave early, to not have to watch their kin die. They took it, brushing Rus's magic like a caress, soft and happy, before crossing into the After with not a single bother.

Rus's shoulders drooped in relief as the earth accepted her magic, whispering understanding. At least that part of this had been easy. The next was going to suck.

The After had always had a pull that Rus didn't care for. She knew it was because she was so close to it, always toeing the line, even more so since she'd cut herself open—metaphorically and physically—and bled to bring Aihuan back. It threatened to suck her under, like a riptide.

There was a caw, sharp and unyielding, then talons dug into her shoulder. She felt the moment Darcy landed, puncturing skin through the thin fabric of her shirt. Pinpricks of pain that grounded her to her body.

"Thank you, old friend," Rus murmured, dragging a deep breath into her lungs, her head swimming with the lack of oxygen from breaths gone too shallow.

There was a garbled gurgle near her ear, and Darcy snipped at the lobe with his beak in reprimand.

"I'll remember to call you next time." Rus shook her head. "Now let me focus."

He huffed a breath but was otherwise silent.

With the pinch of Darcy's claws in her skin, and the ache of the hard ground in her back, Rus had an easier time ignoring the siren song of the After. She could touch it. Call to it. But it would not pull her under. Not this time.

Her blood soaked into the ground beneath her, going to the roots of the tree. A connection. A bond. She felt the moment it tied itself up tight. A knot around her solar plexus that threatened to double her forward, even as she fought against it. Her nails dug into the dirt, and she pushed harder, the green mist of her magic settling with the blood.

What came next started as a low hum. A buzz through her veins. It moved into the ground a second later, making the earth rumble beneath them. The tree behind her creaked and groaned as if a sharp wind had kicked up. A faint green glow drifted around its bark. The connection to the After snapped into place a moment later, ricocheting pain through Rus's body that had her wobbling, screaming, falling, blacking out.

RUS'S SCREAM ripped through the air, and Azure was at Rus's side before she could hit the ground. She fell to her knees, scooping Rus into her arms, and kept her from knocking her head against the tree. She let out a slow sigh of relief that she'd reached Rus in time.

"She did it," Cagney rasped, like she hadn't believed Rus could at first.

Azure turned her head to look at the tree and found it glowing faintly with the aftereffects of Rus's magic. A whisper had started from it, much like how Rus's magic whispered with the dead. A song, a call, begging spirits to come to it. Calling them to come home. A soft green glow, like the first sprouts of spring, pulsed from the bark. It looked more alive than it had before, and yet the whispers grew, one stacking on top of the other until they were no different than the sound of rushing water. And at the center of the tree, where the trunk was thickest, there was a shimmer of something not quite solid. Like looking into a reflection of the world cast on water. The After, Azure realized with a shiver.

"Tell Greer he and his people can bring any spirits willing to leave this plane here," Azure said. Rus shook in her arms, as if a bone-deep chill cut through her, and Azure slid out of her leather jacket to wrap it around Rus's shoulders, protecting her from the air, as best she could.

Cagney pulled out her phone and moved farther away to call her partner while Hunter and Ava shifted from foot to foot in Azure's periphery.

"Is she okay?" Hunter asked.

"She just burned herself out. Dig in my bag and see if you can find the granola bar at the bottom."

"I hate granola," Rus whined. Her eyes were still closed, and there was a thin sheen of cold sweat along her temples, but she was awake, and that was more than Azure had expected, given the circumstances.

"You'll eat it anyway." Azure took the opened snack and pressed it to Rus's lips, not giving her a moment to protest. "You haven't had a real meal in Goddess knows how long. You're practically running on fumes. Idiot." The last word left Azure with such a fondness, she was sure anyone around them would be embarrassed at the display, but she didn't care.

"Love you too," Rus mumbled around a full mouth.

"Now what?" Ava watched the tree warily, keeping a careful distance.

"Now," Cagney said, returning to their group, "we need to get Rus's ass in the car. I'll drive."

"To where?" Hunter frowned.

"The board is meeting early. Apparently, some of them are a little pissed with us for telling Greer to close the celebration down. They're probably going to try to kick Azure off the board." Cagney rolled her eyes, her tone annoyed.

"When are they not pissed?" Rus grumbled, stuffing the wrapper from her granola bar into Azure's purse, where it would no doubt leave behind crumbs at the bottom. "Do Nesta and Phyre know where we're headed?"

"Already on it." Cagney tapped at her phone as she turned to head back the way they'd come, hardly pausing to give the others time to catch up while Hunter and Azure levered Rus from the ground and helped her hobble through the park.

"Ava," Rus called over her shoulder. "You'll stay and make sure no one gets too close to that entrance?"

"Right," Ava agreed.

Chapter 27

The Board of Magic never failed to give Azure a fucking headache.

Honestly, if it wasn't for the fact that Rus had enough on her plate—and shouldn't be forced to deal with morons on the regular—Azure would have said *she* should take the spot as elder of the Coven of the Forgotten. She was much more capable and willing to speak her mind in a room full of people who disliked her, however undiplomatic her words might be. But alas, even if it *would* be amusing to see Rus give this group of curmudgeonly, stuck-in-their-ways fossils the dressing down they deserved, Azure knew that Rus had more important things to do. Like put the finishing touches on her many inventions, the ones proving to the board that their coven was an asset to Moondale instead of an assault. Making them indispensable—much to Brant Ironwood's annoyance.

"We cannot put off the ceremony," Azure said for perhaps the fifth time since entering the room. No one was listening to her. The other elders *never* listened to her, apart from Nixie and Aunt Carmine. It would be insulting if she actually gave a fuck what any of them thought of her. They were all talking over each other. Goddess, she hoped Rus and the others got there soon.

They'd driven over to the board building and dropped Azure off out front so she could scurry in and buy them all some time. What the others were up to, she didn't know. She didn't think she wanted to, either. Nesta had been notorious for knowing anything and everything about everyone, and just how to utilize that information, when they'd been in school. Azure didn't think they were any different now that they were an adult. Phyre was always quiet and collected, but Azure had seen enough of her over the years to know that she had an underlying steel in her spirit, and a willingness to do what was necessary to protect those closest to her.

All Azure could hope was that they got back soon, and that when they arrived Rus would be doing better than she'd been before Azure left her in the car, weak and shivery.

"We have no proof there were any ghosts at all," Brant Ironwood continued as if Azure hadn't spoken. It was amazing, honestly, how someone could act like Azure didn't exist. He refused to so much as look at her, much less acknowledge anything she said.

"That has to be the stupidest thing you've ever said," Azure mumbled half under her breath, but she didn't say it quietly enough that Aunt Carmine missed it.

Aunt Carmine cut her a glare.

Azure lifted a brow in challenge as if asking Aunt Carmine to combat what she'd said. Of course, it was a bit of hyperbole. There was little doubt that Brant *had* said stupider things and *would* say stupider things in the future. But it seemed to have gotten everyone's attention.

"Was there something you wanted to add to the conversation, Elder Elwood?" Nixie asked, but the corners of her lips were turned up, so Azure knew she'd heard her just fine.

"I said, if Elder Ironwood is so skeptical, when my

partner arrives, she'd be more than happy to provide him with the talisman needed to see the dead just as she's done with myself and Evander Greer's force." Maybe they'd even give him a warning about the pain that came with it before the magic flowed through his veins.

"And taint myself with the stink of necrotic magic?" Brant Ironwood snorted. "You must be joking."

Then again, maybe they wouldn't.

"This talisman you and Ashthorne created," Aunt Carmine said, leaning forward with some interest, "is it permanent?"

"No. But we're not sure how long the effects last. There has been little time to experiment with it, as Rus and I had to create it rather quickly." Azure was sure that once they had more time, Rus could perfect it to the point where it didn't hurt the wearer to apply it. Maybe there would even be a method that allowed the folk using it to turn it on without a medium in proximity to provide them with magic to mirror. They would have to input the data into the talisman itself. Tell it what it was meant to be mirroring. But if they could... well, the possibilities would be endless. Any folk could mirror another's innate gift for a short while. It would change the way magic worked for—

"Even if that were the case," Enfys Snowthorn—the head of the Clan of Crescentia, a small clan of cupids of which Nesta and their brother Dillan were a part—said, "the fact still stands that to use necrotic magic goes against the laws of nature. Necromancy is, by its virtue, unnat—"

"Necromancy works *with* the laws of nature, not against them. And even if that were not the case, a medium's ability to see spirits has nothing at all to do with necromancy." Which should have been a point Azure made the first time Brant said it, but she'd been cut off from getting into a pissing match with him by her aunt. Probably for the better. She was less likely to bite Enfys's head off, even if he had been the one to push Nesta into matching Violet with Taryn. On second thought... "The ability to see the dead is as natural as any other gift a folk obtains at birth or upon maturity. It is absolutely no different than my ability to step through the present moment, or a cupid's ability to see the strings of fate. To say otherwise shows a severe lack of magical understanding. And if that is the board's opinion, I'm afraid we have bigger problems in Moondale than an army of disquiet dead."

At the direct scolding to a senior elder, many of the others began to whisper back and forth. The room filled with murmurings about Azure's brazenness, about how she'd learned too much from that necromancer. But also, about how she was right, and how maybe Brant and his cohort were being needlessly biased.

There were eleven clans and covens, total. Eleven elders.

And as Azure lifted a brow imperiously at Brant Ironwood, readying for a fight, they all fell silent to not miss a thing. Gossipmongers, the lot of them.

Brant's face turned violently red. "Now listen here, you little—"

"My partner is correct." Rus's voice floated to the front of the board hall just before the doors burst open on a wind smelling of rotted, fetid things. Goddess, Azure's soon-to-be wife loved to make an entrance.

My partner. It sent a shiver of delight down Azure's spine.

Azure turned toward the door to watch Rus traipse across the yellowed flooring of what had once been the old town hall, Nesta and Phyre flanking her. She'd changed into her trailing green velvet dress, the one she'd worn almost exactly a year ago when she'd barged into this very same hall and demanded the board protect her daughters, and the wide-brimmed fedora with the crows painted beneath it. Somehow, she looked even more beautiful than she had that first time, even for as tired and drawn as she was, and Azure's breath lodged in her throat.

"This is a private meeting," Nixie called. There was no real heat behind the words, though, and Azure wondered if the wards had even been in place, or if Rus just decided to slam open the doors to cause a scene. "You have got to stop barging in here like that."

"Never gonna happen, Nix," Rus said, and had the audacity to wink at Nixie Vernan, the oldest living folk in Moondale. The one most likely to be Chessy—the lochness monster of the Chesapeake Bay. A shiver of delight skittered over Azure's nerves. "Unfortunately, Az is correct. I don't think we can put off the ceremony." She tilted her head to Azure with a fleeting smile. "Sorry I'm late, love, things are getting bad out there."

"How bad?" Aunt Carmine asked.

"Can't you feel it?" Rus frowned, her gaze flicking back to Azure in question. "Have none of the others been able to feel the magic stretching as we have? The chill of the dead dropping the temp?"

Azure shook her head. This realization mystified her as well. There was no mistaking the way Moondale was spreading herself thin to protect them. The wards on the edge of town would be the last thing to go, but if they did... Azure didn't want to think about what was outside. For five hundred years, those wards stood between anything that would happily feed on Moondale's people, and they were turning brittle as the Board of Magic cooled its cauldron.

"Maybe because we're so new," Rus mumbled to herself. Her fingers cupped her chin as she thought. "Maybe because our connection is so fresh."

That wasn't why, at least Azure didn't think so. She thought maybe it had more to do with how, for the first time in five hundred years, Moondale had chosen a coven for herself. There was no denying the way she called Rus home, or how she'd all but thrown Azure and Rus together. Moondale had her fingers in everything Azure and Rus did over the last year, and maybe that was because she knew what was coming. Maybe because she understood that she would need witches willing and able to do what was necessary to protect her and hers. She would need a crow witch and an ink witch who understood the natural cycle and balance of the world. Who were willing to listen to her, and to each other.

"Either way," Azure said, hoping to draw Rus out of her thoughts. They didn't have time for wild theories right now. "Rus is correct. Moondale is doing everything she can to protect us, but the magic is already failing. If we postpone the ceremony until we are no longer under this threat, there will be nothing left of Moondale to save. The Heart will be depleted, our wards will fall, and we will be left to the limited mercy of the Council of Creatures in Ironport to protect us against any incoming threats."

Azure didn't have to say that the Council of Creatures would be just as happy to let every folk that went bump in the night in Ironport cross the boundary into Moondale to feed on their people instead of its own. They all knew that well enough. Relations between the Council of Creatures and the Board of Magic had always been strained. The Council of Creatures was furious that Moondale's heavy population of magical folk tended to draw things like vampires to their borders, but the wards kept them out. Meaning they settled in Ironport and made a mess of things there.

"If we do the ceremony now, there won't be enough energy in the ley lines to power the Heart and the elders," Chelsea Horst protested. She was the elder of the Chesapeake Pack, a small group of shifters that made their home in Moondale generations ago and focused much of their efforts on wildlife preservation.

"She's right." Brant Ironwood took up the argument, not that he needed any help. He was against anything that Azure and Rus suggested, no matter how logical it might be. "Thanks to your intervention, the celebration ended early, meaning we didn't reach the levels we hoped to with this event. It also means there might be negativity in the ley lines we hadn't planned for."

"There would have been more negativity in them had we not done what we did." Rus snarled, baring teeth. "Or did you want us to wait around for when one of the humans got attacked by a ghost? What do you think that kind of thing would do to the energy we were gathering?"

Phyre reached for Rus's wrist and gave it a little squeeze before whispering something to her Azure couldn't hear.

"What would it have done to the town's reputation?" Azure couldn't help but add. Because it was true. If the people panicked, if someone got hurt, the town would never recover. They could say goodbye to any tourist event they might have in the future. And they couldn't afford that, especially not when they had no idea what the unsettled spirits were doing to the ley lines.

"Be that as it may," Gilroy Herne said, tone falsely diplomatic, "what you are suggesting will close the cycle before we have everything we need. And for what? A necromancer's claims that the town is overrun with spirits?"

"Whether you believe me or not is irrelevant." Rus snorted.

"She's correct, it is irrelevant," Nixie said, bringing the arguing to heel. "I'm assuming you've thought about a way to make up for the lost magic, have you not, Elder Elwood?" She turned her attention to Azure so that Azure knew she meant her and not Aunt Carmine.

Azure hadn't, actually, thought much about it. She was too busy trying to keep Rus from fainting again in the back of the car on the way here, but now that she turned her mind to it, the answer seemed obvious. "Many of our smaller events help to fuel the ley lines as well," she offered, licking her lips and giving them all a moment to interrupt her line of reasoning. No one did. "We don't normally hold a winter solstice event, but perhaps it is time that we start. A festival of some kind would draw in tourists and provide good cheer while the veil is thinnest, when we need Moondale's protections the most."

"It would certainly give us a boost," Rus agreed. "Maybe enough to get us through to the summer season when the town will be flooded again with tourists."

"Something low effort," Aunt Carmine joined in, "that the whole town can participate in."

"Then the energy can touch even the furthest reaching lines." Azure nodded. She saw where this was going. "Many in the town already participate in the yearly light competition, and we've always had tourists from the surrounding area who come to see the houses. Why not capitalize on it? Turn it into a week-long festival just before Yule."

"Yes." Nixie smiled, all sharp teeth. "Yes, I think that will do nicely. Elder Elwood, you will be in charge of organizing it, since you did such a good job with the centennial celebration."

Azure's stomach sank. She had no desire to do *that* all over again, but she'd do what she had to. Maybe she could drag Sunila and Indigo in to help. And Violet, if she was feeling up to it. That would take some of the strain off her.

"That's settled then." Nixie turned her attention back to the room at large. "In the meantime, what are we to do about the spirits within our borders?"

The room erupted into more arguing, but one voice, quiet yet firm, pulled them all to silence again. "Before we continue, Elder Vernan," Phyre said as she stepped forward with Nesta at her side. She had a thick stack of packets in her hand, each stapled neatly. "I would like to put it to a vote to have Brant Ironwood removed as elder of our coven."

Brant Ironwood's face turned impossibly redder. Honestly, it was amazing he hadn't yet had some kind of aneurysm. "How dare you! You impudent little—"

"I dare." Phyre stood up taller, her chin lifted as she dropped a packet in front of Brant while Nesta passed the others to the rest of the elders. Azure received hers last, and Nesta handed it over with a wink. A quick glance showed her it was bank account information. "Because it's come to my attention that not only is Elder Ironwood misappropriating funds meant for the coven, but he's also receiving payments from an as-yet-unknown source."

"How did you get access to my private information?" Brant seethed, but Azure noted that he didn't deny the accusation. Probably better not to; it would only make him look more guilty.

"The coven accounts are open to for coven member to see, and Auntie Jalessa was very happy to accommodate our research after Nesta showed her the pictures from your social media." Phyre's smile ticked up a little further. She was enjoying this, maybe a bit more than Azure would have thought.

"You know the ones, don't you, Brant?" Nesta asked, leaning in closer and pulling out their phone. "Of you at the 'lodge' out in Ironport. I seem to remember you met—"

"Enough." Nixie called the room to order again. "We will review the information provided, but before we do, we must do something about the issue we are currently facing. In the meantime, Brant Ironwood is hereby suspended from duty, pending investigation."

Brant let out another irate shout, his chest heaving.

"Go home, Brant," Nixie said in a tone that brooked no argument, the words ringing with power. She was the oldest living folk in Moondale, and most of the time she played at being an old biddy with no magic to speak of, but Azure felt the difference in the air as she exerted her will on the room. "Your niece will take your place this evening."

Brant opened his mouth as if to argue further but was cut off by a cold glare that sent a chill down Azure's spine, even if it wasn't aimed at her.

Chapter 28

"Where did they all come from?" Carmine whispered, fear coating every word.

Rus rubbed the back of her neck, uncomfortable with the way all the elders—apart from Brant, who'd been told to go the fuck home, and honestly Rus was *delighted* by that— turned to her in question. She couldn't believe she'd been able to convince them to come outside and take a look. That they'd let her settle her magic into them for even a moment so they could see what she saw. Even Gilroy Herne, although he'd been the last to agree, and likely only because he felt left out. Nixie Vernan's unwavering faith in what Rus was saying probably didn't hurt.

"My best guess?" Rus shifted back on her heels under the weight of their eyes. See, this right here was exactly why she'd been relieved when Az agreed to become the elder for their coven. This group of folk made Rus uncomfortable. Mainly because they'd been in power when she had been all but driven from Moondale with torches and pitchforks. But who was counting? "They seem to be human. Have none of the clans or covens been taking care of the human dead?"

"How would we know they needed that? We can't see the dead," someone huffed, but Rus couldn't tell who it'd been. Not that it mattered. They made a valid point. They weren't mediums. They didn't know what was going on around them, but even still, the blame for this lay at their feet.

Dhiren scoffed. "Besides, they're human. What's the worst that could—"

"Don't. Finish that sentence." Rus held up a hand. "In this case, what you can't see *can* hurt you." She sighed, running the same hand through her hair. How had these people been in charge for so long and missed what was right in front of their fucking faces? Even if they couldn't see the shades lingering in Moondale, their negativity had to be fucking with the magic of the place. "If it were one or two, it wouldn't be a big deal. But these numbers?" Rus whistled, tilting her head toward the writhing sky as the spirits in her body murmured at her assessment.

They hadn't been humans, which just made this whole thing more concerning. But she still hadn't figured out what type of folk they were. And so long as she was down the mountain, they remained mostly inert. For now. She wasn't sure how much longer that would last. The sun had already set, and the moon was rising. The veil between the living and the dead grew thinner by the second. They needed to get this show on the road.

"Are we sure *you* didn't rip them from their final resting place yourself so you could use this as a way to endear your coven to the board?" Gilroy snorted. He, out of all of them, looked perhaps the most uncomfortable with the dead that surrounded them. Maybe Cagney had a point about his needing to be replaced if he was that out of touch with the natural cycle of the world.

Out of the corner of her eye, Rus saw Az's jaw clench, her lips peeled back on what might have been a snarl. Rus reached down to thread their fingers together and give Az's hand a reassuring squeeze. A silent message to let Rus handle this.

"I'm flattered you think I'm that powerful." Rus scoffed and dropped her hold on Az so she could move closer to one of the spirits at the edge of the path in front of the Board of Magic building. They couldn't get any closer, the wards on the building were too thick for that, but they could get close *enough*. And it seemed that the density of spirits was thicker here. Like whoever pulled them from where they'd been waiting was threatening the board. Or perhaps intended for the spirits to act as some kind of barrier to keep the elders from getting up the mountain to the Heart of Moondale when the moon was at her zenith. "But there are far too many of them for me to have collected and be controlling at the same time."

"What are they doing?" Chelsea Horst asked, terror trickling through her words. She was at the back of the group; since she was the folk with the least magic and the shortest life span, Rus could understand that. She wanted to put as many other creatures between herself and the dead as she could. It was a solid theory, only Rus didn't think it would help any of them once whoever was controlling these spirits decided to set them loose.

"Unclear." And didn't that just make the hair on the back of Rus's neck stand on end? There was too much she didn't know right now. Too many factors outside of her control. Too many things she couldn't account for. She'd run the numbers, tried to sort out the best way to approach this, but she was going in blind, and she didn't like it. "But if we utilize the talisman I created, and everyone pitches in a bit, we can have a number of these spirits sent to the After before the moon reaches her peak. All I'd need would be—"

A loud scoff came from the direction of Enfys

Snowthorn. Rus was getting real fucking tired of him, real fucking quick. Maybe he'd be the next one they needed to replace on the board. She'd had her eyes on Gilroy Herne, but Enfys was quickly climbing to the top of her list. "And you expect us to believe you about this talisman? That it's not some trick you've cooked up to turn us all into zombies or something?"

Rus resisted the urge to roll her eyes.

"You couldn't be a zombie. Zombies are dead," Az answered, because she was too good, and she'd been paying attention when Rus explained the difference between the types of creatures that crossed the line from dead to undead. Also probably as a means to keep Rus from saying something like *you can't be a zombie, zombies have brains.* "Necromancers can't control the living. Their magic doesn't work that way."

"You expect me to believe that?"

Quiet murmurs filled the silence between them. The rest of the elders giving what Enfys Snowthorn said some real thought. Which wasn't good news for Rus. They were quickly running out of time, and she was tired of talking in fucking circles.

"This is all just some—"

"Whatever you think of me"—Rus snarled, her lips peeled back to show too many teeth—"whatever bigoted bullshit is going through your head right now, table it. Put it on a shelf somewhere in that tiny brain of yours, and look at what's right in front of your face." There was the undercurrent of a threat in her words, although her magic didn't lift from her skin to back it up, which was probably for the better. "If you don't let me do something about the unsettled dead, whoever summoned them—which may or may not have been the soul jumper—will use them to tear down the wards. And then an annoyed necromancer will be the least of your worries."

Although an annoyed necromancer was going to be bad enough for all of them, if Rus had her way of things. She couldn't let their current practices stand. Someone needed to look after the dead of Moondale, and she was just one woman. One woman with a family, a teaching job, a business, and a soon-to-be fiancée.

"What do you propose?" Nixie asked, ignoring the murmurs of disquiet among the other elders. Rus wasn't going to convince all of them, but if she could convince enough of them, the others might follow.

"We'll give everyone the talisman," Az said without prompting. "I'll draw it on myself if that'll make you feel more comfortable, and Rus will power it."

"That way you'll at least know what you're up against up there." Rus tilted her chin toward the mountains. "And I'll go first so I—"

"The fuck you will," Enfys snarled.

"You know what, Elder Snowthorn? I think we've heard just about enough from you for one evening," Carmine hissed, stepping forward as she pulled up the sleeve of the peacoat she wore over a beautiful pale-blue evening gown to expose her forearm to Az, who quickly and efficiently drew the talisman there.

They had decided in the car it would be better to utilize the version that didn't connect everyone to each other. It would just be one more thing the elders were likely to take issue with—their magic having the possibility of intermingling like that.

"I'll go first so I can make sure the path is open," Rus continued as if she hadn't been interrupted. "Sheriff Greer and his people are doing the best they can to clear out the spirits down here."

"How?" Carmine raised a brow but didn't pull back as Rus laid a hand on the freshly marked talisman and funneled just enough magic into it to get it started. The pull it left behind in Rus was like the lightheadedness after standing up too quickly. Stars burst behind her eyes, but she breathed through it and focused. Carmine's face pinched in pain. She must have bit her tongue to keep from screaming because there was blood on her teeth when she opened her mouth to exhale. Rus appreciated that. Showing how it hurt would only scare the others off.

"I created a touchstone to the After." Rus spoke carefully, reminding herself that Gilroy Herne—the druid elder of the Grove of Elderwood—was likely to lose his fucking gourd if he found out what she'd tied it to and how Cagney helped her.

There was no point getting anyone else in trouble, not right now, anyway. It would just make the other elders take longer and waste more time they didn't have. The soul jumper could have already gotten through the wards, on its way to the Heart of Moondale. It could wait for them there, ready to steal the energy from the ley lines and— Well. Rus didn't know what it planned to do with all that power. But it couldn't be good.

Carmine raised a brow as if she wanted to ask more, but Az shook her head to silence her.

"That's a temporary solution. No opening into the After can hold without a folk to power it for long," Nixie supplied as she stepped forward next, her arm already covered with Az's neatly drawn talisman. Far tidier than the one Rus sketched on Az's arm. "And Greer will not be able to clean up that many spirits with just his small force."

"No. He won't." Rus knew that. She didn't like it either. It felt like putting a Band-Aid on something that clearly needed stitches, hoping it would stop the bleeding. "But one thing at a time."

Nixie's hum turned into a hiss when Rus funneled some of her power into the talisman. Her graying brows drew together. "Do you think they'll cause problems even after the centennial is passed? Or will they dissipate?"

"I don't know." Which just made matters worse, and Rus was aware of that fact.

"What *do* you know?" Enfys muttered from somewhere farther off. He was making his way to the edge of the crowd, and Rus couldn't tell if he was trying to avoid being given the talisman or if there was another reason. She met Az's eyes, and Az left Chelsea Horst to hem Enfys in so he couldn't leave without drawing attention while Carmine took up copying her talisman onto the others.

"I know that if they don't dissipate, we're going to have one hell of a time when the veil is thinnest around the solstice." Rus shook her head. She'd have to go back over the data from the Ghost Tracer to see if she could find the homes where these spirits were before they'd appeared at the center of town. Maybe, if she got very lucky, she'd find the place where someone was collecting them and keeping them stored. But she wasn't holding out hope for that.

It was as she was pressing her magic into Cliantha Greer—Evander Greer's grandmother? Great aunt? Rus couldn't remember—that an idea struck her. An idea she'd keep to herself for the time being, because she'd already thrust enough on the elders. But the more she thought about it, the more sense it made.

A class to teach folk to help the dead move on. They'd have to find another way to use the talismans, maybe some kind of stone that could hold a magical charge. A piece of ore from the Heart, perhaps. Younger folk would be better; they weren't as set in their ways. And it would be good for every clan and coven to have their own group ready and able to tackle a negative force. Then the cleansing wouldn't fall to just a handful, who might be quickly overwhelmed. Even if she was slowly building a coven equipped to handle it.

They'd have to start small, of course. Rus didn't want anyone going into a situation with this many unsettled dead without her or Az there to protect them.

But this... this could work.

"What are you thinking?" Az asked, pulling Rus from her thoughts just as Rus was finishing up with Enfys, who let out a sharp cry of pain as if she'd hurt him on purpose, hamming it up while he blew on the burning talisman.

"We'll talk about it later." Rus shook her head. One thing at a time, like she'd said. "For now, let's get up the mountain. We should take as few cars as possible."

"Good thing I'm here, then!" Cagney called across the parking lot, where she was standing in front of a beat-up school bus painted in a riotous rainbow of colors, twirling a ring of keys around her finger.

Rus barked a laugh and led the group forward. "Do I want to know where you found this thing?"

Cagney shrugged. "Evander likes vintage cars." Then she turned to climb the steps and drop into the driver's seat. "Hop in!"

Chapter 29

The sky darkened further as the bus rumbled up the mountain road. The trees around them disappeared into a darkness so thick, it was blacker than a starless night. A chill raced down Azure's back.

"That's not good," Rus murmured from where she was pressed so close to Azure's side, her warmth warded off some of the cold emanating from the window.

"More ghosts?" She wasn't sure if the talisman was fading and so she was unable to see them, or if this was something worse. Much worse.

"No." Rus leaned ever closer, pressing Azure's shoulder hard against the window, but she didn't mind. It was good to have Rus next to her like this. Good to know she wasn't alone. "That's something else."

"What is it?" Although she didn't think she wanted the answer.

There was a weight in the air the closer they got to the Heart of Moondale that had nothing at all to do with the altitude. It settled heavy over Azure's shoulders, threatening to slump her in her seat. Only the warmth and life of Rus breathing beside her kept her upright, alert.

"I don't know," Rus admitted. Her voice shook as she pulled Azure into her chest and pressed her face into Azure's neck.

"We'll figure this out," Azure promised. Because there

was nothing else they *could* do. They either found a way to combat the darkness, to keep the soul jumper from enacting its plan, or they lost Moondale. That wasn't an option. Never would be. Not so long as Rus and her family called Moondale home.

Rus sighed. Her breath tickled the sensitive skin under Azure's ear, sending a more welcome shiver up her spine as a companionable silence blanketed them. A peace that Azure knew could not last, however they might have wanted it to.

The bus jerked to a stop in the small, gravel parking lot alongside the path that led through the woods to the Heart of Moondale. While the others stayed in their seats, looking out the windows with faces full of trepidation, Rus rose and held her hand out to Azure.

"Shall we?" A smile tipped up one corner of Rus's mouth, looking more smirk than grin, and Azure's heart stuttered in her chest. Rus was never as beautiful as when she was casually cocky.

"You should have brought a coat," Azure chided lightly, her eyes flicking over the short-sleeved green velvet dress in reprimand.

Rus shrugged, and Azure let her pull her to her feet and down the narrow aisle of the bus as the wind howled outside. The bus rocked with the force of it.

Rus tsked lightly, shaking her head. "I'll be fine. But I should probably leave my hat here."

"Very likely."

Rus set the wide-brimmed hat on one of the empty seats. "Besides, if I wore a coat, I'd have to cut my hands again."

Azure let the subject drop, her jaw twitching with the need to scold Rus for how freely she spilled her blood. If she wasn't careful, she might cut through something important in her hands and make them unusable. Better then, that Rus had her arms free for easy use. Although Azure hoped she wouldn't feel the need to open a vein again.

When she stepped down from the bus with Rus's help, the wind outside was biting cold, sinking past skin and into bone as it cut through Azure's woolen peacoat. She pulled Rus in closer, wanting to wrap her in her coat to protect her bare arms and chest from the wind. Not that Rus would ever allow that.

Self-sacrificial dumbass. The words echoed with fondness, even in her own head. Goddess, she loved this woman so much it hurt sometimes.

Without prompting, she unwrapped the thick scarf from her neck and wound it around Rus's. It had warming charms crocheted into it, thanks to Indigo, and would help ward off some of the chill. Not much, but some.

"I'm fine, Az. Really." Rus protested weakly.

Azure didn't pay her any mind, just knotted the scarf and pulled her in by it, soft and leading, until their lips could meet. It was a tender kiss. No teeth. Hardly any pressure. A reassurance that they were both there. That they had both made it and would continue to make it. A vow.

"Marry me?" Azure asked again when she finally pulled away, her breath shorter than it'd been in a long time, her skin warm despite the wind.

"You know," Rus laughed, panting as well, "I think I'm gonna."

"Is that a yes?" Hope blossomed, burning hot in Azure's chest, warming even the tips of her fingers, which had gone numb from the chill.

"Ask me again. When we come out on the other side of this thing."

When. Not if. Because Rus knew they would be fine in the end, just like Azure did. It washed away some of the anxiety that had settled into a knot in her stomach. A relief.

"And then you'll say yes?" Azure pressed. She already knew the answer. Of course she did. Whatever doubt might have clung to her the first time Rus gave an excuse had disappeared quickly when she realized what Rus was doing. It was why she'd made the deal, why she'd decided to keep asking. Why she might ask for the rest of her life, even if Rus never agreed.

"You sure you don't want someone respectable?" Rus teased, nipping at the tip of Azure's nose. "Someone who has *natural* magic?"

"Death is natural." A fact the rest of the folk in Moondale would have to come to accept, even as they railed against confronting their own mortality. Next came a quiet truth, one she hadn't discovered until recently. She whispered, "And it is beautiful."

Rus let out a noise like a teakettle come to boil and pressed her forehead against Azure's. "That was so sexy. We don't have time for you to be sexy right now."

"Apologies." But she wasn't sorry at all. How could she be when it earned her another hurried kiss before Cagney beeped the horn of the bus?

"Are you two just going to stand there making out or what?" Cagney shouted, clearly annoyed. No one else in the bus had moved to follow them. Willing to let Rus and Azure be the first to scope out the dangers of the area. Cowards.

"We're going. We're going." Rus flapped her wrist, pulling away from Azure but not letting go as they turned toward the forest beyond the parking lot, a duffle bag of supplies in one hand, Azure's hand in the other.

It, too, was *too* dark. Azure knew the wood and the trail through it were there, because she'd been here enough times to remember what it looked like, but there was nothing beyond the short distance of the bus's headlights. And even those didn't cut more than a couple of feet through the dark. As if whatever had come to Moondale was eating up all the light. Building a wall of darkness to keep them separated from their destination.

Rus squeezed her hand, whether to lend Azure strength or to find it for herself in the knowledge that Azure was there, she wasn't sure. It didn't matter. She squeezed back.

Then they stepped forward.

The trees didn't materialize until they were almost right on top of them, Rus's nose so close to the bark of the nearest one that it was amazing she hadn't run headfirst into it.

"What fresh hell is this?" Rus muttered, tugging Azure so she was further behind her back, shielding her from whatever lay ahead with her own body.

"What?" Azure moved onto her toes to look over Rus's shoulder. What she found made her wish she hadn't.

Ghosts lined the path ahead. They'd left the way open for anyone to walk to the Heart, but the meaning was clear. There was not a part of this forest that was not covered. There was nowhere to run, nowhere to hide.

"Were they like that before?" Not that it mattered; they were there now. And even if they weren't standing in the way of reaching the Heart of Moondale, it was only a matter of time before they were set in motion.

"No." Rus's grip tightened to near painful around Azure's hand, the knuckles grinding together. A chill had settled into her fingers, either from anxiety or the wind, Azure couldn't tell. Rus's shoulders expanded with a deep inhale, then she turned to face Azure again. "I'm going to go on ahead, to make sure it's safe."

"You shouldn't go alone." There was no reason for her to, not when Azure was right there, ready and willing to face whatever came next. Not when the soul jumper was likely lingering nearby. Waiting.

"Darcy will be with me." Rus tilted her head up, and there was a flapping of wings before the crow melted out of the dark and alighted on her shoulder.

"It could be out there. It could—"

"It probably *is* out there." But Rus didn't sound scared. An arrogant smile ticked up one corner of her mouth again as Rus leaned in to press her forehead to Azure's. "But I need you to watch that pack of jackals." She tilted her head. Her gaze cut back to the bus, which still rumbled where it idled.

Azure glanced over her shoulder to see if it was visible, but now that they'd stepped out of the light provided by the headlights, the bus had disappeared, the darkness swallowing it up. That couldn't be a good sign. "How long should I wait before I follow?"

The skin stretched over Rus's jaw as she chewed on the inside of her cheek. Her hand twitched like she wanted to lift it to rub at her nose, but she refused to let go of Azure. "Ten minutes."

"Will that be enough time to pull the soul jumper from Taryn's body?" It didn't sound like near enough time. Rushing things would only make them worse. More dangerous. It would mean Rus would do something reckless, likely to get herself hurt in her hurry. Azure didn't want to think about what kind of plan Rus would come up with in such a situation.

"No. But it'll be enough time to lead it away from the

path, and possibly enough time to lock it in an array so it can't get away from me."

"What will you do once it's in there with you?" They hadn't talked about this part of the plan, or if they had, Azure lost the information in the rush of everything else. But she had a gut feeling she wasn't going to like the answer.

"Let me worry about that. You worry about getting those idiots to the Heart so we can complete the cycle. Yeah?" Rus pressed another kiss to the tip of her nose, then pulled away before Azure could stop her, spinning on her heel to disappear into the dark. "Ten minutes," she called, as a reminder, just before her voice was swallowed with the rest of her.

"Fuck," Azure hissed under her breath and turned back toward the noise of the bus. Rus was right, of course. The sooner she and the elders closed the circuit, the sooner they could cut the soul jumper off at the knees. And if Rus was going to be facing it largely alone, Azure wanted to ensure it had less of a power source to draw from.

The bus came into view a few moments later when she was close enough, and she dragged her shaking legs up the steps to face the rest of the elders.

"We're following after her in"—Azure checked her watch—"nine minutes. Whatever fears you have, you need to get over them, and quickly. We don't have time to waste."

"What about the soul jumper?" Aunt Carmine asked, already gathering her things. She was still too thin and a little slower from her last experience with the thing living inside Taryn Addington, but Azure appreciated that her aunt didn't back down. Didn't falter. Never had. It's where Azure herself learned it from.

"We didn't see it, but Rus believes it's in the wood somewhere. We'll stick to the path, and she'll draw it away.

But..." Azure flicked her eyes back to the forest through the dark. She couldn't see it, or the ghosts standing vigil inside, from here, but that didn't mean she didn't know it was there. Looming. Waiting. Would it eat them whole as soon as they stepped off the bus? Or would they be able to fight it off? Only time would tell. "There are ghosts lining the trail. For now, they're inert like those in town."

Fear rippled through the group again. Goddess, how could creatures who were so old be so afraid of a group of shades? They all were powerful enough to dispel a single spirit without a blink, and yet...

Shaking her head, Azure dug into her purse to pull out another notepad and began to work without a word, enough pressure on her pen that she cut through the paper in places. It might not work, but she had to try.

"We'll place these talismans along the path as we go," she said, passing a small stack to her aunt as Carmine got closer to look over her shoulder. If the spirits were activated by whoever was controlling them before their group reached the Heart, the talisman would do no good, but... "They should push the spirits back a bit further, give us some breathing room."

"When did you come up with this warding talisman?" Aunt Carmine asked, pride warming her tone.

Azure shrugged, not slowing her progress in creating talisman after talisman, four to a page. "I merely adapted the one I created for Rus to wear when she exorcises a building."

Aunt Carmine hummed her approval and took another small stack to hand to Nixie Vernan so they could separate them and pass them out.

By the time ten minutes passed, several of the elders had small stacks of hastily scrawled talismans and instructions on how to ward off spirits. Some of them had only taken a single sheet for themselves, probably hoping it would do the job if the ward on the path failed. Azure didn't tell them that it probably wouldn't, as the talisman had been created to work with the nature of trees, not bodies.

They gathered before the trail, murmurs of unrest traveling through them.

"I'll bring up the rear," Cagney said, falling behind as they started into the woods.

Chapter 30

The soul jumper was waiting when Rus stepped off the path into the suffocating dark. Just as she'd thought it would be. She couldn't see it, but she could feel it. It's eyes on her like a cold winter chill, cutting straight to the bone. Her heart kicked up a notch, but she breathed through most of the panic that threatened to freeze her to her spot. Still, it took her time to pinpoint its location without the use of her eyes, to circle around it so she could push it back with her movements. More time than she had to spare.

She took a step further, forcing it away from the trail the elders would use to reach the Heart of Moondale. Every movement measured, and careful as she forced herself to stay calm, to not run when fight or flight kicked in.

"They won't thank you for this," the soul jumper said, its footsteps crunching on the forest floor as it melted from the dark in front of her. Its voice had grown echoing and strange since the last time Rus spoke to it, even as it remained inside the body of Taryn Addington. Almost as if it were breaking apart, losing control of the dead it used over the centuries to maintain its hold on life. "Nothing you do will ever make them respect you. Will *ever* make them think of you as anything other than *less.*"

Rus rolled back her shoulders and pushed forward. The soul jumper stepped back almost in time with her movements, a careful dance. It seemed nervous about letting Rus close enough to touch. A perfectly valid concern as Rus's magic roiled just under her skin, the disquiet spirits possessing her whispering their displeasure, their hate. Even if the soul jumper wore a different face, had a different voice, they knew what it was. And they wanted the freedom and the power to destroy it.

"I don't care about them," Rus answered, her voice unwavering, calm. She had about five minutes before Azure and the others took their first step onto the trail, by her estimate. Finding and moving the soul jumper out of the way was taking longer than she'd have liked. Mainly because it insisted on monologuing. Which was just kind of annoying, not dangerous. "They're not who is important to me."

It was the truth.

Rus had come to an understanding over the last year, and she knew that what the soul jumper said wasn't far from reality. A reality she ran from once. The Board of Magic, the stuck-in-their-ways and the bigoted, would always look at her as something dark and twisted. They would always think of her magic as unnatural and wrong. And if given half the chance, they would try to run her from town all over again.

If they did, they wouldn't get very far. Not this time. Because Rus understood herself and the people around her better now. Azure accepted her. Her family, her coven, her friends, accepted her. They would fight for her, and they wouldn't let Rus turn tail and run when things seemed like they might be getting too hard. They would stand *with* her.

"How romantic." The soul jumper snorted, taking another few steps away from the trail as Rus pushed it back farther with her unhurried pace.

It was too dark in the forest to tell if she had enough space to put her plan into action. She was going to have to take a shot in the dark, literally, and hope the Goddess and luck were on her side. Both seemed to have been for the last year, despite all the hauntings, and possessions, and other problems. Or maybe that was just Moondale doing what it could to keep her here. Rus was beginning to suspect there was more at work in her returning than just witch hunters chasing her toddler.

"And one woman is enough when your entire community would turn against you?" There was an underlying vulnerability to the question that gave Rus pause.

"It's not one woman," Rus said, power heating the sentence. She'd known it, of course, but saying so out loud made the truth of it run deeper. Yes, she had Az. She would always have Az once this was all over and they got married. But she also had Nando, Cagney, Phyre, and Nesta, her family forged in the cold fire of the dead. She had a coven now, however small, in Hunter and Ava. She even had people like Brenton and Greer willing to help where they could, despite them not being much more than acquaintances, and in Greer's case literal frenemies.

She had her *own* community.

A chill ran down Rus's spine, like someone had walked over her grave, but she kept moving. Pushing the soul jumper back and back and back. The noise of the people in the wood was muffled by the darkness, but she was attuned to it, listening for it. Proof that Az and the other elders were making their way to the Heart of Moondale.

Good.

Now to put the second phase of her plan into motion. Her hand twitched for the nail gun weighing down her bag.

"Not one—" The soul jumper scoffed, clearly disbelieving and annoyed, for it faltered for a moment. Just one.

Just enough time to let Rus hem it in close and grab on to Taryn Addington's wrist.

A scream rent her mind. Anguished and fearful. So loud Rus dropped the grip, and the soul jumper was given time to shove her back. She stumbled, her foot caught on a fallen tree in the darkness, and went down hard. The landing jolted her tailbone, but when she reached out to catch herself, Moondale answered. Moondale sent a subtle buzz up along her skin, an unmistakable sign that *this* was where she was meant to make her stand.

Either there was a fairy ring or a gathering of ore—something Moondale knew would help her when she needed it.

Lucky.

Rus didn't wait to see if she was right about what she thought she'd stepped into. She turned to sneer up at the soul jumper, the nail gun gripped tight in her hand. "Is that what happened to you?"

Her magic twisted around her, glowing faintly in the looming darkness, but she caught moon-pale mushrooms out of the corner of her eye—a fairy ring—as her magic circled the small clearing, settling at the soul jumper's feet. Still, for the moment, but waiting. A subtle rustle of wings from above, a reminder that Darcy was there to pull her out if she went too deep.

"Did Mazarin leave you? Did she bring you back only to abandon you? Did she turn on you?"

"She wouldn't!" The soul jumper lunged forward, all sharpened nails and viper-like reflexes. There was hurt there, in its words. Heartbreak and loneliness. Rus didn't like to manipulate people, especially not the dead. Many of them had been through enough. But she needed the soul jumper as off balance as she could get it.

Pain ripped through Rus's nerves. The wound on her

hand tore open on something in the dark as she scrambled farther into the ring, leading the soul jumper after her. Blood spread over the leaves, lending Moondale more power. Then she lifted the nail gun and shot a series of iron nails into the ground to close the soul jumper in with her.

Green magic, like mist, like poison, clung to the soul jumper's stumbling steps, following, chasing, then settling into the lines of the natural array Moondale had left for her. The soul jumper was inside, and there was a moment where Rus thought maybe it wouldn't work. It had been a long time since she'd used a naturally forming array, and they were always fickle at best. But then the mushrooms and nails glowed green and bright through the black, near blinding with how used to the dark Rus's eyes had become.

"Wha—what did you *do?!*" the soul jumper screamed, its own magic whipped out from the hands of the witch it had been inhabiting for over a decade at this point. Red and violent. Like blood in water.

It lashed against Rus's ankles as she scrambled to her feet to put some distance between them. She just needed a minute to catch her breath, to get her phone from her pocket. The list Hunter provided burned her eyes when she began to read the names, already having memorized them on the trip up the mountain but wanting to make sure she got them correct.

"Aster Donovan." The first name sat thick in the air, heavy. It landed like a blow.

The soul jumper stumbled back, its face twisted, snarling. Something alive and parasitic shifted under the skin of Taryn Addington, making her flesh ripple. Its head jerked from one side to the other, and for a moment, there was an overlay of another face overtop of Taryn's. Like bad CGI in a horror movie.

"No. No. Be silent!" Its hands flew to its head, covering its ears, as it hissed.

Whispers started up from the earth, the dead gaining ground against something that shouldn't be alive to begin with.

"Aster Donovan," Rus repeated with more force, letting her magic trickle into the name. The neon-green light of her power flashed like a camera in the dark, the After calling to the soul trapped within Taryn with the soul jumper.

Another scream. The sound was chilling, raising every hair on Rus's body.

"You were the first," Rus said, pushing to her feet. Blood dripped from her palm onto the ground. She lifted her hand and turned it over. Magic gathered in the deep wound, heedless of the debris that had settled there, catching at the blood to drip onto the ground with it. "You didn't even know what it was when it first spoke to you, did you?"

I thought she was a friend. The whisper on the wind was hollow, like it came through a tin can instead of appearing in Rus's mind. A sadness there made Rus's heart clench in her chest. It wasn't fair, the way the soul jumper had taken over these people's lives. Wasn't fair how it used them, manipulated them.

"I'm sorry." Rus reached for the soul jumper, heedless of the violent, sparking magic that lit its arms, threatening to burn her up right along with the forest around them. All it took was a touch. A single brush of fingers. And something tore in Rus's nerve endings, making her shout in surprise as the spirits from before helped to rip Aster Donovan from Taryn Addington's body.

Welcome. Welcome. Welcome. They invited her in, and she settled uncomfortably under Rus's skin.

It's getting a little crowded in here. Rus didn't like

having so many piggybacks at once. But there wasn't time to send Aster or the others to the After when there were four more spirits to free from the soul jumper. And besides, she might need them still.

It stumbled back, putting as much distance between itself and Rus as it could, before bumping into the edge of the array, the barrier gifted to her by Moondale herself. The magic flashed again, trembled under the force, but held.

"Eden Elias." The ground shook beneath them. Goddess, Rus hoped that meant the elders had made it to the Heart, and not that the soul jumper brought something worse with it to stir up more trouble. "What did she promise you?"

She didn't! the man screamed, anguished and pained. *I hadn't the choice! I hadn't the means to escape!*

Rus lunged for the soul jumper and grabbed onto its wrist, holding fast even as its magic lashed against her bare skin, opening old scars. The cold stung her wounds. She needed to be quicker. This was taking too fucking long.

"Freedom." Rus pressed the word through clenched teeth that threatened to chatter. "Vengeance."

Another ripping through her chest sent both her and the soul jumper to their knees. The ground and the branches and twigs on the forest floor dug into her skin through her dress.

Join us. Help us. We will avenge you.

The wind picked up and tore at the scarf Az had tied around her neck. It was doing little to ward off the cold that sunk deep into Rus's bones, making every joint ache.

"Carson Forrest." The name tore from Rus in a gasped breath. How much more of this could she take? She'd never had to work through so many forced exorcisms in such quick succession. Never under such extreme conditions.

Blood dripped, cooling and sticky down her arms, even as the magic of the soul jumper grew weaker. Less cutting, more scratching. Rus's head spun from blood loss. "Find peace. Rest. It's done now."

Her skin was stretched too tight over her bones. Her lungs squeezed with all the metaphysical space the spirits in her body took up.

"One more. Just one more." Her teeth chattered around the words. All she could hope was that once she ripped Julian Bennet free, she'd be able to send all of them to the After without too much of a fight, because she didn't think she had the energy for one right now.

"What are you *doing?*" The soul jumper snarled, baring teeth dripping with saliva and blood in Rus's face, and struggled weakly against her hold. It had to know now, though, what she had planned for it. "Do you know what will happen if you do this? Do you understand the consequences of your actions?"

"Spirits *lie!*" The first rule of necromancy. The one Rus had recited over and over again to her girls, to Nando, to Az, to anyone who would listen. The reminder that the dead could lie just as easily as the living. Especially dead like the soul jumper that had already proven it would do anything within its power to cling to life, to not heed the call of the After and what was waiting for it. They would do anything to manipulate Rus into believing them.

"You'll set *her* free!"

"Julian Bennet!" The name rang through the wood like a gong. It vibrated off the trees, echoing. And with it, everything stopped. The ground was still. The wind was silent. The magic that had lashed at Rus, cut her arms, her legs, her torso to ribbons, sputtered weakly.

Julian slipped beneath Rus's skin, and she groaned at

the feeling of her flesh being pushed beyond its limits. What little food she'd managed in the last few hours crawled up her throat. She coughed, blood coating her tongue, but didn't stop. Running her hands down her burning arms, she gathered the blood and clapped her hands together as she dropped back onto her ass in the dirt.

The After was so close now, the veil so thin, it was easy to open a pathway. She felt the foot she had in the grave sink a little deeper. She might never be able to do this again. But it didn't matter. Not so long as she managed it this once.

Six spirits.

Six unsettled shades crawled under her skin like bugs, causing it to ripple and shiver. Her nerve endings lit up with pain, and she let her focus narrow to that, the soul jumper forgotten for the moment, weakened as it was. The real threat now was the ghosts possessing her, ripping her apart from the inside out because there wasn't enough room for them inside of her.

A caw, and Darcy landed on her shoulder, his talons digging in through the fabric, lending his strength and his magic. Providing the space and the power she needed for one last push.

Rus breathed in deep and forced her lungs to expand, even as the pressure on them threatened to squeeze the life from her body. The air smelled of damp earth and decomposing things. It was good the soul jumper had come to her during this season, when so much of the world around her was dying, passing into the next phase of the cycle. It made this easier.

"Rest," she whispered, her voice jagged and broken from how tight her throat was. But she managed just the same.

The spirits inside her shivered, like maybe they would

deny her order. Cling to her insides and fight to stay. But at least four of them knew what became of folk that did that. They'd seen firsthand how it had twisted the soul jumper beyond recognition—made it into something closer to a demon than things of this world ought to be. And so, they let go. Slipping through into the deep, calm darkness of the After.

Before they went, they whispered a name.

Elodie Ronen.

And once they were gone, Rus slumped forward. Sweat cooled along her brow, burning her eyes. Her whole body was weak, shaky.

"What did you do?" the soul jumper asked, voice trembling. "Do you know what you've done? What you've unleashed?"

Chapter 31

The wind around the elders settled, no longer tearing at their clothes and threatening to send them stumbling, but it wasn't *quiet*. The darkness lifted, revealing the Heart of Moondale that stood at the center of their circle, but the spirits did not leave.

Fear hemmed the elders in. Made them shift closer to one another.

It was still frigid up on the mountain, the cold biting into Azure's fingers. Her breath puffed out of her in thick clouds.

"Do you think she defeated it?" someone asked, their voice so soft and hopeful. Azure couldn't tell who it was.

"The ghosts are still here," someone else answered.

Fear spread like wildfire through the group of elders. Valid, but all it was going to do was make them easier targets. Azure knew that from experience. She'd seen the way the dead and the living alike could prey on the fears of the folk. Could use them to drag folk into positions they never thought possible. Make them do things they wouldn't normally. It was how the soul jumper had come to be, after all.

"We must finish the ritual. Close the cycle," Azure said without a trace of the same terror shaking her voice.

Was she afraid? Yes. But not of what the soul jumper would do. Not of the ghosts that lingered, so plentiful they almost outnumbered the trees. There was little to fear from the dead. What she was more afraid of was what could happen to Rus if this ritual wasn't complete. What could become of her family, her coven, her friends, if they didn't see this through. She would not have the squeamishness of a few ruin what she and Rus had begun to build for themselves.

"If you do not wish to join me, please step outside of the circle." Although Azure knew every elder in the clearing understood what that would mean. To not participate in closing the cycle, to not offer their blood and their power... Moondale would offer little, possibly nothing in exchange. The blessings Moondale had given their clan might die on the vine.

Someone inhaled as if to argue, but Azure hadn't the time for such nonsense. Whatever was happening in the woods beyond her sight could be killing Rus, pushing her the rest of the way into the grave. Azure would not tolerate cowardice causing her to lose the woman she loved.

She pulled her athame from her pocket and cut into her palm.

Whether the others followed suit did not matter to Azure as she stepped forward and pressed her bloody hand to the Heart of Moondale. The moss-covered stone dug into the wound, making her hiss and clench her jaw around the words that must come next. The spell that would tie her blood, her magic, her coven to the land beneath them for another hundred years.

The words themselves were a mirror, a reflection of the pledge a folk took during their ceremony to be inducted into a clan or coven of Moondale. The offering of magic and blood the same. But the feedback that came when Azure pressed her magic into the Heart, and the Heart answered, was so much *heavier,* burning through every nerve in her body the way nothing else ever had.

She was a live wire. A conduit. Her hair floated around her. Her feet lifted from the ground. Her eyes squeezed shut as her mind raced through Moondale, along the ley lines. Image after image of the town where she'd been born, raised, fallen in love, found a family, flashed one after the other. Almost too quickly for her to see.

Main Street. Necromancer's. Elwood & Co.

Her aunts' house—154 Mourning Moore.

The coven house—155 Mourning Moore.

The park. The woods. The board building. Town hall. The courthouse.

157 Mourning Moore.

Home.

The vision seemed to settle there, flooding warmth through her veins. As if Moondale approved and was happy to have her and her family living there. As if Moondale welcomed them.

Then there was a voice in her ear. A whisper.

Growing increasingly loud the longer she held on.

No. *Two.*

One leading, calling. A siren song in the dark.

The other was so soft she could hardly make it out, but she thought it might be a warning.

"There you are," someone said, and when Azure was finally back inside of herself, no longer traveling the circuit of Moondale, she met the eyes of a woman crouched atop the Heart, her feet almost disappearing into the vibrantly purple moss on the stone. It was difficult to see anything beyond her, though the other elders must have been there too.

"Mazarin?" Azure struggled to focus on her. Her shape

shifted and blurred, vibrating with something Azure didn't understand. But the nose, the jaw, the spacing of the eyes... they all harkened back to the Elwood lineage. "Mazarin Elwood."

Mazarin crowed in delight, and like that, she solidified. As if naming her was all she'd needed to cross the divide between the living and the dead. "Do you want power, Azure Elwood?" She leaned in closer, her gaze narrowing in assessment. Now that she was in something closer to living, breathing color, Azure could see that Mazarin Elwood had the same color eyes she did: a rich mahogany brown. The same warm, russet-brown skin. She could see now how Rus knew immediately that they were related.

"What sort of power?" Azure asked, although she was already sure she knew the answer. It sat heavy on the tip of her tongue. She'd seen enough of the dead over the last year, listened enough to Rus, to understand what was happening.

Moondale's warning was still in the distance, a nagging buzz at the back of her mind drowned out easily enough by Mazarin's power. The lure she cast shivered along Azure's shoulders like a fisherman throwing out a net. "The *unlimited* sort. Immortality, for you and your coven. Invulnerability. The strength to protect, to care for those you love. I can give it to you."

Azure didn't even have to ask what it would cost her, because it didn't matter. Any such promises came with a high price. A price she'd already seen people like Taryn and Violet pay. Some things were too good to be true. And so, her answer was simple. It echoed something she'd been told over and over again since getting back together with Rus.

"The dead. *Lie.*"

She reached out to grab Mazarin, not even thinking for a moment what might come next but knowing that she couldn't let this ghost get away and perhaps weasel her way into someone else's body. She had likely started with Azure because she thought she'd be the easiest to fool, and they were related by blood. But she would move on if given the chance. Choose someone else. Someone who was weaker to such promises. Azure couldn't give her the opportunity.

Mazarin shrieked, wheeling back in a futile bid to escape Azure's seeking hands. She wasn't quick enough. It was like trying to grab onto a bag full of cold water. Azure's fingers chilled instantly, quickly growing numb, and Mazarin's shape threatened to slip from her grasp, but somehow Azure held on. The extra magic in her veins from Moondale lent something to her that Azure had never had before and might never have again: the ability to touch the dead as she would the living.

It was a skill she'd seen Rus display numerous times but had always found impossible for herself. For the dead were nothing more than shadows, projections. They did not have a physical form.

But something had shifted. Either in herself or in the world around her, and she could touch Mazarin. She could hold her.

"You little bitch!" Mazarin snarled, her words losing much of their old-world accent, her free hand coming up to scratch talon-like nails into Azure's skin. "Let me go!"

"No." Azure didn't know what possessed her, what gave her the idea that she could do what she'd seen Rus do so many times. Maybe because she knew the steps. Maybe because she finally understood what Rus had been trying to teach her for decades now. But in a voice ringing with power, she said, "Tell me why you're here, Mazarin Elwood."

It was a demand that the dead could deny if they

wanted, but it would be difficult. The draw of wanting to be understood was too great. "Let me go!"

Azure gritted her teeth and pulled a pen from her bag, all while fighting against Mazarin's thrashing. Spitting the cap onto the ground, she started writing, fast and furious, down her arm. The characters were not balanced. The mere idea untested, untried. Thinking up things on the spot as she was, putting them to use immediately, had never been Azure's go-to.

Moondale's warning grew louder in the back of her mind, though she still couldn't make out words, just the vague understanding that she had to do *something*. She had to put a stop to this before Mazarin could leave the clearing and enact whatever she'd returned to this plane for.

When the talisman was done, the magic rocked through her like an earthquake. Her knees weakened, and she trembled but held tight.

"What did—what did you do?!" Mazarin screamed, struggling harder against the pull of the improvised spirit box she'd just turned herself into. Rus was going to have a fit about that, but Azure didn't have time to fuck around with coming up with another way.

Mazarin disappeared a moment later, and Azure felt the squeeze of another spirit shift inside her body. *How does Rus do this so often?* It was so uncomfortable. Her skin stretched too tight like when she forgot to put lotion on during winter and it dried out. She shifted.

Let me out of here! Mazarin hissed in the back of her mind, slamming her spirit against the walls of Azure's chest, testing her hold. She wouldn't break free. Not right away, at least. Azure had Moondale's blessing racing through her veins, a hum of approval from the earth tickling at her nerves, and all the knowledge she'd acquired from a year at Rus's side.

"Tell me why you're here." Azure kept her voice calm, closing her eyes so she could focus on the spirit inside of her instead of the wood around her. She didn't know what the elders were doing, if they were even still standing, and it didn't matter. She had to deal with this first. One thing at a time, as Rus said earlier. "What is your unfinished business? What is tying you to this plane? Tell me your purpose."

A snarl ripped from the spirit inside of her. A threat.

"You can tell me," Azure said, steady and sure. "I can help you move on." Although she'd never done it before, and she wasn't sure that she'd be able to. Could she touch the After like Rus did? Use herself as a bridge the way Rus always had? There was no reason she couldn't... Not when she'd already been able to touch a spirit. It was just a matter of—

Or what?

"Or we can wait here until Rus finds us, and she will force you through the veil, unfinished business or no. But just know that if I send you into the After, you might be able to return to the reincarnation cycle. You may be able to try again. If Rus exorcises you, I cannot make any such promises." Hopefully Rus would get there soon and not be so burned out from dealing with the soul jumper that the threat of her was a valid one. But Azure couldn't count on that. She wouldn't. It wasn't right to expect Rus to always be there to drag her out of trouble. She was an Elwood, for fuck's sake. The elder of the Coven of the Forgotten. She could handle this on her own. "Tell me what you want."

Revenge.

How cliché. "On?"

On the Elwoods. On the family who cast me out. Those

who burned me from their line. Who cast me adrift in limbo, with no roots, no way back into the reincarnation cycle. I want them to suffer.

"Your actions with the soul jumper have already made my sister and aunt suffer. There are no other directly related Elwoods in Moondale. The others are related by marriage. I will not allow you to have vengeance on those not from the bloodline." But there was still—there was still *Azure.* "If you must curse someone to move on, let it be me."

Mazarin didn't say anything, but Azure could almost feel her shifting uncertainly, as if trying to better understand the witch who had trapped her inside her body. That was perfectly valid. This method was not one any Elwood, including Azure herself, would use. But she had a feeling that whatever Mazarin could do to her, it wouldn't be the worst possible outcome. Curses could be broken, and if anyone could see to that, it was Rus.

You'll never know peace, Mazarin threatened.

Azure swallowed around a smile. "I plan to marry a crow witch. Peace is not something I ever counted on."

This decision will haunt you for the rest of your days.

"My soon-to-be wife is a medium and a necromancer. Many things will haunt us. What's one more?"

There will be pain. Loss. Darkness.

"Life is a cycle of all of those things." Rus taught her that.

You are a strange one, Azure Elwood...

"Thank you." The grin on Azure's face grew.

Mazarin let out a long, annoyed sigh. *If that is your choice, fine.* Her magic rippled through Azure's body, the curse locked into place, a grinding ache in her chest. She didn't know what it would do. Wasn't sure what kind of havoc it would wreak on her or her life. But she did know that she and Rus could handle it. As they had handled so much else.

Azure pressed her hands together in front of her, the blood spreading from one palm to the next, and she felt the After open like a door. A creak. A groan. On unused hinges. Darkness lay beyond, even if she could not see it. "Now go."

Then Mazarin Elwood was gone. Passed on to the After, Azure hoped, possibly to her next life. Only time would tell.

And Azure stumbled under the weakness of her body as the world swam into focus around her.

Chapter 32

The spirits had gone, the soul jumper was weakened, and Rus turned her attention to the shriveled, torn shade in front of her. Its hold on Taryn Addington was tenuous. A single, fraying thread.

With Darcy's magic in her veins and the name the spirits had given her on her lips, it took almost nothing for Rus to lean forward and grab Taryn Addington's wrist again. For her to whisper the name gifted to her.

"Elodie Ronen."

Elodie came away from Taryn's body with no resistance, and Taryn slumped forward, her head landing on Rus's shoulder only because Rus angled herself to catch her. Rus breathed a sigh of relief. One problem was solved. Just one. But one thing at a time.

"You should move on now," Rus told Elodie, holding up a hand to the flickering spirit of a blond woman that was torn around the edges. Centuries of wear appearing all at once. The harsh green glare of her magic showed that the blood from her wounds had slowed, at least. Probably a by-product of the magic Darcy was cycling into her without so much as a sound.

Elodie's head turned to look off into the forest that surrounded them. The woods were no longer pitch black, but there was a silence to it that was oppressive, pressing down on Rus from all sides.

She's back.

"Who?" Although at this point, Rus would wager she knew the answer. She'd always been a betting woman, and there was only one witch that Elodie could possibly fear. Mazarin Elwood. The question was, what was she doing? What were her motivations? What secrets had she hidden when she'd lied to Rus's and Az's faces? Had this been her plan all along?

Mazarin. Elodie said the name like it broke her heart to even utter it. Like it was a wound, raw and blistered, pus slipping from beneath the skin. All the confirmation Rus needed to know that Az's ancestor had been full of shit this entire time. Goddess, sometimes Rus hated it when she was right.

"Let Az and I take care of Mazarin." She wasn't sure how they would. Not until she saw what the fuck Mazarin was there for. Whatever it was, Rus was sure it would be some kind of revenge against the Elwood family who'd banished her.

She brought me back. Elodie's voice shook.

Like this, drained of her power, and with nothing but sadness clinging to her incorporeal form, Elodie looked like any other shade Rus had ever known. She was just a person who had been through something horrible. Traumatized and broken, just as Rus might have been had she not returned to Moondale and learned the truth of Az's love for her. Like this, Rus almost felt bad for her. Whatever Elodie Ronen had done to stay alive over the years, she had done it because of something that had been done *to* her. Rus understood that now.

"You should move on, before you fade." She was hardly holding on to this plane as it was, and should she fade, Elodie Ronen would be no more. No reincarnation. No afterlife. Just gone. A truly unnatural death, for nothing in this world was meant to stop existing altogether. Everything was meant to cycle back through into something else. Matter—spiritual or otherwise—was not meant to be destroyed. It went against nature.

Maybe fading would be better. Than whatever awaits me on the other side.

That was, in all likelihood, true. Elodie had done terrible things in the hundreds of years she'd been alive. She'd hurt people. She'd ruined lives. Her After would not be one of grace. It would be one of punishment of her own making. Rus could hardly blame her for thinking that nothing at all was better than that.

"In the end, that is your choice." And Rus would never take that choice from someone. Not like this, at least. Kaytee had been a different discussion; she'd been power hungry and mad. Hell-bent on dragging Rus into the After and inhabiting her body as revenge. Elodie wasn't like that. She was just... sad. "But you need to hurry and decide," Rus warned, her voice still soft. "You don't have much time."

Will I see her again? Mazarin?

"Maybe." Rus adjusted her hold on the unconscious woman in her lap. Taryn had yet to stir. Ahe wouldn't for several days, after what Rus had to do to set her free, if she did at all.

I cannot tell if that would be a blessing or a curse.

"A bit of both, I'd wager." And boy, did she understand that. Seeing Az again for the first time after over a decade had been the worst and best kind of torture.

I loved her once. And she loved me.

"I know." That was the worst part in all of this—how Rus could see herself and Az in Mazarin and Elodie. They were so similar. Maybe if they'd been born in another time, this would have been their fate too. But Moondale was on their side now. "Do you love her still?" She didn't know why she was asking. It wasn't like it mattered. It wouldn't change what Mazarin did to Elodie and what Elodie did in response. Neither of them was blameless in this.

I think I might. Somewhere. Under all the hurt.

"Then I hope you're able to sort this out."

Elodie seemed to sigh, her shoulders lifting and falling with the movement, even though she didn't need to breathe. Then she nodded to herself and reached for Rus's hand. It took nothing at all for Elodie to cross over, as insubstantial as she was, as tired, but still when it was done Rus was hardly holding herself upright along with the weight of Taryn against her.

"Rus," Cagney breathed her name like a relief as she ran through the wood, dodging fallen branches and downed trees without even looking at where she was going. The perks of being a druid who was deeply connected to the forest. "You have to come quick."

Rus was immediately on alert, Elodie's warnings of Mazarin Elwood echoing through her like bats in a cavern. "Why? What's happened?"

"It's Azure." Cagney scraped a foot through the edge of the warding array, breaking off a couple of the mushrooms from their stems, and dropped down in front of Rus, already scooping Taryn up without having to be told. "She's done something intolerably stupid."

Well, that didn't sound like Rus's Az at all. But the fear in Cagney's eyes made Rus's insides squeeze. "What is it? What has she done?"

"She invited a spirit into her. So she could—"

Rus didn't wait for Cagney to finish that sentence. She thrust Taryn fully into her arms and rolled to her feet. She ignored the way her legs trembled under her as she ran in the direction of the Heart. Darcy flapped beside her, a caw coming from his beak. "Fly ahead. If she needs you, pull her out of there."

Darcy gargled something that sounded like annoyance but did as instructed, swooping through the trees at a speed Rus couldn't keep up with.

By the time she reached the clearing where the Heart of Moondale resided, her entire body was trembling from the strain, sweat coating her skin in a thin sheen despite the chill in the air. But she didn't stop. She couldn't. Not until she dropped to her knees next to where Az was sitting on the ground, looking around, dazed, her back propped up against the Heart.

"You beautiful fucking idiot." Rus launched at Az, pulling her against her chest and pressing her face into her hair. Grabbing her by the shoulders, Rus pushed Az away from her to look into her eyes. They were heavy lidded and tired, but when she stared deeper, there was no hint of a spirit hiding behind them. Az had exorcised Mazarin Elwood without any help from Rus. Goddess, would Az ever stop amazing her? "Who said you could go off and do something so reckless, huh?" She wagged her finger in Az's face, and Az caught it in her hand, threading their fingers together. "You stupid, astounding, wonderful woman."

"You're one to talk," Az said, her voice scratchy and strangled.

"Yes. Yes, I am one to talk." Still, she couldn't hide the wonder painted plainly across her face as she looked at Az. This woman. Her partner. Her fiancé. Her best friend. How had she ever gotten so lucky? "How did you even manage that? You've never opened a portal to the After before, and I've never shown you—"

"I listen." Az shrugged, a teasing smile creeping up one side of her mouth. She was exhausted, drained from the strain of whatever she'd done, but she was still there. She was still Az. "To understand the nature of necromancy," Az said, leaning in closer so the words brushed against Rus's ear, whispered low and slow enough that only she would hear them even as the elders in the clearing began to regain themselves and mill about, "one just has to see the beauty inherent in life and death."

A shiver raced down Rus's spine, and her fingers fisted in Az's coat involuntarily. "Marry me?"

"What?" Az pulled back, eyes wide, cheeks slightly flushed where they'd been pale a moment ago.

"Will you marry me?" Rus repeated the question, her heart in her throat. She thought she knew the answer, but that didn't mean asking wasn't scary. Goddess, how had Az done this so many times and not lost her nerve?

Az threw herself forward into Rus's arms, and they both flopped back against the cold, hard ground with a thump. "I think a winter solstice wedding would be perfect," she whispered, breathless.

"Is that a yes?"

The answer came in the form of a kiss that left them both dizzy and gasping after everything they'd been through the last hour or so. They were both covered in sweat and grime. The scent of ozone, the sharp tang of blood, still hung in the air. But it was perfect. It was everything Rus had scarcely allowed herself to wish for. She bundled Az closer and breathed her in.

"Don't think this gets you off the hook for your recklessness," Rus chided gently around a half-formed chuckle as they both lay on the ground, unwilling or unable to move. Even Rus wasn't sure by this point. "You should never have opened the veil to the After without a more experienced necromancer, or at the very least, Darcy here."

Az snorted and struggled to sit up, grabbing Rus's arm as she went to show off the still-bleeding wounds from the soul jumper. They were no longer a danger to her, but from the way her skin was stained red, it was clear they had been not that long ago. "And this is not recklessness at its finest?"

"Is my wife sassing me right now?" Rus gasped, happiness fizzing in her veins. Goddess, she loved this woman so much. How had she ever thought that Az wouldn't accept her for all that she was? Wouldn't love her, flaws and all? She'd been such a fool for so long. But they got there in the end, didn't they? That was all that really mattered. "I love you."

"I love you too. But in all seriousness"—Az pulled away so she could better examine Rus's arms—"what the fuck did you do to yourself?"

Rus shrugged. "The soul jumper didn't want to go down without a fight."

Az released a sigh that was all annoyance and struggled to her feet, pulling Rus up with her. "Come. Let's go home and get cleaned up." She gave Rus's hand a squeeze that was perhaps weaker than normal, but the smile that split her face as she added "wife" was wide and self-satisfied.

Rus nearly melted on the spot, stumbling along behind Az as they ignored the rest of the elders in their bid to escape the woods and return to their family waiting for them at 157 Mourning Moore. At *home*.

Chapter 33

"The ghosts haven't gone away," Gilroy Herne said, his tone accusing.

Azure resisted the urge to roll her eyes and make a snarky comment about stating the obvious. She was trying her best to be *diplomatic* and play *nice*. At least until they could get a vote from the Grove of Elderwood to have Gilroy removed the way they'd had Brant Ironwood removed. A thing that was still very much in process, even a week later. Campaigning, Azure had been informed by Phyre, took time.

Brant Ironwood's seat sat empty tonight, the Circle of the Silver Flame unrepresented. A reminder that things were changing. Slowly but surely. Azure breathed easier every time she looked over to find the vacant chair.

"Rus never said they would leave when the threat passed," Azure responded, doing her best to keep her words from sounding clipped and irritated. "She said that Sheriff Greer and his force could usher some of them over, and he did. The population of disquiet shades in Moondale is far lower than it was at the height of the centennial. But there are still many left."

It was the truth. Rus didn't know where the spirits had come from. Didn't know if they were summoned for the express purpose of distraction or attack. Nor did they know, at this point, which of the threats that they'd faced had done the summoning. Neither Elodie Ronen nor Mazarin Elwood copped to it before being sent to their rest. Azure didn't suppose it much mattered at this point.

What *did* matter was that the dead still lingered in Moondale. Drifting through the streets. They weren't hurting anyone. But they would become more of a problem if they were left to ferment further. No matter how weak the Board of Magic might think the spirits of humans were, they could still cause chaos.

"And Icarus Ashthorne has proposed a solution," Aunt Carmine added. There was a layer of annoyance there that most wouldn't catch, apart from someone like Azure, who had known her a lifetime, but it was there just the same. Azure wondered if Aunt Carmine had finally learned to respect Rus after all she'd done. Or if she saw Rus as family, as she should. Maybe it was a combination of both.

"Yes. Send our underprepared youth into the field with a *necromancer*." Enfys Snowthorn rolled his eyes, practically spitting Rus's title like a curse.

This song and dance was quickly becoming stale to Azure. All she wanted was for this fucking meeting to be over so she could go home and curl up with her family on the couch. It was movie night, and she was missing it for these idiots.

"From what my witchlings tell me, they're learning a lot under Ashthorne and Elder Elwood's tutelage. More than just how to send the dead to their final rest." Cliantha Greer —Evander Greer's grandmother—it seemed, was also losing interest in this same tired argument.

Azure appreciated that Evander Greer was able to convince his grandmother to allow some of the young witches of the Crimson Tide to aid in the cleansing of Moondale. His testimony that their efforts were slowly turning a tide of darkness no one had noticed in the town were invaluable. He was the sheriff, after all. He had the statistics to back up his claims. Not that Moondale had ever been a high crime area, but there was a notable difference. Slight as it may be.

"Agreed," Aunt Carmine said. "They've learned to think creatively and on their feet. Skills that extend to use beyond dealing with disquiet spirits."

Others nodded their agreement. Not all of them had sent folk to help in Rus and Azure's first excursion into freeing those tied to this plane, but it was only a matter of time before they did. Azure felt settled to know that Rus had gained the trust of so many, finally. It had taken much too long, but at least they were here now.

Gilroy and Enfys were quiet, clearly sensing that they were outnumbered.

"We can only do two groups at a time," Azure said, as if this might calm some of the fear. But the reminder that she, too, was able to create an opening into the After now seemed to make people uncomfortable all over again. Ah well, they would just have to get used to it. She wasn't a necromancer and none of them could call her one, as she'd never reached into the After and pulled someone from it. She'd never coaxed the dead back to this plane to help her fight. Or pulled their bodies from the ground and reanimated them. And she likely never would. She didn't want, nor need, that kind of power when she had Rus. But the ability to give peace to those who lingered, unable to let go? That, she was proud of.

If she and Rus managed to teach enough of the young folk in their care to respect the cycle of life as Rus had taught her, maybe they would have others soon. *Also* not necromancers. It would be good for every clan and coven to have at least a few folk able to cleanse a haunting without having to call on Rus all the time.

"But we are making progress," she finished her thought. "We hope to have many of them crossed over before the veil is at the thinnest come the winter solstice."

Before their wedding, because Azure didn't particularly want a bunch of uninvited ghosts fucking up something she'd been waiting nearly twenty years for at this point.

There was some grumbled agreement. More silent seething. But the meeting progressed after that. More clans agreed to send a few of their own to help Azure and Rus in their efforts, and there was some discussion about the festival of lights planned for around the winter solstice. But nothing much of note happened, and Azure was relieved when she was free to wrap her scarf around her neck tightly and step out into the chill late-October air.

Rus was waiting for her, propped up against the passenger side door of Blue, where she'd parked on the curb next to the hydrant. It was illegal. There was a whole parking lot with plenty of empty spaces. Rus seemed to know this, because there was a little smirk on her lips, a challenge that asked someone to report her to the sheriff and have Evander come out there and write her a ticket. Because she was a bitch like that.

"You didn't have to wait for me," Azure said instead of lecturing her, then stepped up close and leaned in to brush a kiss to her lips.

"No, I didn't. But I wanted to." Rus shrugged. She pulled Azure in closer by her hips, her hands warm through the fabric of her skirt, fending off the cold air with a touch that made Azure shiver for a whole different reason. "Can't have my future wife walking all the way home by herself."

Rus's eyes flicked over Azure's shoulder, a pointed

explanation about the ghosts still lingering in Moondale. Azure could see them now, even without the talisman. Rus said it was because she had dipped her toe into the After, and it left its mark on her. It wasn't the only thing that had. But Azure had yet to discover what Mazarin's curse would entail.

Azure hummed. "I appreciate it."

"Anything of note happen?" Rus raised her chin to gesture to the Board of Magic building behind her.

"Not really."

"All right, then. Let's get home." Rus stepped away from the car and opened the door for her. "I think Nando picked up *more* wedding magazines today."

Azure laughed softly and let the happiness at the reminder that they'd be married soon chase away a chill that threatened to settle into her bones. Something hovered over her, an axe about to fall, but whatever it was, they'd deal with it when it came. Eventually. For now, she was going to let herself be happy. Let herself bask in the excitement their entire household felt for the incoming wedding.

"What are we watching tonight?" Azure leaned back in her seat, grateful for the warmth of the car.

"*The Addams Family*." Rus fixed her with a sharp smile and pulled away from the curb. Then she reached over to take her hand and pulled it into her lap, where she could thread their fingers together.

"Perfect." Azure smiled to herself, watching the first flakes of a late fall dusting float to the ground.

The coming winter would be cold, but also... *beautiful*. She had little doubt.

GLOSSARY

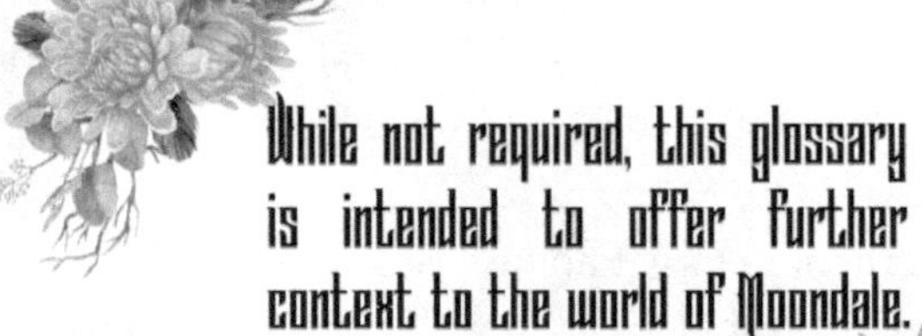

Pronunciation Guide

- **Aihuan:** Aye-hoo-wahn
- **Meiling:** May-lee-ng
- **Jiejie:** Gee-ay-gee-ay

Terms Guide

<u>Witch Terms</u>

- **Athame:** A ceremonial blade used in ritual magic.
- **Aura:** An emanation surrounding the body of a living creature , regarded as an essential part of the individual.

- **Covenless:** A witch who does not belong to a formal coven.
- **Familiars:** A living creature (traditionally a cat) attending and obeying a witch.
- **Folk:** A word used to reference any person of magical lineage.
- **Moonmother:** A witch assigned by a child's parents to take responsibility for the child in the event the parents are unable.
- **Poppet:** A small figure or doll used in sorcery or witchcraft.
- **Possession:** The act of having one's body inhabited by a spirit.
- **Reanimated:** A being that has been brought back to life through magical means.
- **Soul Eater:** A spirit that has consumed another spirit as a means to gain power.
- **Spellcraft:** The act of creating new or using existing spells.
- **Talismans:** An item, or paper, inscribed with magical characters or runes to perform a specific spell.
- **Wards**: A magical barrier set using either spellwork, talismans, or runes to protect a specific place.

Chinese Terms Guide

- **Jiejie:** A familiar way to refer to an older sister or older female friend, used by someone substantially younger.
- **Niang:** Mama

- **Baba:** Papa
- **A-:** Familiar diminutive
- **-Er:** A word for "child", added to a name to express affection.

<u>Circle of Jade Waters</u>
WITCHES
best known for scholarly pursuits

Elder: Carmine Elwood

Members:

- Carmine Elwood
- Maureen Beecher
- Violet Elwood
- ~~Taryn Elwood~~
- ~~Azure Elwood~~
- Indigo Elwood
- Sunila Elwood

<u>Circle of the Silver Flame</u>
WITCHES
best known for weapons & wand makers

Elder: Brant Ironwood

Members:

- Brant Ironwood
- Brenton Ironwood
- Phyre Ironwood

<u>Circle of the Crimson Tide</u>
WITCHES
best known for security & ward work

Elder: Cliantha Greer

Members:

- Cliantha Greer
- Evander Greer

<u>Clan of Crescentia</u>
FAIRIES - Cupids
best known for their skills in matchmaking

Elder: Enfys Snowthorn

Members:

- Nesta Holyore
- Dillan Holyore

Grove of Elderwood
DRUIDS

best known for their agricultural skills

Elder: Gilroy Herne

Members:

- Gilroy Herne
- Cagney Cashel

Chesapeake Pack
SHIFTERS

best known for their efforts forest preservation

Elder: Chelsea Horst

Members:

Circle of the Emerald Forge
WISH GRANTERS

best known for preservation of the Moondale lei lines

Elder: Dhiren

Members:

Ladies of Nimue
WATER FOLK

best known for their efforts in bay preservation

Elder: Nixie Virnan

Members:

Clan of the Unseen Moon
UNSEELIE FAE
best known for

Elder: Yaereene

Members:

Sisters of the Meadow
SEELIE FAE
best known for

Elder:

Members:

Coven of the Forgotten
WITCHES
best known for their advancements in magical technology

Elder: Azure Elwood

Members:

- Icarus Ashthorne
- Azure Elwood
- Fernando

ACKNOWLEDGMENTS

I always start these things but thanking the reader, and this one is no different. I want to thank you—whether you're a returning reader or Lou is new to you—for picking up my little indie published book, supporting my dream, and following along with Rus and Az on their journey. Without readers, I can't do what I do, so I greatly appreciate the support.

If you loved every moment of Rus and Az's story (as I hope you did) please leave a review, follow me on social media, or give me a shout out. I love hearing from you guys, it's really the best part of writing.

Next I'd like to thank my family who supports me in this weird journey I'm on to become an established author. They show up to my signings, they listen to my rants about my characters, they look at my covers and tell me when they're complete shit (I design my covers FYI), and they're the best people to have in my corner, no joke.

Then there is the small hoard of beta readers I had look at this bugger to tell me if any of it actually made sense, and if I'm as funny as I think I am (turns out I am). Thanks Meg, Val, and Nancy! You guys provided so much helpful feedback, and I'm super grateful.

And of course my editor, Brenna. Who continues to give The Bay of the Dead 'verse her love, and enjoys these books as much as I do.

And last but certainly not least, thank you to my small writing support group. Tiss, Meg, Whitney, Nancy, Jasmine, and the rest of my MTP family—without you there would be no Lou.

ABOUT LOU WILHAM

 Born and raised in a small town near the Chesapeake Bay, Lou Wilham grew up on a steady diet of fiction, arts and crafts, and Old Bay. After years of absorbing everything, there was to absorb of fiction, fantasy, and sci-fi she's left with a serious writing/drawing habit that just won't quit. These days, she spends much of her time writing, drawing, and chasing a very short Basset Hound named Sherlock.

When not, daydreaming up new characters to write and draw she can be found crocheting, making cute bookmarks, and binge-watching whatever happens to catch her eye.

Learn more about Lou and her future projects on her website: http://louinprogress.com/ or join her mailing list at: http://subscribepage.com/mailermailer

facebook.com/LouWilham

instagram.com/lou.wilham

Also By Lou Wilham

The Witches of Moondale
    The Hex Next Door
    The Ghost of Hexes Past
    Home is Where the Hex Is
    A Hex To Remember

The Hunters of Ironport
    Overkill
    Fresh Kill
    Kill Your Darlings

The Fae of Eventide
    An Offer Fae Can't Refuse

Sanctuary of the Lost
    Of Loyalties and Wreckage
    Of Love and Ruin
    Of Hope & Blight
    Of Blight & Ruin

Completed Series
    The Heir to Moondust
    The Tales of the Sea Trilogy
    Villainous Heroics
    The Clockwork Chronicles
    The Curse Collection
    Benvolio & Mercutio Turn Back Time

Lineage by C. Vonzale Lewis

On Tulare Island, Magick is a way of life, but for smart-mouthed Nicole Fontane, it's a curse to be avoided at all costs. Yet the legacy she was born with and her failure to live up to it isn't so easy to bury.

With less than two hundred dollars in her bank account and rent looming overhead, Nicole is forced to take a job at Tribec Insurance. Corporate, stuffy, and nothing like what she wanted for herself. It doesn't help that the company's proprietors, the Stewart family, harbor a morbid fascination with the Naqada, a mysterious pre-dynastic Egyptian society. Between the eerie atmosphere, heightened security, and the stench of blood wafting through Tribec, Nicole suspects the Stewarts are dabbling in a dark art she never thought she'd encounter:

Blood Magick. Deadly. Forbidden. Unnatural.

Despite spending a lifetime avoiding Magick, Nicole unwittingly becomes a pawn in the Stewarts' nefarious schemes. To save her home and those she holds dear, she must confront her troubled past with Magick and unlock her latent abilities, even if she's terrified of the outcome and what it might spur.

The way of life Nicole shunned is her only lifeline—one covered in thorns—but it's all that stands in the way of an Old God's resurrection.

Available Now

Those We Couldn't Burn by Whitney L. Spradling

Worlds collide when an ancient vision brings a witch and witch hunter together.

Prince Tyberius Berkshire, witch hunter extraordinaire, has been set with an impossible task—discover the truth of an ancient vision to keep his family on the throne. His world crashes down around him, when an intricate piece of the vision's puzzle falls into place in the form of a purple-haired witch.

Neave Paker has spent the past ten years quietly taking revenge against the witch hunters. Until the prince of the hunters captures her. Taken to the palace, she's given the choice to either work for the enemy or burn at the stake.

Together, they set out to discover the truth. But difficulties lie ahead as they fight attraction and animosity. When they uncover more than they bargained for, the unlikely duo must determine what is more important to them: their beliefs or their hearts.

Available Now

Dead Rockstar by Lillah Lawson

Stormy Spooner is at her wits' end. Careening towards bitter after a nasty divorce, she sometimes wonders what her life is becoming.

After unearthing a cryptic set of lines from a dusty album cover, Stormy tries the impossible: to resurrect Phillip Deville, enigmatic former frontman of the Bloomer Demons. Stormy's love for her favorite dead rockstar knows no bounds...but it was all supposed to be a joke.

When she answers a knock on her door the next day and finds herself face to face with the dark-haired rock god of her every teenage fantasy, her entire world is turned upside down.

Turns out, she's awakened more than just Philip, and Stormy will have to do battle against a cast of strange characters to keep herself and her new undead boyfriend safe.

Available May 15, 2024